The Free Trader of Warren Deep

Free Trader Series
Book 1

By Craig Martelle

Craig Martelle Major USMC retired
2016

Cover Illustration © Tom Edwards
Tom EdwardsDesign.com

Editing services provided by Mia Darien – miadarien.com

<u>Other Books by Craig Martelle</u>

It's Not Enough to Just Exist (Jan 2016)

Free Trader Series Book 1 – The Free Trader of Warren Deep (Feb 2016)
Free Trader Series Book 2 – The Free Trader of Planet Vii (Mar 2016)
Free Trader Series Book 3 – Adventures on RV Traveler (Apr 2016)
Free Trader Series Book 4 – The Battle of the Amazon (estimate Oct 2016)

Rick Banik Thriller Series

People Raged and the Sky Was on Fire (May 2016)

For my friend Bill Rough

Table of Contents

ACKNOWLEDGMENTS i

1 - Ass 3

2 –Binghamton 5

3 - Detour 8

4 – A New Goal 12

5 – A New Plan 15

6 – Cameron 17

7 – Upset the Trade 19

8 - Jail 21

9 – Run! 22

10 – Not Going 26

11 – Good Hunt, Bad Hunt 28

12 – Smoked Venison 32

13 – A Cold-water Surprise 34

14 –Like an Eagle 37

15 – The Hawkoid 44

16 – Grasslands 48

17 – 'They come' 50

18 – Now They're Three 54

19 – Lift the Dark Cloud 57

20 - Saffrimander 62

21 – Running from the Fight 65

22 – The Caravan Rests 68

23 – Heading South 70

24 – Other Hawkoids 72

25 – Hawkoid Disdain 74

26 – The Camp before the Storm 78

27 – Bonding 81

28 – The Pain of the Great Desert 83

29 – Healing Time 86

30 – The Plunge 88

31 – Into the Great Desert 90

32 – Moment of Truth 94

33 – Half Way 96

34 – The Tortoid 98

35 – A Rough Night 102

36 - No More Water For You 106

37 – Tonight's the Night 109

38 – Preparing for the Oasis 110

39 – Just a Scratch 113

40 – The Oasis Pacified 117

41 – It Sucks 122

42 – The Lake 125

43 – Development Unit 128

44 – Distance Check 132

45 – Moving On 135

46 – Oasis Zero Two 137

47 - Restored 140

48 - Hope 142

49 – Oasis Zero One 144

50 – Dinner Awaits 146

51 – Repair Shed 149

52 – A Venison Meat Pie, Please 152

53 – Masters of Water 157

54 - Feeding 160

55 – Get Up 162

56 – Puke...164

57 - Endless Questions 167

58 - Maps...169

59 – Feeling Bad 171

60 – Leaving the Great Desert Behind................................173

61 – She's Hungry...175

62 - Micah...177

63 – Dinner Tales 180

64 – The New Caravan 182

65 – Everyone Adds Strength...185

66 – You Really Should Have Talked...................................190

67 – He's a Pig 197

68 – Freedom's Taste 200

69 – Helping the Village...206

70 – Introducing a Friend 208

71 – Villagers Prepare..211

72 – The Road 214

73 – The Lizard Men...217

74 – A Celebration Like No Other 221

75 – Safe Now, Safe Forever..227

76 – Too Much Power...229

77 – A New Oasis 232

78 – What To Do...234

79 – All of Us..236

80 – Where You Go, We Follow 238

81 – Nothing to Fear, Everything to Fear............................240

82 – Everything to Fear, Nothing to Fear............................243

83 – Leave or Stay? 247

The Free Trader of Planet Vii..251

1 – The Companions..251

2 – The Power of Old Tech....................................253

3 – Back to the Oasis...256

ACKNOWLEDGMENTS

This journey started a long time ago when my brother Guy bought me the original Dungeons and Dragons® boxed set. This was early in TSR®'s existence, so we had to build our own dungeons, run our own campaigns. Then I attended GenCon in 1979 where I met James M. Ward. I bought Metamorphosis Alpha™ and Gamma World™.

I like the bio-engineered approach, the lost high-tech of modern worlds. Is there an Atlantis? Once I saw MA and GW, I was hooked. I read Aldiss & Heinlein. Post-Apocalyptic became my favorite genre.

Thank you James for inspiring this world and Guy for introducing me.

I also want to thank my good friend Bill Rough who is always there whenever I need a sanity check. This was the first sci-fi novel he's ever read and he did it to help me out. He is the wisest man I know.

My better half Wendy had a great deal of input on the characters of this story. She was quick with ideas for what kind of animals she'd like to see and how she felt they could contribute. She wanted a companion snake, but I couldn't do it. Snakes creep me out. We live in Fairbanks, Alaska, where there are no snakes.

1 - Ass

'Ass!'

"You are such an ass!" Braden lay by the fire in the blanket he'd been using since he was a child. The young man's long braid was wrapped around his neck like a scarf. He looked at the Hillcat, a scowl darkening his face.

'It makes noises but no sense,' the 'cat responded over their mindlink. The 'cat's orange back, even with a man's knee, had black dots and a black slash toward his tail. He was called a Hellcat by those who'd seen him make a kill, but not by Braden, his most loyal friend.

When he was a child, Braden saved a Hillcat kitten from drowning. At that moment they bonded, and instantly, Braden knew he had a lifelong partner. Many called the joining the ultimate pairing of friendship and joy.

It hadn't taken long before Braden's bond with the 'cat felt like the relationship his parents had. Together their entire adult lives - annoyance, bickering, surrender, friendship, then more bickering, and intertwined throughout was a fierce loyalty. The old man would say anything about his partner, but if anyone else said something, the fight was on. Braden called the 'cat an ass ten times a turn of the sun, but they fought their enemies together. They were there for each other.

And so it was, the relationship between a Hillcat called Golden Warrior of the Stone Cliffs, or simply G-War as Braden called him. The Hillcat had his own name, but even after ten cycles of the seasons, he hadn't told Braden what it was. He insisted that Braden wasn't mature enough to know his true 'cat name.

As Braden glared at the 'cat, G-War raised one paw in his mocking way of giving Braden the finger. The 'cat turned around a couple times, sniffing the air, then faced away from the young man and dropped to the ground. G-War's head was up, sphinxlike, his eyes closed. The 'cat cut their link.

The 'cat listened in on Braden's thoughts, but Braden only 'heard' what the 'cat wanted him to hear.

"I hate it when you do that," Braden retorted, but knew that he could sleep now, without fear of surprise, as he did every night when the 'cat watched over him. Without G-War, Braden would have never survived his life as a Free Trader in Warren Deep.

2 –Binghamton

Braden always stopped where he could take a look, see how things were before he entered a community. Binghamton was hit or miss. Sometimes it was the best place to trade, other times, it was a great place to avoid.

Braden nudged his team of two water buffalo to a halt. He climbed down from the buckboard and walked to a small rise on the side of the road. He crawled the final few feet, not wanting to highlight himself. He took out his telescope, a gift from his father, nothing more than rough hide rolled with polished glass set at both ends, and scanned the road in front of him. He stopped at the collection of buildings that made up Binghamton. He looked from one to the other, not seeing any activity aside from the market square.

In the central square where the traders conducted their business, people gathered. Braden didn't see any traders or their stalls. Everyone watched what looked to be a lynching. One person, probably a man, stood on a block of wood under a makeshift tripod, his hands behind him. Braden thought he could make out a rope tied to the man's neck.

"Hey! Come over here," Braden said to G-War.

'So my name is Hey? Is it giving me a new name?' Braden was never surprised how the 'cat fixated on the trivial, when Braden was serious. He set himself up for it every time.

"Could you please come over here and take a look at this? I would like to know what you think." Braden's voice was laced with sarcasm. He even bowed slightly, as much as he could from his position on the ground.

The 'cat padded lightly from under the wagon. He had been enjoying the shade. He stopped half way there and squatted. Braden wrinkled his nose. He would never get used to the smell of 'cat pee.

'If that's what it wanted, why didn't it just say so in the first place? It knows how I

love to say yes to its distractions.'

"Ass," Braden said under his breath. He knew the 'cat heard him. It heard everything. It saw everything.

G-War pinned his ears against his head as he crouched and looked over the rise.

He soon changed his position to sitting, with his ears up. He was longer than a man's arm, not counting his tail, and had a slightly oversized head, necessary to hold a large mouth of spiked teeth and two sharp fangs. People not paired had an innate fear of Hillcats. Braden always warned potential customers to keep their dogs inside. G-War had a tendency to go after them if they barked at him. For anyone who saw a Hillcat make a kill, they would never forget the ferocity of it.

'So the humans are killing another human. What of it?'

"But why?" Braden asked, expecting the 'cat to have an opinion.

'He cheated them, or so they think.'

"Did he?" Braden knew that the 'cat could touch other minds on occasion, especially when a person was distraught. It made sense that the man's thoughts were coming through loud and clear.

'No.' With that, G-War took a particular interest in licking his paw, then using it to groom the fur around one ear.

"That's it? No?" He asked, hoping for more. No answer. "Do you think we should go down there?"

G-War stopped his grooming, looked back at the town briefly, and then turned to pad back to the wagon. *'No.'*

He didn't think so, either. If Binghamton took to killing traders for a simple case of mistaken cheating, then he wanted no part of it. Braden would miss trading with them though. Binghamton made for a nice way point. There was always something they needed and something they had that could be traded elsewhere at a nice profit.

"Oh, well." Braden took one last look through his telescope. "Let's get outta here." Braden turned his team around, facing them away from Binghamton before he climbed aboard. What he saw bothered him. Not death. He'd seen plenty of that, probably too much in his twenty cycles on the planet. What bothered him was how a town could unite against a trader. When he passed that word, no other traders would go there.

Traders were the life-link between the communities of Warren Deep. Binghamton just cut itself off from the rest of humanity.

3 - Detour

Braden back-tracked his team, then headed south on what looked to be little more than a game trail. It would take time and be slow going, but he knew it led them where he wanted to go. He grew up on the roads with his trader parents, where they showed him the ways around Warren Deep. They never allowed themselves only one way in. They never knew when they would need to avoid an area, or just disappear.

Braden's water buffalo would never help him make a quick escape. His parents had used horses, but he couldn't afford those. Not yet anyway. He counted on G-War's senses to help them avoid trouble. And if all of that failed, he counted on the magical bow beneath the seat of the wagon. It wasn't really magic. It was a relic of the past. It was a relic of the past, made in the before time. It was the Rico Bow. Its like would never be made again.

The bow was a black that seemed to absorb the light. It had a second curve at the top and bottom that helped guide the string, magnifying the power of the pull. He had seen a couple other bows like this one, but the others were modern-made of fine yew, and much longer. Very few people had the strength and size to wield one properly. Braden was not a tall man so he could never use a full-sized long bow. His Rico Bow, though, gave him a significant advantage over others in Warren Deep. No adversary could get close to him.

And that was the last thing he wanted. He preferred to be with his 'cat, trade for a profit, and enjoy each town's unique offerings. He liked to have a woman in each town. Many he happily paid for a few hours of their time. He was not yet ready to take a mate, for he was not wealthy enough to treat her properly.

Braden pulled out the bow as the wagon bounced along the trail. He heard G-War express his discontent with a low-throated growl as he scrabbled to regain his position on a small desk inside.

'Stop. There are a couple rabbits that require my attention.' With that, G-War was out the back and in a silent flash of orange, disappeared into the trees alongside the trail.

"I guess we're stopping," Braden said as he pulled back on the reins. Rabbit sounded good. He took out two of his precious hardwood arrows and jumped down, looking in the direction G-War had gone.

When they hunted together, a kill was almost always guaranteed. Most of the time, that meant Braden drove prey toward a waiting 'cat that would strike from nowhere, going straight for an exposed throat. Using claws and teeth, the 'cat made quick work of wild game. G-War avoided protracted fights or posturing. He said that was for mating rituals, not eating. When killing for food, quickest was best. When killing to survive, then kills needed to be even quicker.

Once in the woods, Braden stalked quietly, earning a harsh rebuke from the 'cat. Braden's idea of quiet was far different than that of a Hillcat. He stopped moving and watched. He couldn't see where G-War was, but he could feel him close by.

The 'cat had taught him to use all his senses. Braden sniffed the air. High country pines. Musty undergrowth. He closed his eyes and listened. A branch moving, tree bark disturbed. He looked toward the sound, squinting his eyes. About 30 strides away, a squirrel stopped running down a tree, motionless, head raised. Braden nocked an arrow, slowly took aim, and pulled back. He sighted in on the squirrel, then raised the point of the arrow slightly to account for the distance. He let go the bowstring. With a muffled twang the arrow split the air, driving through the squirrel's neck. The body went limp, falling to the side, hanging where the arrow pinned it to the tree.

A heartbeat later, the high pitched scream of a rabbit pierced the forest calm. It was instantly silenced. A second animal ran wildly through the leaves and undergrowth as G-War closed the distance. Rabbits will bolt, zig-zag, run some more, then stop. G-War didn't try to overtake the rabbit. He only wanted to be within striking distance when it paused. This rabbit had a little more spunk than most, possibly the smell of fresh blood and the size of the creature chasing it added fuel to its fire. But in the end, it hesitated and the 'cat did not.

G-War collected both of his kills and headed back toward the wagon.

"Oh, you're sharing with me? What a good kitty!" G-War hesitated for a second and then continued toward the wagon. The 'cat didn't waste time answering his ridiculous human. He wondered if all 'cats had bipeds that were so inane. *If only he had never fallen into that river,* but alas, he was a kitten, young and unwise in the way of the world. He could have done worse, though. *What if his human couldn't hunt for itself? What if his human was a farmer - how inglorious would that have been?*

Braden carefully removed his arrow from the squirrel and carried the kill to the edge of the woods. He used his trusty skinning knife to make short work of it. He used a notch in the tree to help him remove the fur. Squirrel hide is extremely tough. You have to wedge the tail into something and then pull for all you're worth.

Once finished, it would make for a nice meal. With two rabbits, he figured G-War would have something left over. He watched the 'cat tear into them. G-War had a particular affinity to the entrails. Braden didn't mind as that meant there would be meat available for roasting.

He built a fire with a spit and put the squirrel on it. He checked back to see that the 'cat had finished and was now cleaning himself. "Do you mind?" No answer. One carcass was almost completely intact. Braden made quick work of cleaning it and put it on the spit behind the squirrel.

On a full stomach, the world always looked like a better place. He heard a floorboard in the wagon creek as G-War jumped in, probably to curl up under the desk for a nap. The wagon was mostly enclosed, on the sides by boarding and the top by a rough canvas cover, greased to keep the rain from getting through.

It was home. He could sleep inside the wagon, when they weren't carrying a full load, or sleep outside, depending on the weather. The world was his oyster, or so his parents had told him, before they went to the great beyond. He wasn't sure what an oyster was, but his mom made it sound wonderful.

The bow was a gift from his dad. His dad never shared where he had gotten it, even though he hounded him about it until his death. Braden didn't like unanswered questions. Like Binghamton. What happened there?

Braden wanted knowledge. He also wanted wealth. He wasn't afraid to take risks to achieve either.

It came to him clearly as he held his Rico Bow. He needed to find Old Tech. His routine trade route wouldn't get him what he wanted. He needed to step outside of the norm, maybe even leave his wagon behind. A trader without a caravan. That would make him unique!

Maybe even poor and quite possibly dead. But he would be the envy of the other traders. No one traded solely in Old Tech. There are people who spent their entire lives trading and never handled a piece of Old Tech.

It had to be out there. Time to dig out the maps and recall the campfire tales.

He knew that Hillcats passed knowledge down the generations. Braden wondered if G-War knew anything. Then, what would it take for G-War to share what he knew?

4 – A New Goal

Braden laid two maps on his desk. They were the only maps he owned, but they weren't the best resource he had for the geography of Warren Deep. He had his rudder, handed down to him by his parents. A rudder was how sailors documented their navigation of the seas. They protected the rudder more than the treasures they carried, for the rudder was the navigator's key to his existence.

And Braden had one for the trade routes. It was rough-pressed thick paper, the best that could be had in Warren Deep, and he meticulously kept it up to date. He made the latest entry regarding Binghamton in small script, as a side note to the page dedicated to this area. He added a couple lines to his family's sum knowledge of the town of Binghamton.

If they followed the current trail, he would end up at the main road between Binghamton and Cameron. He could then continue east to Cameron. From there, he had three choices. His finger traced the routes on the hand-drawn map. Which route would take him closest to an area that was open, yet unknown?

G-War smoothly jumped to the desk from the floor of the wagon. He looked at the map, appearing to study it, then sat down in the middle of it. He immediately curled his paw toward his face, exposing his claws, where he started to nibble and pull on them. Every now and then, the claws needed to have old growth removed, leaving only the sharpest and smoothest points.

"Really? You need to do that right here?" These weren't questions. They rarely were. The 'cat did as he pleased, much of it seemed calculated to make the most mischief for Braden.

Braden poked the 'cat in the side, pulling his hand away quickly. Then he pointed his finger and slowly moved toward G-War's side again. The 'cat fixed his unblinking glare on the finger, raising his paw, claws out, ready to strike. Braden wisely stopped.

"You wouldn't?" Again, not a question. Braden had razor thin scars on both arms and legs from where he was on the losing end of play-fighting with the 'cat. He was told that he had rather nasty scars down his back. He told people this was from a mutie that jumped him, but didn't live to brag about it.

That wasn't true. It was from a play-fight where G-War ended up in a tree and pounced on him. Braden had turned just enough to keep the cat from landing on his face, and the 'cat scored his claws down Braden's back. That was the only time the 'cat had been apologetic. Probably more for being unable to control his jump than for clawing his human's back.

It wouldn't have been a problem if it had more fur on its back, like any respectable animal, G-War thought.

Braden changed the trajectory of his hand so that he ruffled the fur around G-War's neck, scratching a couple places he knew the 'cat liked. The 'cat opened the mindlink. 'Ohh, right there. Yeah, that feels good. Don't stop. Okay. Stop now.' To punctuate this, G-War slapped Braden's hand with a paw, claws retracted.

Braden smiled and laughed. He knew the game. Petting G-War was therapeutic for both of them, as physical contact between them kept the bond strong. The power of the bond was not in owning the other, but in their commitment. Neither could be described as clingy. Braden was friendly, the 'cat aloof. Neither could depart this friendship no matter the circumstance. Neither wanted to. Even after the 'cat injured Braden, that same 'cat comforted him, even finding numbweed for the human's wounds. Unprocessed numbweed could only be made potent by chewing it. The 'cat complained about the taste and that it made his mouth feel funny. The 'cat also contended that Braden owed him for finding, chewing, and applying the numbweed.

"Old Tech, my friend. To make our fortune, we need to find a source of Old Tech. Imagine if we could bring a wagon load back to Jefferson City itself!" Braden imagined himself at the head of a parade, being rewarded with money, power, women, maybe even a seat on the Council.

"Whaddya think, G?"

'I think that I don't like being bored for the few hours a turn I am awake. I don't like being hungry. I really don't like the rain, because that leads to the thing I detest the most, being wet.' The 'cat locked eyes with Braden, then blinked slowly. *'Whatever. Wake me when we get there.'* He got ready to jump off the desk.

"Wait. Do the Hillcats know if the ancients had any hidden outposts and where they might be?"

'Yes.' The 'cat jumped down and wriggled past Braden's feet to wedge himself under the desk.

"Thanks. Now tell me which way we need to go."

'Fine. South. South out of the hills, through the trees, across the desert, along the coast, and back into a forest. It is close to there. Maybe thirty turns away?' The 'cat curled up as he closed the mindlink.

"But Warren Deep ends in the desert, which we can't cross. It's too far." Braden thought for a minute. "It's too far…"

5 – A New Plan

Everything else forgotten, Braden focused on what it would take to overcome the obstacles in reaching an Old Tech outpost. First, they had to cross a desert. How could they carry enough water and food to make the crossing possible? As he thought about it, that was the only real obstacle he saw. If they reached the other side and there was water, he could fish and the buffalo could graze. If there was a forest, they could hunt. Crossing the desert. Water. Food. Speed.

He had time to think. It was another two turns to reach Cameron, then four turns south to reach Whitehorse, the last town before the Great Desert. He would fill up on water and information, then take the plunge.

He was in great spirits riding high on the buckboard as the water buffalo ambled mindlessly forward. He needed to make a successful trade in Cameron, but he had always done well there. It was a crossroads between the east/west and the main north/south trade routes. They had a high turnover which meant they always needed goods. Braden had boxes of the finest flint arrowheads, some so small, they could be used in a blowgun to pierce the eye of a pigeon. He also carried bolts of rough cloth, a few tortoise shells shaped as breastplates for protection, and the smallest of his load but with the most potential for gain, he carried five vials of the spice saffrimander.

Saffrimander was coveted by the wealthy to season any dish. It was produced in only two places, one of which Braden had passed through half a moon back. He traded a complete load of swords and knives, but knew it was well worth it.

The weapons had been scavenged from a small battle between two neighboring communities in the western high-tree forests. Braden hadn't done the scavenging but he made the trade, then put as much distance between him and the battlefield as he could. The trade of the weapons for Saffrimander had been a lucky one. Regardless, it would help to make his name in the business.

Braden was a Free Trader. That meant he was not a member of the Caravan Guild. His parents had been members for a while, but they didn't frequent the Jefferson City area. They had little interaction with the Guild and most importantly, the Guild could not provide them with protection, a main reason to pay the tithes. Guild trades protected both sellers and buyers. Guild prices guaranteed a certain quality.

Braden would meet Guild Traders, for he was one of their suppliers. This was how the system worked best. Free Traders took more risk, but earned all the value of their trade. The Guild Traders paid the tithe, but risked far less. They knew what they would make from a trade. They knew that the trade was guaranteed. They lived boring lives of routine and comfort.

That wasn't for Braden. Although the Hillcat often made comments about wanting more servants.

6 – Cameron

Braden rolled slowly into Cameron, a smile on his face as he thought of Ava. She was a friendly school teacher. He had not yet been successful in sharing more than a meal and drink, but maybe this trip, he would see more of her. He smiled broadly at that.

G-War departed the wagon in a flash. Braden could never shut out the sexual antics of the 'cat. G-War took it as his personal mission to never let a female domestic cat in heat go unserviced. He shared of himself as far and wide as possible. It was a bit disturbing for Braden. The 'cat was so sedate, until females were around, then he became a one-'cat dynamo. It could be an immense and intense distraction.

This also left Braden most vulnerable, for the 'cat provided a distinct edge when negotiating. G-War could feel when someone was rejoicing in the terms of the trade and this helped Braden to get a little more. He wanted people satisfied with their trades, not ecstatic at how they had out-bargained the Free Trader.

Braden continued driving his team to the market square. Every town had one where the traders could set up their wagons, where local vendors plied local products, and where buyers came to buy. Stables were located near the markets so the beasts pulling the carts could be readily tended to. For a fee, of course.

It was the law of the trade.

As Braden unhooked the water buffalo, a couple of local vendors asked what he brought. He politely declined, waiting until he had more people around. Not having competing offers often led to getting a lower price, a less lucrative trade. Although Braden was young, he was no fool.

As he was delivering his two stalwart buffalo to the stable, he was inundated with flashing images of a long-haired calico, the target of G-War's affections. Then a small gray cat entered the picture. Another suitor, judging by how quickly G-War drove it away.

The stable master took Braden's delay as a counter to his offer. The prices were standard, so it wasn't a tactic although the man lowered his fee to a single silver piece for both animals. Braden realized what the man was saying as the 'cat reached his post-affections purr.

"That's a great deal and thank you. I'll throw in five arrowheads for your kindness." Free Traders needed to maintain good relations. No trade this turn was worth losing next turn's deal. Traders who ripped people off went out of business very quickly. By out of business, he meant they were killed, like the man who had mistakenly perished in Binghamton. The stable master seemed nervous, but pleased with Braden's addition to the agreed trade.

Braden returned to his wagon, thinking that he would talk with the stable master later. He wanted to figure out what was amiss. He loved answers. Not so much the questions.

7 – Upset the Trade

Once his wagon was prepared for the trade, he stood on the buckboard and howled in his trader voice, "Come ye, come ye! See treasures from distant lands available for trade at prices so low you'll be amazed! Cloth and arrowheads, breastplates and more! Are you safe? You will find peace of mind here! Come ye, come ye!" It didn't take long before a small crowd surrounded his wagon, asking to see the wares.

He pulled his items out, one by one--the cloth, each tortoise shell, a few arrowheads, and finally, when the haggling over these items tapered off, he stood back on his buckboard.

"Saffrimander! Who has tasted this magical spice? You will never go back to average fare! Do I have an offer for one vial of the best saffrimander available?" He had been in town long enough to know that this was the only saffrimander available, so his statement wasn't untrue. He didn't know how it tasted so couldn't personally attest to its quality. Never sample the wares, his father had taught him.

There was a bit of jostling as people tried to get closer. Excitement always generated better deals. Scarcity also drove up prices. He would not reveal that he had four more vials unless the price went nice and high. He could trade vials and two water buffalo for two horses. The horses would get him closer to his goal, but that would be a lofty price indeed.

There was more jostling and then the people parted, allowing the town's security officer through. Everything got quiet.

"G-War! I need you," Braden whispered.

'Right here,' the 'cat responded directly into Braden's mind. He looked to his left, where the 'cat was sitting calmly at the back of the wagon, watching everything.

"How are you in this fine daylight, good sir?" Braden asked with a flourish and bow.

"Hey, you! Come on down here. I want to talk to you." He turned to the crowd. "Go on, all of you. That's it. Trading is done for this turn." He stepped back, looking at Braden with his hand on the pommel of the sword at his side. He was slightly overweight with a ten-turn growth of a straggly black beard. Beady eyes glared at Braden.

The security officer ushered people away, waving them off with one meaty hand. He waited until they had gone before getting to the heart of it. "Give me the saffrimander," he said without preamble, holding his hand out for the vial.

"I don't understand. This is for trade."

"Not anymore. I suspect it's fake and as such, we can't have it in the market. Now, give it to me."

Braden was torn. He had run into people before who tried to take his goods, but that was in less civilized places. Cameron was the last town within the Caravan Guild's territory. As such, trades were always protected.

"How can we sort this out, good sir? I guarantee that the saffrimander is real. I acquired it far to the west, near Lightning Creek."

The security officer seemed uninterested in Braden's claims. He grabbed Braden's arm and steered him toward the city government building.

"There's no need for that!" No answer from the gruff man. "G. Watch our rig. I'll be in touch." The security officer looked around to see who Braden was talking to. He couldn't see anyone so he shook his head and continued on.

Two men had been lurking in the shadows. After Braden and the security officer passed, they casually strolled toward the wagon.

8 - Jail

Once Braden and the security officer made it to the jail, any pretense of civility dropped. The man shoved Braden roughly to the floor. He took his gold coins and a few silver shekels, which Braden kept in his belt pouch to make change. Thankfully, he dropped most coins through a slot in the buckboard to a heavily secured chest hidden within.

The man put Braden in manacles against a wall. In an imperious voice, the security officer proclaimed, "For violation of the rules regarding Fair Trade, you are sentenced to one turn in the manacles, no food, no water. Property on your person is confiscated. Your wagon will be searched for other contraband, which will also be confiscated once it is discovered."

Braden was furious. He was being robbed. "For any violations of Free Trade, a Guild representative is required to be present at the hearing! But this isn't about that, is it?" The security officer laughed as he waddled away, holding the vial of saffrimander up to the light.

Braden had no idea what the man thought he'd see in the spice. Braden was also happy that he only advertised one vial. He wasn't sure that anyone would be successful in searching the wagon. G-War would hurt people, but they could overwhelm him with numbers. Braden needed to get himself out of this jail and out of town.

9 – Run!

The first man, lean with wicked eyes, put his hands on the wagon's back gate in order to haul himself in. He screamed in pain as two claws lashed out, raking his arms and slicing tendons in the back of his hands. He doubled over in pain.

The 'cat leapt from the wagon onto the man's back, immediately springing into the face of the second man. Before he could stop the 'cat, it was claws-deep in his face and neck. He managed to grab hold of the cat's tail, trying to fling him away, but that only ensured that the 'cat could dig his claws deeper into the man's throat. Blood spurted as his jugular was severed.

G-War dropped to the ground and jumped back up, landing on the first man's back. This time, he stood up and tried to shake the 'cat off. G-War wrapped one paw around the man's throat from behind and with his long claws, ripped through the man's windpipe. The dying man reached for his neck as he went to his knees.

'Be there in a few bounds,' G-War sent to Braden. The 'cat measured time in heartbeats or turns of the sun, but also in distance he could cover.

The orange tabby extended his body fully during his run to the jail. People barely noticed as he flashed by. He never hesitated as he leapt onto a ledge and squeezed his body through an open window. He saw the security officer seated at a table, looking greedily at the gold, silver, and saffrimander. The man didn't notice the 'cat until he landed on the table, upsetting the small treasure before him.

The 'cat made one powerful leap into the man's face, knocking him backward off his chair. The 'cat pushed off hard as they approached the stone floor. The security officer's head smacked loudly when it hit. The 'cat deftly rolled away, turned, and went into a crouch, ready to leap again. The man lay still.

"The keys are in the pouch on his belt," Braden offered. Although the 'cat could work magic with his claws, he didn't have hands. He ended up using his teeth to pull the pouch off and brought the whole thing to Braden. "Nicely done," he said with a nod of thanks. "Is he dead?" The 'cat didn't answer. Braden quickly removed the key, then the shackles. He dropped it all on the filthy floor.

He checked the man while G-War leapt into the open window and looked out. He was still alive. Braden took his money and vial of saffrimander, and without a further look, opened the door and strolled into the street as a free man.

A free man who would be wanted shortly. They walked quickly back to the market square. A number of people had gathered and were looking at the two corpses behind the wagon. "What did you do?" Braden asked in a whisper.

'I kept the thieves away. I knew that I had to leave to save it, as usual, so I couldn't leave them maimed and angry. Of course.'

Braden angled away from the wagon and into the stable. The stable master was surprised to see him.

"Just a little misunderstanding. Everything is cleared up now." Braden nodded reassuringly and smiled at the man. "What kind of deal can we work where I get two horses? The wagon and water buffalo are a given, but what else will it take?" Braden rolled the vial between his fingers. The stable master looked at it hungrily, licking his lips. He stroked his short beard.

"If you had another one of those," he said, nodding suggestively at the vial. "I think we can seal the deal."

"Consider it the trade done. Saddle them up. I'll be right back with the second vial." Braden forced the man to shake his hand. Braden started walking away, stopped, then looked at G-War. The 'cat took a few steps toward the stable master, then sat down and stared at him with his unblinking 'cat gaze. Braden hurried outside and shooed the people away from the wagon, telling them that security was on its way and they'd want to talk with everyone there. That hastened their departure. That also told Braden that he wasn't the only one who suffered from security's power grab. He wondered if there had been a coup.

He systematically yet quickly took everything of value and rolled it all up into a blanket, then rolled that into a second blanket. With his Rico Bow and quiver of arrows across his back, he tried to throw his worldly possessions over his shoulder. It was too heavy. The life of a trader with a wagon wasn't lived lightly.

He ended up dragging his blanket rolls to the stable. His time had to be getting short. He figured he wasn't the only target of Cameron's new security office, so the average person probably wouldn't turn him in, but there were two dead men on the ground in the square.

He also figured the stable master was in cahoots with security, judging by the surprise on his face when Braden showed up. And fear. He didn't expect Braden to have another vial of saffrimander. The trade was always sacrosanct. When he agreed, they shook hands and sealed the deal.

The stable master prepared two horses as per their agreement. The 'cat was stalking along an overhead beam, staying above the stable master. He glance furtively over his shoulder, confirming that he was always only a second away from getting slashed.

"Call your Hellcat off. I've done as you wished," the stable master demanded in an angry voice, laced with bits of fear.

"Two points, my good man. First, he's not mine. It doesn't work that way. And second, we made a deal. It isn't as I wished, but as we agreed. You are only fulfilling your part of our bargain. I will not be maligned. This was a Fair Trade and, as such, is protected." Braden handed the stable master a second vial of saffrimander. The trade was concluded.

"Now, if you'll help me put my blanket on my pack horse, I would greatly appreciate it." G-War dropped into a crouch where the stable master could see him. It was clearly a threat, but not one that Braden had overtly made. They each took an end of the blanket roll, then walked it over the horse's back. Braden quickly tied it down and climbed onto his mount. G-War jumped onto the blanket roll and dug in. With the reins in one hand

and the second horse's lead in the other, Braden looked down on the stable master. He flipped two shekels on the ground in front of the man. "A tip, for your assistance. Be well." Inclining his head slightly to the stable master, he prodded his horse to a walk. Once out of the stable, he turned sharply away from the market square and headed toward the school.

10 – Not Going

He tied the horses to a post behind the school, a single-story building with numerous rooms on both sides of one main hallway. He stalked down the hall until he saw Ava. She was in her classroom. He waved her to come out, but she shook her head and kept lecturing. The motion made the students turn and look at him. He smiled and waved at them.

As his father had taught him, there were two types of people: customers and potential customers. The children were the latter. One never knew when they'd be working their own deals. Wasn't it always better to deal with a trader with the winning smile?

The students made ooh and ahh sounds. They knew their teacher was not yet paired, so they were always looking out for her to find that special someone.

Since she had lost control of her class, she told them to practice writing on their boards while she attended to the distraction.

"What are you doing here?" She was not amused.

"What happened? What's with the security office?" Braden asked in a heavy whisper.

She sighed. "Some men came. One of them became the senior advisor to the mayor. Next thing we know, the mayor's gone and these men are in charge." She looked down and shook her head. "Why do you ask?"

"They tried to steal my stuff. The security officer, of all people. They put me in manacles. I'm sorry to say that a couple men died when G refused to let them into the wagon. I need to leave, and I can't come back." Braden lifted her chin so she would look at him. "Come with me!" He blurted out. He didn't know why he asked that. That wasn't what he planned when he came here.

"I can't. The children need me." She hesitated, then said in a lower voice, "This is my home. I can't live on the road, or worse, on the run." She blinked quickly to keep the tears away. Braden knew the tears weren't for him. They were for herself. She wanted out, but Braden wasn't going to be the one to take her away.

He bowed down and kissed her hand. "My lady. May the sunshine bring you joy." He turned and strode out without looking back. He needed to go.

11 – Good Hunt, Bad Hunt

South to Whitehorse they went. G-War grumbled incessantly as his perch on the pack horse was hardly comfortable and his trip was not restful.

To the east, the rugged Bittner Mountains created the perception of an impenetrable wall. In the blink of an eye, Braden had gone from being a trader to being a nomad. With the loss of his wagon, he lost the means to support himself. Although he had three vials of saffrimander and a healthy pouch of gold and silver, he was hardly poor. But that wasn't enough to retire in comfort.

Once on the road south, Braden decided that he didn't want anyone to see him. If other travelers brought word of a man and a 'cat traveling south on horses, the officials might come after him. He urged his horse Max into the brush. The other horse's lead was tied to Braden's saddle. Pack followed mindlessly.

He headed east, driving hard through the scattered trees and brush to get far away from anyone who might see. He pressed forward, long into the fading light, only stopping well after dusk.

G-War jumped down from his perch on their blanketed goods, sat, and stared at Braden.

"What?"

'Hungry,' the 'cat replied.

"I know. I am, too." Braden tried to play it cool, looking back at the 'cat with a sideways glance.

'There's a deer. That way.' G-War nodded to show the direction. He then

jumped to a low tree branch, spread eagled, allowing his legs to dangle. He rested his head and looked at Braden through half-closed eyes.

Braden quickly hobbled the horses so they could graze without running off. He took his faithful Rico Bow and a few arrows and headed in the direction of the deer.

He expected the deer was not far. The 'cat knew what Braden would tolerate.

What Braden didn't know was how the 'cat knew where the wildlife was. He'd asked, but G-War couldn't or didn't want to explain it. The 'cat accepted what was, without question. Braden didn't push it. He appreciated the fact that his hunting consisted less of searching and more of killing.

It was almost dark, which could make the shot difficult. Braden hurried as much as he dared. He was hungry too, his mouth watering at the thought of roasted venison.

He crouched as he stepped carefully along a game trail, seeking to make no noise. He looked for any movement to show where the deer may be. His arrow was nocked. All he needed was to aim, pull, and release.

As he had hoped, the deer was using the same trail. He stopped silently, slowly raising his Rico Bow. The deer gave him a thirty degree shot from the front. He aimed carefully and let it fly. The arrow buried itself to the feathers and the young buck jumped straight into the air, then bound into the brush. Braden heard the crashing as it continued its headlong flight.

'Damn!' He thought. He had counted on a clean kill. He hated to see an animal suffer. He also greatly disliked chasing after a wounded animal, especially in the dark.

He tried to run after the deer, but something held his foot. He almost fell and reached down to free himself, while not losing sight of where the buck had disappeared. His fingers fell upon a vine wrapped tightly around his ankle. He pulled on it. It pulled back.

This time aloud, "Damn!" A mutant tree. He threw his bow to the side and pulled his long knife. Two hand-spans of new steel, sharpened on both sides slashed downward through the vine. A second vine snaked toward him, then a third. He slashed them away. He ducked his head to the side and retreated away from the tree. Crawlers generally couldn't take on a human with a knife, for their vines weren't fast enough. If you fell asleep against one or had no way of cutting yourself free, you would have a tough time.

He picked up his Rico Bow and walked backwards away from the Crawler. They were solitary creatures, so he didn't worry about running into another one. Not this close anyway.

He turned back along the game trail, getting his bearings, then jogged after the deer. He followed the trail of broken brush, until the blood trail on the ground grew in size. As the deer ran, the arrow caused more and more damage.

There! Twisted in among the brush as it tried to leap one final obstacle, but failed. Braden's shot had barely missed the heart, but by running, the deer drove the arrow home. The buck was probably dead before he made his final leap.

Even though Braden made quick work of cleaning the buck, it was nearly pitch black by the time he shouldered the carcass to make his way back to his camp. He went slowly, hunched close to the ground to find his way to the game trail.

Even though the buck had only gone about fifty strides, it took Braden a great deal of time to make it back to the trail. He spent most of his time waiting and looking. Finally, the moon cast enough light that he could see. At that moment, he was only one stride away. Once on the trail, he looked for the Crawler, but couldn't find which tree it was. Speed was defense. The buck had gotten heavy. Field dressed, it weighed far less than he did, but there was a limit to how long he was going to carry it.

With an adrenaline surge, he leapt forward and jogged along the trail, watching the side where the Crawler had come from. Then, he broke through into an opening where two hobbled horses were startled at his appearance, the smell of blood adding to their fear.

He dropped the carcass and went to the horses, making cooing sounds to calm them. He rubbed each along their necks. He needed the horses, and he needed them to trust him. That was something he still had to earn. He had no sugar crystals for them, but was determined to trade for some next chance he got.

He turned back to find G-War fangs deep into a haunch.

"Really? Ass!" Braden was surprised only for a second. The 'cat never failed to take care of itself. "Leave some for me, you furry little ingrate." Braden busied himself making a fire. He was even hungrier now.

12 – Smoked Venison

The morning came, bringing fog and dew. It smelled as only a forest can after a spring rain. They had all slept well after a filling meal of venison and some berries from bushes alongside their impromptu camp. The horses had grazed well, too. He found them curled up among the bushes, enjoying the sleep of the dead tired.

Braden was a little sore. He had ridden horses before, but never for long, so yesterday's ride had taken its toll on his legs and rump. He figured that more sitting would be painful. Maybe he would walk, leading the horses for part of the daylight.

G-War started this turn of the sun with more venison. He grumbled a bit as it wasn't fresh, but at least it hadn't spoiled. The 'cat could eat something long dead and foul beyond what a human could tolerate, but he didn't like it. That was for survival feeding only.

Braden re-stoked the fire and put more venison on. He used his knife to cut a number of branches, slightly thicker than his thumb. Then he cut pine branches, heavily laden with needles. As the fire cooked his breakfast, he fashioned a four-sided pyramid where he tied the branches, creating a number of racks.

Braden removed his nicely cooked venison and chewed contentedly. He waited for the fire to die down and leave a bed of coals. He put his rack contraption over the coals, not where it would catch fire but where it could hold the venison for smoking.

He stripped the carcass into long thin strips of meat. He took all the choice cuts, not worrying about cleaning off the bones completely. He placed the strips on the rack until it was full, then piled the pine branches around the outside of the pyramid. He scrounged in the brush until he found choice plants to include with a cherry tree branch. He chopped these up and put them onto the coals to make smoke.

He let the smoke build, feeding more leaves onto the coals at small intervals. One G-War nap later, he pulled down the pine branches, releasing all the smoke into a big puffy cloud. He tucked the hot and smoky strips of meat into a big carrying bag. The smoked meat was now cured and would last for weeks, if need be. It was important to always have a stock of food and water. For now, water wouldn't be a problem as numerous creeks ran from the Bittner Mountains. He only had two flasks. They needed a way to carry more water. Much more.

Braden adjusted the loads, putting some of the weight behind him. He spread the load and widened their blanket roll on Pack, giving G-War a better place to ride. Braden knew the 'cat would still complain, but having a full stomach would ease his discomfort.

"G! You ready to go?" Braden asked. The 'cat looked at him from his seat at the base of a tree.

'I am considering killing it while it sleeps.' The 'cat closed the mindlink and padded over to Pack, who shied away as the small predator approached. With two quick bounds and a leap, G-War was on the horse's back. Pack pranced and settled down as it accepted the 'cat and his place on its back.

"Ass." Braden adjusted himself in his saddle, trying to find a position that was less painful. It was going to be a long turn.

13 – A Cold-water Surprise

They stopped early in the daylight. Braden's seat could not take the saddle any longer. He walked for a while, but that provided little relief. They found a stream where the horses, the 'cat, and Braden lined up and drank their fill. They followed the stream toward the mountains until they came upon a small lake, little more than a pond.

The rule in Warren Deep was the bigger the lake, the bigger the things that could eat you. Braden stayed close to where the lake emptied into the stream. The approaches there were shallow and the water moved quickly.

He undid his long braid and shook his head to let his hair flow. He got to his knees at the edge of the water, where he wet his hair and his head. With sand from the small beach, he rubbed his body, one arm at a time, then each leg. He rinsed each as he finished. He let the water flow over and through his hair. Then cautiously, he waded into the water, a little at a time until he was waist deep. He ducked down quickly until he was completely underwater. The cool water was refreshing.

He stood up and made to back out, but in front of him, two eyes appeared out of the water and watched him. *A cold-water croc*, he thought. These weren't as big as their warm-water cousins, but they could still kill you. Braden was in a bad position. The croc had the upper hand. Why hadn't G-War seen this creature? He was surprised. He knew the 'cat couldn't sense fish, but he should have known about the croc.

Braden stood rock still. He moved painstakingly slow, trying not to disturb the water. The croc was capable of great bursts of speed, but mostly in a straight line. Braden did not have any weapons with him as he was naked. His clothes and knife lay on the beach.

As he watched, smaller crocs appeared behind the big croc. Braden stopped counting at ten. These were just a few hand-spans long, nose to tip of their tails. The croc had a brood. Was she protecting them or waiting for them to make the kill? Braden hoped the latter as he could probably outrun the offspring.

He was mid-thigh when the big croc surged forward, forcing a wave of water in front of it. Braden backed two steps, but fell down as the water prevented him from running as fast as his mind was telling him to go. He pushed hard to the side as the croc opened its jaws for a bite. The croc snapped down, grazing Braden's leg. The small crocs swam toward him with all the energy their little bodies could muster.

A golden streak flashed by, landing on the big croc's snout, raking the beast's eyes in an instant before attempting to leap off. The 'cat was thrown toward the shore, landing upright in shallow water.

Braden rolled once more until he faced the shore, then high-stepped out of the water. He made an arc toward his clothes, snatching the knife as he ran past. A few of the small crocs on the shore raced after him. He slid to a stop and made a broad swing, parallel to the ground, hammering a couple of the little creatures. They fell aside, broken bodies unmoving. The others came on. Another broad stroke and two more went down.

Braden backed up slowly, hoping the others would come forward. Half of them did. He slashed them to death from a rocky perch that the small crocs couldn't climb. He jumped down and dispatched the rest of them with reckless abandon.

The large croc continued to thrash about at the water's edge, infuriated at losing its eyes. He'd heard they were good eating, but had never had the opportunity to try one. Now was his chance. He crept to the side of the croc as it churned up the water and the sand of the shore. With two hands on his knife, he timed his swing as a downward chop to the exposed throat of the croc. Although this was the vulnerable underbelly, it was still far tougher than Braden imagined. He thought he had delivered a killing stroke, but it only made the croc angrier. It was hurt and dangerous.

Braden jumped out of the way as it leapt in his direction. He hopped a couple more times as the croc backed into the water. It struggled to swim, and then it submerged and disappeared from view. Bloody bubbles appeared above what was probably the deepest part of the small lake. Braden didn't think a dead croc would float, and there was no way he was swimming in there to retrieve it.

He still wouldn't have the opportunity to try some croc.

Braden put his clothes on, angry at himself for going that deep into the water. He knew better, but it felt too good.

Once he put the knife through his belt, he looked up. In front of him was one very wet Hillcat. G-War's eyes were slits as he glared at the human. "Whoa. You've looked better, G."

Braden took the shirt off that he had just put on and rubbed the 'cat to help dry him, until G-War scratched his hand, letting him know that there was nothing he could do to redeem himself.

'Why did it go into the water?' The 'cat's question burst into his mind.

"To clean off the dirt of the road! It's been how long since we've been able to clean up? Believe it or not, humans like to be as clean as any 'cat." He nodded emphatically to drive his point home. "By the way, why didn't you let me know it was there?"

'There was no problem as long as it didn't go into the water.' The 'cat wasn't forthcoming with information unless it was clearly needed. Like his help last night with the deer, which showed that self-serving information was the most readily shared. And that was the end of what passed for a reasonable conversation between Braden and the 'cat.

14 –Like an Eagle

As they continued south, staying far from the road, they spotted a couple more Crawlers, no more cold-water crocs, and plenty of deer. They saw a mutie Bear a ways off, but the horses were able to gallop past before he became interested. The Bears were the most dangerous creatures known in Warren Deep. They could paralyze a creature with their mind. Not that they needed that edge to overwhelm something so insignificant as a human. They couldn't see very well, but they were smart. Most people were fortunate enough to never see one.

The civilized areas of Warren Deep had been mostly cleansed of mutants, the kind that would kill a person anyway. When the weather changed or the ground shook, some would appear. Everyone lived with a certain amount of fear. Fear that you wouldn't bring home enough food for your family. Fear of fire, life, pain. Anything. Animals had an even greater base instinct for fear, even intelligent ones.

But Braden had never sensed any fear from G-War. Maybe the 'cat lived completely without it. He was deadly, quick, and prescient. He knew when a fight was coming. Braden suspected that he also knew how it would turn out. G-War seemed surprised that he ended up in the lake during the fight with the croc. Still, surprise wasn't fear. He looked back at the orange fur ball curled up in a nest that he made within the blankets on their pack horse. Braden expected that his claws were embedded to keep him from slipping off and getting another unwanted surprise.

Braden smiled. He had been incredibly lucky meeting the Golden Warrior. The 'cat had saved his life numerous times. The bonding was supposed to be a partnership, but Braden felt more like an honored servant. For providing food and basic services, Braden received one forever guardian that questioned his competence at all times, while occasionally delivering life-saving support.

On cue, G-War lifted his head and looked at Braden. The 'cat blinked and rose to a sitting position. *'As it should be,'* he sent over their mindlink, then added, *'Hungry.'*

They entered an area of rolling plains in the foothills of the Bittner Mountains. Rocky islands broke the monotony of the flowing grasses. It was serene. Braden wondered why no humans had settled here, for it looked like it needed nothing to be fertile. Maybe it was because they were a long way from the roads.

The ancients had laid out a system of roads that tied together the important places. These were still the main travel ways, although the road surfaces themselves were cracked and overgrown. New roads had been made in the dirt alongside those of the ancients. Although the ancients had been long gone, people were still hesitant to move into the wild.

Braden led his small party to a rocky outcropping, dismounted, and gave the area a good once over. He didn't like surprises any more than G-War. "Anything?" he asked the 'cat, trying to avoid another croc crashing the water party incident.

'Yes,' he answered almost instantly. And so began the twenty questions of their conversation.

"Will it kill me?"

'Not if it doesn't go into the water.' Braden gave the 'cat a hard look. His demeanor hadn't changed. His whiskers flicked back and forth, before settling back. Was that a laugh? Had G-War actually made a human-quality joke? Braden should have been offended, but he was impressed. Maybe in another ten cycles he would be allowed to learn the 'cat's name.

'No, it won't.' The 'cat started to scruffle around on the blanket, gave up, and jumped down, startling the horse. Pack settled down quickly. *'Follow me.'*

Another first. Even when the 'cat knew Braden was getting himself into trouble, he let him walk headlong into it. Braden couldn't remember a time when the 'cat volunteered to lead them into danger. Braden wisely followed, an arrow nocked on his Rico Bow. On the other side of the rocks, near the top, an eagle was perched. Braden had never been this close to an eagle. It was impressive and different from any other bird he'd seen.

It glistened, its feathers shiny in brown and white. It looked like he was seeing the bird in the reflection of calm lake water. It looked at him and screeched a long, awe-inspiring cry. G-War sat down and looked intently at the eagle. Their eyes locked and to someone else, it would seem as if they were in a stare down. Braden knew better. The 'cat and the eagle were talking.

'Meet Skirill,' the 'cat finally opened his mindlink. The flood of images was overwhelming and Braden fell to his knees, dropping his bow in the process. The eagle and Braden were linked through the opening that G-War created. Seeing how an unprepared mind communicated, he finally understood why G-War kept their mindlink closed most of the time. Did his mind do this to the 'cat?

"I'm Braden," he finally said after regaining some control over his own thoughts. "I am very happy to meet you." No matter what role he filled at present, he would always be a trader, always congenial to new people. Or creatures.

Images of injuries became the focus of what Skirill sent to him. Braden closed his eyes and concentrated. He saw what the eagle was looking at. Injuries to his body, a wing, and one leg. Braden opened his eyes. He could barely make out the damage from where he was. He climbed the rocks to get a closer look. The eagle's appearance was menacing, his hooked beak ready to tear flesh. Braden stopped and looked back at the 'cat. The human held out his arms, palms up in the universal what-the-hell gesture. The 'cat slightly inclined his chin, indicating that Braden should go on.

"I think you need another dip in the water." Braden concentrated hard on his memory of a dunked G-War from yesterday. The look on the 'cat's face. Their mindlink snapped shut.

Braden laughed to himself as he resumed his climb. The eagle bobbed its head. Had he seen that image?

He took a seat before the eagle with his palms outward in what he hoped showed calm. The eagle was far more impressive close up. As it stood, it was taller than G-War was long. It was easily as wide. Its wingspan would probably be as long as his old wagon. The beak was rough, with small notches marking where it had tried to rip through something hard. Maybe it had succeeded. The injuries on the eagle's body suggested that maybe it was not.

It looked like a Bear claw had caught the eagle unaware. Braden wondered if it was from the one they had seen to the north. Maybe the Bear had frozen the eagle's mind and then attacked. It was a miracle the eagle had gotten away. The great bird nudged Braden's head. He recoiled, until he realized that the eagle wasn't interested in a long examination. It was interested in the help that the 'cat probably promised.

"I have numbweed. I have a needle and thread. I have something to use as a bandage. I can help you." Braden started climbing down, over his shoulder he told Skirill, "I'll be right back."

After applying most of his stock of numbweed, Braden decided that it would be a step too far to try and stitch up the worst of the wounds, the one on the eagle's leg. He asked for G-War's help in communicating.

The 'cat harrumphed, then opened the mindlink. The images were calm, not overwhelming this time. Skirill must have been in a great deal of pain. Braden formed an image in his mind of sewing the gash together. He focused on that image, then asked politely, "Good sir! May I sew up your wound? It will greatly speed the healing process and maybe even save you a few feathers." He waited, not knowing what kind of reply he would get.

After a couple moments, the Eagle started squawking. Braden thought it sounded like he was trying to talk. "Ssssack Soooo. Esss." The "s" was pronounced as a mini screech, the "ck" as a click of the eagle's tongue. The vowels were expelled air, with the tongue shaping how it sounded, instead of non-existent lips.

"One more time, please." Braden asked.

"Sssack sooo. Esss," the eagle replied.

'He said, Thank you, yes,' G-War interjected in his thought voice. Braden was surprised that the eagle was trying to speak directly. Maybe the images from Braden's mind were too much for Skirill, as his were mostly unintelligible to the human.

Braden took out his thread and the smaller of his two coveted needles. He threaded it carefully and, taking a deep breath, plunged the needle between two feather shafts and into the skin. He pulled the skin up so he didn't dig into the muscle, then pulled the thread through. He did the same to the other side, pulling the skin tightly across the gash. He looked up to gauge the eagle's level of pain.

Skirill gave no indication that he felt the pain.

"Just a few more and we'll have it closed up. Then we'll put numbweed on one more time, say after sunrise? Then you should feel a lot better. By the way, how did you learn to speak our language?" Braden was thinking out loud rather than trying to carry on a conversation with an eagle. He continued working on the wound.

"Ohhh Kay," Skirill said. "Anngaage eee aaaeeeend. I saw. I learrr."

"You learned our language from my mind?" He was getting easier to understand the more he talked. He couldn't believe what he was hearing. "Are humans the stupidest creatures on Vii?" Warren Deep was the land north of the Great Desert on the planet the inhabitants called Vii.

'It sees truth,' G-War purred softly into his mind. He still couldn't believe it possible. The eagle had learned to speak from a few heartbeats worth of contact with his mind. What had he learned?

He saw pretty pictures of the land as the eagle flew.

Once finished sewing the wound shut, he tied off the final knot and bit through the string to cut it. The eagle giggled at this.

"Come on, Skirill. It's all I have. I didn't want to use my knife so close to your body, which is magnificent, by the way." Back to trader platitudes. He saw an eagle with his eyes, but in his mind he saw a creature that was probably superior to him. Braden had no special powers. He counted on Old Tech, his Rico Bow, to give him his edge. He practiced a great deal with it to be as deadly as possible.

He pulled the string with his right hand and he nocked the arrows on the right side. This was counter to how he had been taught as a youth, but he discovered that he could shoot far faster and just as accurately doing it his way. He could loose three arrows in the space of a single heartbeat.

Maybe that was his special power, the ability to work out problems and then act. As he was doing now on his journey to find Old Tech.

"Come on, G, you have to like something about me, don't you?"

Thumbs,' was all the 'cat said.

"Yup. That's all I am to you, opposable thumbs. And you know what, G? Don't you ever forget it!" To emphasize this, Braden waggled his thumbs around and then touched each of his fingers in turn with each of his thumbs. "Somebody's got thumbs and somebody else got no thumbs…" Braden sang out loud, dancing as much as he could from his perch on the rocks.

"I go too," Skirill said slowly, but clearly.

Braden stopped taunting G-War and turned back toward the eagle. Braden could not have hoped for better. The eagle could help them navigate the Great Desert. "Are you sure?"

"Yessss. 'rends. Hacky 'rends. Don't want 'or yoursells. Good 'rends."

"Happy friends," Braden repeated. "Don't want anything for ourselves? I want plenty, I'll have you know! Why do you think we're going to cross the Great Desert?"

"You 'elee you can. I 'elee you. You seek knowledge, not 'ower."

"Yes, I believe we can. And yes, I want knowledge. But if we find some righteous Old Tech, I'm bringing it back to make a profit, so I can settle down with a good woman."

G-War sat up straight and cocked his head while looking at Braden.

"Did you just make a dog face at me?"

'Don't be so insulting,' G-war harrumphed and haughtily strode back toward the horses.

As it got dark, the eagle hopped down the rocks, flexing his injured wing but unable to fly. The numbweed took away the pain and sped up the healing process, but they still needed time. Braden started a small fire, sheltered on three sides by the big rocks. Braden pulled out a large handful of venison. After seeing the look in Skirill's eyes, he pulled out two more gracious servings.

After eating their fill, they sat back, enjoying the warmth of the fire and the silence of the plains. "Skirill, maybe you can tell us how you got all that?" Braden asked, nodding toward the eagle's injuries.

"Sit 'aack. I tell you a story…"

15 – The Hawkoid

Skirill talked for a long time, starting with his unfortunate encounter with the mutie Bear. The fire had to be re-stoked a couple times during his monologue. By the end, Braden had to admit that Skirill was getting quite good at speaking in the human tongue and that he was an intelligent, magnificent creature.

He said that he wasn't an eagle at all. He was known as a Hawkoid, a species developed by the ancients after their arrival to help with the colonization once technology was systematically removed. The humans believed that they had to develop their self-sufficiency independently.

Braden thought this was the stupidest thing he'd ever heard. His Rico Bow was Old Tech and it made Braden's world possible. Why would they do away with it? He'd heard stories that the ancients had arrived from the stars, but he didn't believe that. How could anyone travel through the sky? Humans didn't have feathers, at least those he knew didn't.

He believed it was a war that destroyed the ancients. War always left the people and the land shattered. He had seen it not a moon ago in the west. He made a good trade with the swords, but he didn't like how he got them. It wouldn't bother him to not see that again. When would humans get enough of fighting?

He couldn't answer that. He wore a long knife and carried the Rico Bow. Who was he to throw down his means of self-defense? Someone else would have to be first to go without weapons.

And that person wouldn't last long in Warren Deep. Even in Cameron he had been forced to fight, well, G-War had anyway. And Cameron was supposed to be civilized. Maybe war was coming to set the world back even further.

What kind of Old Tech would he find? Would it make the world more peaceful or more dangerous? Maybe more comfortable, but for whom?

Braden had stopped listening to Skirill as he struggled with all the questions that entered his mind. He hadn't heard a story with this perspective. Since he had been in the Hawkoid's mind, he believed everything that Skirill said.

Skirill eyed Braden patiently. He knew that the human's attention had gone elsewhere.

Braden looked up and mumbled an apology. He regained his focus so that Skirill would continue, but the Hawkoid hesitated.

"You ha' questions?" Skirill finally asked.

"Yes and no. I have questions, but they need to make sense to me before I can ask them." Braden looked around. Maybe his real question was, who? Who were the ancients? "What do you know about the ancients?"

"They were wise and skilled. They were like gods. They created us. They created this land. They are the ancestors o' all creatures here. Their ti'e ended and they turned the world o'er to you. Us. All creatures. I ho'e they are 'roud of us, 'ut I don't think so."

Braden thought about what happened in Binghamton, in Cameron. His battle with the croc. It seemed like everyone and everything was carving out their niche with no regard to anyone else. That was not the world he envisioned. He grew up a trader. People trusted each other. People welcomed strangers, especially traders.

Not now. That didn't mean Braden had to embrace the fear.

"How do Hawkoids greet and treat members of their own family?" Braden asked. "Tell me about your family."

"We ru' our 'eaks together and 'ow." Skirill was intrigued that the human had asked. "Our nesties are our 'rothers and sisters fro' one hatching. Our click is all the nesties fro' our 'arents, 'ates for li'e. I ha'e two nesties and there are thirteen in our click. My 'arents are gone. I do not yet ha'e a 'ate."

"Hawkoids mate for life. Two and thirteen." Braden repeated back key points from a conversation in order to help him remember. His father had taught him that trick so people would like him more. It had served him well in his life. The older he got, the smarter his father was.

"Thank you for that, Skirill." Braden got up and leaned down to put his nose against the Hawkoids beak. Since he was bent over, there wasn't much of a bow left, but he tried it. Skirill chuckled and bowed back. Braden didn't know if that showed humor or joy. "And this is how humans do it." He put his hand on the uninjured shoulder of the Hawkoid, where the muscles of the breast connected with the joint to the wing, leaned in and gave Skirill a kiss on the top of his feathered head.

Braden pointed to G-War and himself. "I hate to break it to you, my new friend, but traveling with us, you probably won't find a mate." Braden turned his point into a palms up sign of submission.

'It speaks for itself,' G-War interjected.

"Are you two linked?" When it came to G-War, Braden asked a great number of questions where he already knew the answer. If his mind was disciplined enough, would he simply know, like Skirill had been able to learn his language directly from his mind? He would have to work on that.

Skirill bobbed his head once as he had already learned what that meant to the human. He had also gotten quite adept at shaking his head no.

"Your little trysts don't count, G!"

'I'm a 'cat. Has it learned nothing in the past ten cycles? Humans…'

"You get me, don't you, Skirill?" Braden pleaded. The Hawkoid nodded, then shook his head, then nodded some more. Braden looked confused.

"I don't know what that means, but it appears that I'm outnumbered."

'It has always been outnumbered.' With that, the 'cat moved away from the fire, faced the darkness, and assumed his sleeping/watching pose.

"Time to get some sleep, Skirill. With fresh minds, we will see what the daylight brings."

16 – Grasslands

The fire burned down during the night. There was no more wood and sod to burn, so they ate a cold breakfast.

Between bites, Braden shaped a plan for them to discuss. "We can continue heading south through the prairie until we get back into a more wooded area. The horses are well fed on the prairie grasses and should be up for a nice walk, plus we need to hunt and we need water. Our supply of venison is going fast. Skirill? How are you feeling this morning?"

The Hawkoid flexed his wing, stiffly and slowly at first, then a little more vigorously, ending with what Braden thought was a wince. "Good, 'ut can't 'ly this daylight." Braden opened a pouch with the numbweed and applied the last of it to Skirill's wing. If his leg or body took longer to heal, that was fine. The Hawkoid needed his wings to fly.

"I'm not sure we can make it to the woods this turn, but I know we won't if we don't get started. Which horse do you think you can best ride?"

Skirill didn't want to balance himself with his wings as that would prevent his wing from healing and maybe even set him back further. He settled for riding behind Braden with the human's braid held tightly in his beak. His claws dug into the saddle as he stood a full head taller than the human. Braden held one arm back, helping the Hawkoid balance. G-War opened their mindlink just to share his 'cat chuckling.

"Don't make me come back there and pet the good kitty!" Braden's juvenile threat did nothing to dampen the 'cat's mirth. He could feel a rumble behind him as the Hawkoid's massive chest heaved in laughter. Braden really was outnumbered.

He didn't care that they looked a strange lot, he was just happy that they covered a lot of ground on that turn. When they came to a thin creek, barely more than a trickle of water, they drank their fill then refilled the skins they had.

They pushed forward into the early evening until they reached trees sprinkled outward from the woods. It was a perfect camp for their group. A little cover, woods close by for hunting, and the open plain where Skirill could freely fly.

"I can 'ly in the woods, you know. When 'y wing is 'etter."

"Of course you can," Braden conceded. He stroked the Hawkoid's feathers absently as he looked around where they might camp. No Crawlers. No signs of animals. "What do you think, G?"

'Hungry,' the 'cat replied.

"Would you look at that! Smoked venison right where we can get it at," Braden replied sarcastically. "Unless, you might know where we can find something a little more fresh?"

The 'cat unfocused his eyes then shook his head. *'No. Not tonight.'*

"Sorry, Skirill. Maybe tomorrow." He broke out the venison for the other two as he set up the camp. He hobbled the horses so they could graze. He gathered a small supply of firewood and prepared to light a fire.

'No fire. Not tonight.' Braden trusted the 'cat implicitly. The 'cat knew there was a threat out there somewhere. If the cost of being safe was sleeping without a fire, then the price was easily paid. They would look at things again with the sunrise. He was sure it would be better after a good night's sleep.

17 – 'They come'

It wasn't. It wasn't a good night's sleep at all. And things didn't look better.

G-War tapped him awake when it was still quite dark.

'Get ready. They come,' the 'cat said directly into Braden's mind.

"Ready for what, for who," Braden whispered while trying to shake off the fog of sleep. He pulled on his long knife, put on his quiver, and readied his Rico Bow. It was dark, the moon either hadn't risen yet or had already set. Braden didn't know how long he'd been asleep. His brain wasn't fully engaged yet.

He was surprised at how hard it was to wake Skirill. A simple shaking wasn't enough. Braden grew more vigorous as the moments passed, until the Hawkoid awoke with a start and drove his beak into Braden's leather jacket. The human fell down with a crunch and loud "ow."

The 'cat's loud exasperation penetrated both their psyches. *'They come for the horses. This way.'* G-War bounded off past the horses, expecting the others to follow him. Braden ran to get in between the horses and whatever 'they' were. Skirill hopped, rather awkwardly, then broke into a run, shooting past Braden. To better protect the horses, Braden grabbed them and pulled them back toward the tree under which they camped. They were hobbled, so it was tough getting them to move.

As he was tying them off, he heard the scream of a Hillcat as it attacked something. The Hawkoid's screech followed. His friends had joined the battle. A deep snorting rumbled through the grass. An image from G-War flashed in his mind, and Braden finally knew what was coming.

A wild boar rushed at him out of the dark, the dirty tusks the brightest feature of the pig's head. Braden jumped straight up and as the boar passed beneath him, he drove his knife downward, into the back behind the shoulder blade. His knife was wrenched from his hand.

He tripped as he landed and rolled, bringing his Rico Bow in front of him. The next boar took an arrow through its eye. The third turned to avoid the human, presenting a perfect side shot from just a couple strides away. The shaft disappeared into the beast. The boar furrowed into the ground as it died while it was still running.

Another Hawkoid screech, but this time from in the air. He glanced up as Skirill made a tight wheel turn directly overhead and dove toward a target that Braden couldn't see. Braden let the bow sling across his back as he leapt two steps and pulled his knife from the dead boar's back.

Another boar rushed past. It had a Hillcat clinging to it. The 'cat was trying to get a claw into the boar's throat. He knew that boar would die and turned back just in time to avoid another beast's charge. He danced a quick sidestep to dodge the boar's tusk. He struck with his knife, but only raked a slash along its ribs. It snorted and screamed in pain, but continued charging toward the horses. Max whinnied and reared, driving its front hooves into the boar's head. The beast staggered away, stunned and bleeding.

Yet another boar ran at him from the darkness. Skirill dove in from nowhere, landing on the boar and pulling it a few strides from the ground. The flesh ripped out of its back as it fell from the Hawkoid's claws. It fell with a thump and tried to get to its hooves, but Braden was there, stabbing his knife into its side. He pulled it out, ready for the next beast to attack.

But there were no more.

Skirill dropped out of the darkness and back winged to drop lightly to the ground. His chest heaved from his exertions, and the wound on his wing trickled fresh blood. Braden took a deep breath and slid his long knife back into his belt.

They were out of numbweed, so Braden pressed his fingers against the Hawkoid's wound to stop it from bleeding. He looked around for G-War, seeing him at the extreme range of his night eyes, maybe five strides away, sitting calmly next to the tree where the horses were tied, casually licking the blood from his paws.

Once the bleeding stopped, Braden rubbed some of his own saliva onto the wound. It helped him when he was hurt, so maybe it would help the Hawkoid. Skirill cocked his head as he watched Braden work.

As he finished, Skirill head butted him and said, "You 'ought well, human 'riend."

"You fought well, too, my Hawkoid friend." Braden hesitated for a heartbeat. "My friend." He put his hand on Skirill's shoulder.

"Hey! You okay, G?"

'Why wouldn't I be?' Braden didn't have an answer to that. He would always ask, just in case. He knew that he needed the 'cat far more than the 'cat needed him. When the time came, he would be there and do what he had to do for the 'cat.

Skirill head butted Braden one more time, then moved away from the tree. He didn't want the horses to step on his tail feathers.

"Time to make a fire! We've got some pork to smoke." Braden busied himself with banking wood for the fire. He didn't have evergreen branches to build a smoker, but he had a blanket. He needed branches to make his lattice work to hold the meat and keep the blanket out of the fire. He started to climb the tree, then had an idea.

"Skirill. Can you fly to the top of the tree and break off some branches for me?" The Hawkoid flexed his wing a few times. He hopped and ran forward then with a couple strong strokes, he was airborne. He disappeared into the darkness, then reappeared a few heartbeats later, back winging to land in the top branches. Braden heard snapping and the limbs started to fall.

He waited until Skirill called that he was done, then he gathered the wood. Peeling some strips of the soft bark, he used it to tie the thin branches together. He built his framework, then started the fire, letting it dry the lattice work with its heat. He let the fire build on itself, then went to work butchering the more choice strips of meat. When all was said and done, he probably had more than his own body weight in pork strips. He filled his field smoker about a quarter of the pile. He added some leafy branches to the fire and let that build into a heavy smoke. He wrapped it all in the blanket to keep the smoke in.

Braden took some raw slices of meat to Skirill, who thanked him before tossing it down whole. Hawkoids didn't chew. They ripped. Braden was happy not to be on the receiving end of that beak. Again, anyway. If he didn't have on his jacket earlier, he wasn't sure how much damage the Hawkoid's beak would have done to him. He felt his chest. He had a bruise, but it was minor. That probably equated to a Hawkoid love tap. That last head butt was harder. He'd have to talk to Skirill about the Hawkoid's expression of affection. It hurt!

18 – Now They're Three

It took the rest of the night to smoke the meat. Braden saved a little for Skirill and G-War, who both preferred their meat raw. They could enjoy a breakfast more to their taste.

The 'cat and the Hawkoid slept soundly while Braden worked. He was dog tired when morning came, but their food problem had solved itself.

Although the boar pack had been small, the horses would have stood no chance alone, their soft bellies vulnerable to the boars' tusks. If Braden had been alone, he would have climbed the tree and picked off the boars one by one using his bow. Who knew what G-War would have done by himself, maybe take over the pack, leading them to take over all of Warren Deep. Braden laughed to himself at the thought of the 'cat riding the lead boar.

By protecting the horses, the three of them had secured their ride. They had a long way to go and walking would take all the fun out of it.

Braden shook out the blanket the best he could, but it would reek of smoke for many turns to come. He used that blanket to wrap the smoked pork.

He saddled one horse and prepared the blanket pack on the saddle of the other. With one blanket now filled with pork and the other with the rest of their goods, there was no room for the 'cat. Could the three of them ride one horse? Probably, but it would not be comfortable.

Skirill solved this problem by saying that he could fly.

"Me and you, G. Just like old times." When Golden Warrior of the Stone Cliffs was still a kitten, he rode in Braden's lap in the back of the wagon. The boy and the 'cat were inseparable, mostly because Braden had never had a friend. They were traders. They met different people every turn.

He played with all the kids they ran across, but they never stayed long. Stop. Trade. Get back on the road.

He wouldn't trade his life for anything. The town people were soft. The nomads weren't friendly. The farmers were always digging in the ground. No, the life of a trader was what he loved. And he traveled with the creature he cared most about. Plus he was on a journey to find the biggest and best trade ever.

G-War covered the space from the ground to Braden's lap in a single smooth leap, landing softly, yet still using his claws, just enough to let the human know his place. He settled in on Braden's lap and Braden's new caravan was off. He thought of the group as the caravan, no longer needing the wagon to anchor their trade.

Skirill perched on top of the tree and waited for a long time before he took to the sky. In no time at all, he overtook the horses and flew on, gliding gracefully above it all. He soon became a mere speck on the horizon.

G-War opened their mindlink and instantly, he could see through the Hawkoid's eyes. It was disconcerting and Braden had to grab two handfuls of the horse's mane to keep from falling. The view was incredible, the entire world laid out before him. Braden sharpened his focus and let his mind become one with the Hawkoid's. Other Hawkoids, all larger, flew around. A nest with eggshells. Overwhelming hunger! Mother! A rabbit. Joy! Cliffs. Falling. Flying! Soaring.

Braden bounced awake with a start. They had only gone a few steps, but he had lived half a lifetime as his Hawkoid friend. He understood what the screeches and calls meant. He could recognize Skirill's nesties and click. He had a map of Warren Deep in his mind from the viewpoint of one high above the ground. He knew which way they needed to go to get to Whitehorse because he had seen it. It was not far off. A little more than a turn on horseback, a fraction of that on the wing.

G-War settled into his lap and even started purring. Maybe the 'cat was proud of the progress the human made with the mindlink. Once it became clear what was possible, Braden actively sought it and found it.

Braden attempted to open a link with G-War, testing his thought speech. *'You are the best friend anyone could ever have.'*

'I know,' the 'cat responded in a friendly tone.

'Ass.'

19 – Lift the Dark Cloud

Between G-War and Skirill, Braden would never have to enter an unknown area. He could see and feel what was ahead. Whitehorse seemed safe. He saw nothing out of the ordinary from Skirill's viewpoint high above the town. G-War felt no immediate threat, but when many humans were in one place, the 'cat couldn't be sure.

They needed to get better storage for water and then buy some grain to take with them. Maybe a two-wheeled cart to pull behind the pack horse would make life a little better for everyone. He had three vials of saffrimander that should get him everything he wanted. He also had gold and silver.

He didn't want to stay long in Whitehorse. Only as long as it took to secure what they needed for their attempt to cross the Great Desert.

Skirill stayed on the outskirts of town, perched high in a tree. Braden and G-War rode on Max while Pack trailed, carrying two large bundles. They headed straight for the market square. Braden didn't need to create a persona to try and fool these people. He was a trader and that was the role he played best.

He tied the horses to a hitching post and walked to the center of the square. From deep within, he summoned his biggest voice. "Hear ye one, hear ye all! Saffrimander! From the western wilds, the finest spice in all of Warren Deep. Saffrimander! This daylight, someone will own this vial of the spice. I am Braden, sanctioned by the Caravan Guild as a Free Trader. This daylight, at midday, I begin the auction." The usual merchants took notice of the announcement and he saw how they calculated ways to win the saffrimander. His real targets were the servants and regular people in the square. He needed them to take word to the well off, to the wealthy.

Leaving G-War to protect their goods, Braden went in search of water flasks or casks and a two-wheeled wagon.

The water flasks were common and readily available, so Braden bought one trader's entire stock – a cool dozen flasks for a silver shekel each, but Braden worked the best deal in buying them for a single gold piece. Ten silver to a piece of gold. He wanted a couple casks as well so they could carry water for the horses. The horses would drink everything they could get and then some. The rest drank little in comparison. If Skirill could find an oasis or two, their chances would greatly improve. The Hawkoid had quite remarkable vision, as Braden had seen for himself.

Braden started with the stables. He took smoked pork and smoked venison with him. It never hurt to ply the hired hands with food. Home baked cookies were best, but he didn't quite have any of those. Braden's plan was thwarted when he ran into the stable master before meeting any of the stable hands.

"Greetings, good sir!" Braden started with his routine. "My compliments to you on your fine establishment." The stable master stopped him right there with a hand held up.

"Who the crap are you, you stinking dung heaping pile of slime?" Braden had too often dealt with hostile customers to be perturbed at the stable master's rude diatribe.

"Free Trader Braden. I am very pleased to make your acquaintance…?" Braden held out a hand for a shake and a name, but the stable master spit on it.

"That's what I think of your Free Trader, boy. Crap off, you crapping pile of crap!"

"I will leave you to your thoughts, then, good sir. Please to have a fair turn of joy." Braden knew there would be no deal here this daylight. The stable master turned and lifted one leg, forcing a heinous fart in Braden's direction. Too late as he was already rapidly exiting the stables. Using his newly discovered ability to talk with the 'cat without talking aloud, he exercised his thought speech, '*G, did you get any of that? Are we in danger here?*'

'*Yes. No. He is simply a foul creature.*'

Braden laughed fully at that. A lady pulled her young daughter close as they hustled past, their eyes averted. "Sorry," Braden mumbled, still smiling. Next stop, the blacksmith.

The blacksmith was far more congenial, and welcomed Braden to his hot and stuffy workshop. The heavily muscled man was covered in dirt mixed with sweat, forming channels running down his chest and back. He had a warm smile and readily offered his oversized paw. They shook heartily, and Braden was pleased the man did not crush his hand.

"Good sir, I'm looking for two casks to hold water and a two-wheeled cart to carry them. After a most unpleasant conversation with the stable master, I am no further in my quest. Would you be so kind as to point me in a direction where I may find what I seek?"

"The stable master! Ha!" He started to laugh and slapped Braden's back with a massive man paw. "He's in a right foul mood this daylight, isn't he?"

"How did you know?"

"Because he's that way every turn. Ha!" The blacksmith's voice boomed. The stable master could probably hear him, as he was only two buildings away. "You've come to the right place. My partner next door is the woodworker. We make casks together. And I'm working on a cart in the back. It's older, but the owner might consider a trade. See? Everything you want." Braden nodded indifferently. Now that he knew what goods were available, the delicate dance of give and take began. If one seemed too needy, he would pay a higher price.

"Let me see the cart and then we'll talk about casks." They went behind the blacksmith's shop, back into the fresh air that was only a little less warm. A rickety old cart stood there, its axle broken. Braden looked at the blacksmith through narrowed eyes, instantly wary. He looked around to see if it was a trap, see if he was going to be robbed.

The blacksmith put up his hands to show good faith. "No, no, no. Don't worry. I'm not out to steal from you. The cart is mine. I wasn't working on it as I don't have anything to pull it. I can have my partner shore up the wood here, and here." He pointed to a couple areas that definitely needed help. "I won't bother trying to fix the axle. I can replace it before the sun reaches its height," he offered.

"How long for the woodworker to do his work?" Braden asked noncommittally.

"A little longer, just past midday. Look here," he said as he crooked a finger at the underside of the cart. Braden walked around the cart to put it between him and the blacksmith. Then he leaned down to look underneath. The carriage and frame were in far better condition than the rest of the cart. Braden could see the blacksmith's legs and that he had not moved. For some reason, he didn't trust the man, so he remained wary.

'G, what are you getting from this guy?' The 'cat didn't answer right away. Braden opened the mindlink carefully. G-War must have let him in. He saw clearly through the 'cat's eyes. He was watching a female cat with great interest. *'G. G!'*

'I don't think I like its new ability to talk. It interrupts important thoughts.'

'I'll leave you alone if you can get something from this guy. I don't trust him and I don't know why.' He looked up at the blacksmith and nodded his head as he continued his examination of the cart.

'He is thinking of murder. It darkens him. Not us. Make the trade.' G-War cut the mindlink with a nearly audible snap.

Braden was pleased that he had sensed something amiss.

"What are you willing to trade for the cart, repaired as you described, and two casks?" Braden opened. The dance had begun.

When it was over, the blacksmith and woodworker were standing together, pleased with the deal. Braden had gone deep into his purse because he started to like the big man and his partner. He wanted him to be happy and maybe avoid the dark path he was considering going down.

"Thank you, kind gentlemen! I look forward to coming back, soon after midday, to pick up my cart and my casks." He handed over half of the gold and silver agreed to, with the rest to be exchanged upon final delivery. They all shook hands, then both the woodworker and the blacksmith started taking measurements to complete their part of the bargain.

Braden watched for a few heartbeats, then put his hand on the blacksmith's shoulder. Their eyes met. "Don't do it. You'll be different if someone dies. It's not worth it." The big man looked at him oddly, gave him a single nod, and went back to work.

Braden felt the dark cloud lift.

20 - Saffrimander

At midday, Braden was standing tall in the market square. There were more standing around than before, but not anywhere near as many as he hoped. As a Free Trader, he had committed to starting the auction at midday and so he was obligated to live up to his commitment.

Without saying a word, he pulled a vial of saffrimander from his belt pouch and held it high. He let everyone take in the sight.

"Saffrimander! You all know what it is. Magical! Mystical! The rarest and most exotic spice in Warren Deep! Who will make the first offer?" He bellowed over the small crowd. The bidding was started by another trader.

"Ten pieces of gold," a bearded man shouted hopefully.

"Twenty."

"Thirty."

"Five platinum!" A newcomer offered. It was the equivalent of fifty gold pieces or five hundred pieces of silver. It was still a low price for Saffrimander. Far below what Braden traded to get it.

He would take a loss! But there was no loss. He was no longer a trader. He was a nomad, a searcher. Anything he received was an investment toward crossing the Great Desert. An investment in the biggest trade ever. Braden smiled as the price climbed agonizingly slowly. He would always be a trader.

"Ten platinum and that's my final offer!" Another newcomer chimed in. This man was older and wore fine clothes. Braden didn't care what this man's final offer was, he only cared what THE final offer was, but the older man must have been someone as everyone deferred once he spoke. There were no more bids. Braden read the body language of the assembled people and determined to play to the man's ego.

"This is the lowest price I've seen in all my turns. My compliments to you, sir, on your deal. Ten platinum it is!" Braden jumped down. He handed the vial to the man, who turned to go without paying.

"I'm sorry. Ten platinum, please." Braden reached to stop the man from leaving, but was himself stopped by another man he hadn't noticed. This man pulled a small purse from his belt and dropped it into Braden's hand.

"And that's the end of it," he said as he too turned and walked off. Usually, the buyer counted the money in the open, reinforcing the trader's trust in the bidder. Braden thanked people for attending and bidding. As the last walked off, he opened the pouch to find two platinum pieces and fifteen gold. He'd been ripped off, as he suspected he would be by the way the crowd treated the older man, but Braden hadn't thought his duplicity would stoop so low as to pay a third of the agreed-to price.

He saw the second high bidder, a man who had bid eight platinum, at the edge of the market. He went to him.

"Are you still interested in a vial of saffrimander?" The man's eyes perked up. "Eight platinum and it's yours," Braden said pulling the vial partially from his purse, shielding it from any other prying eyes.

"I'll give you five," he replied. Braden appreciated the man's shrewdness, but acted insulted nonetheless. He put the vial back in the purse at his belt and walked away. He knew that G-War was watching them as he had returned to his perch on Braden's horse. He felt a hand on his shoulder. "Wait. Eight is all I have. Would you take my last shekel?"

"I'll take your eight and a loss, and give you five gold back. Final offer." Braden wanted the power of platinum. If he ran into trouble, money could buy a way out. The more he had, the better his chances of surviving. Then again, that was how a trader in the civilized world thought. He was heading into the Great Desert.

"Done," the man said before Braden could further refine his "final" offer. They made the trade, huddled closely together. With one last handshake, the two went their separate ways.

He'd keep the last vial to himself. The trader in him refused to take a further loss. And if he ever ran across the old man again, he would set things straight. The man owed Braden six platinum and five gold. That was non-negotiable. The turn would come where he would pay. It was the law of the trade.

21 – Running from the Fight

When the cart was ready, the blacksmith found Braden in the market buying dried greens and hard cheeses. The big man seemed excited about how the cart had turned out.

Braden also found himself pleased with the final result. The woodworker had performed magic with the cart, transforming it into one that was twice as high as the rickety old version. It contained no buckboard, so a driver would have to balance across two added boards and a leather strap.

Braden hadn't intended to drive from the cart, but the braces and leather strap were a nice touch. He thanked both the men profusely and gave them a couple extra gold pieces for their efforts. Once the trade was made, going above and beyond solidified one's reputation, but it generally earned the craftsman no extra gold. Their reputations for high quality helped garner greater value in future trades. Call it better marketing, as long as the buyer shared the information.

The casks were sturdy and new. He tied these within the cart using some rough twine. He brought the horses over, tying his mount to the back of the cart and hooking up the pack horse to the harness and leads. The horse seemed indifferent to pulling or carrying, and Pack took his new task as stoically as his last. Once hooked up, Braden waved at the blacksmith and the woodworker as he drove through the square. He headed north out of town. No one needed to know his intended destination.

Once out of sight of the town, he turned his horse east toward the Bittner Mountains. The pack horse, pulling the cart with their two blanket packs and two empty casks, was behind him as they disappeared into the trees.

We are being followed,' G-War passed via their mindlink.

"I thought so," Braden answered out loud. *What do you see, Skirill?* he said with his thought voice. He was answered with a picture from high above of four men on horses, trotting along without a sense of urgency. They turned where Braden had turned from the road, following the cart's tracks toward the woods. Skirill took flight, gaining altitude by making a wide circle, keeping the men in the middle of his vision.

They had a good lead, but with the cart, they could not hope to long outdistance the men. Braden didn't want to fight. He did not know why he was having such a streak of bad luck. He was used to being welcomed to towns, treated well, and given a happy send off. The last three towns had been nightmares.

This confirmed his decision to seek Old Tech. He needed to get away until things settled down. If he had to fight, let it be the unknown. The last thing he wanted was to be an outcast within his own land. If he killed these men, he wouldn't be able to return. He doubted that he'd be able to return to Cameron or Binghamton. Memories were short; time would be his only friend.

He needed to buy more of it. So he doubled back, taking a wide route to the south and then west to the main road. Through Skirill's eyes, he saw when to stop and let the men pass him, still following his tracks to the east. He then raced his team to the road, heading north as fast as the horses could run. He kept going until he could conceal a turn back to the east. He headed into the trees once again, stopping the horses well off the road.

He went back and erased their tracks, leaving no sign for the men to follow. He slowly walked the horses deeper into the woods. Skirill floated to the south above the men, who picked up their pace when they saw the track leading back toward the road. He watched through the Hawkoid's eyes as the men reached the road, frantically looking about. When they picked up the track of the cart, one among many that had recently traveled the road, they galloped north.

And they kept going straight past where Braden had turned off. Skirill glided east, directing Braden along the best route until he could get into the open and put more distance between them and the men. G-War didn't sense anything near them, so they pressed on.

Skirill made one last sweep toward the road, going higher and higher until he caught sight of the men as specks far to the north. Braden's maneuver had lost them. He wanted to find out why they were following, but not badly enough to fight. Something was happening in Warren Deep, something unpleasant and dangerous.

If traders stopped trading, the towns would become outposts. Distrust would grow. Then fear. Fear drove people like a stampeding herd that couldn't be turned. They couldn't be stopped. All Braden wanted was to ply his trade, enjoy his life, and in some future cycle of the seasons, settle down. He couldn't do any of that if he was constantly on the run. He breathed a sigh of relief. He was happy that he didn't have to ambush the four men. The only way he could have won that fight was by killing them at a distance using his Rico Bow.

If they had no evil intent, then Braden would be the one in the wrong. He was certain that wasn't the case, but was glad he didn't have to find out.

They pushed forward until the horses were exhausted, even though daylight remained. Skirill winged away for one last look and saw that no one followed. They were safe, for the moment anyway.

22 – The Caravan Rests

They camped by a small stream, where they drank freely. Braden filled the casks and his new stock of flasks. This increased the weight on the cart, slowing them down, but they had no other choice.

This part of the forest teemed with wildlife and shortly, G-War, Braden, and Skirill had killed a mix of rabbits and squirrels. Skirill ate his kills after ripping them apart and swallowing the pieces whole. Braden thought the Hawkoid must have one hell of a stomach to digest all of that. It made his stomach churn just to think about it. G-War avoided the bones when possible, preferring the softer parts of the flesh.

Braden liked his meat cooked. He cleaned two squirrels and one rabbit, letting them hang until nightfall. He wouldn't risk a smoky fire in the daylight.

He searched the underbrush of the surrounding area. They needed more numbweed. He wanted some tubers, and maybe other wild vegetables if he could find any. Skirill and G-War were carnivores. Braden needed more, wanted a great deal more than just meat, but was willing to settle. His last two trips into town weren't long enough for him to get a bed and a good home-cooked meal. He would have been happy with a bad home-cooked meal.

When Braden returned to their camp, Skirill was asleep on a branch overhead. G-War was asleep in the back of the cart. The horses were even down and out cold. Braden was instantly alert, adrenaline surging through his body. He'd heard of mutants who could put people to sleep with their breath. The mutie Bears could freeze beings with their mind.

'Is it too much to ask that it is quiet?' G-War asked via their mindlink.

A certain amount of paranoia was healthy as it kept a person on his toes.

Braden felt like he was going a little too far. G-War would have let him know if anything was wrong. Skirill probably would have, too. The horses should be sleeping; they worked hard this turn.

And Braden felt fine. He had not yet eaten, so he wasn't burdened with digesting the huge meals of his companions.

'Sorry, G. Too many weird things lately,' he responded to the 'cat, in his quietest thought voice.

He went to work building a small fire where he could hang his one pot and make a rabbit stew. His mouth watered thinking about it.

While his dinner was slowly heating, Braden pulled out his rudder. It had been at the bottom of the one blanket pack for many turns. He needed to update it. Carefully, with his fine pencils, he updated his entries, especially those regarding the path he had taken from Cameron to Whitehorse, back to his current position. In another half turn, he should cross the trail he made previously. This was the value of the rudder, keeping the trader on the best path. He smiled to himself. He would remain true to his craft.

23 – Heading South

The night was thankfully uneventful. Come morning, man, creature, and beast alike were well rested. They found their earlier track and followed it south, until the point where it turned west toward Whitehorse. They turned east instead.

Skirill scouted far ahead. He flew to the northern border of the Great Desert, looking for the easiest way south. Skirill found a stream in the foothills of the Bittner Mountains, close to the Great Desert. They determined that would be the best place to camp and get their fill of water before plunging into the barren wasteland.

Braden looked at the two horses and the cart. G-War was crouched in the cart, on the softest place he could find, the blanket pack of smoked meat, watching as the group passed through the forest and into the grassy plains. Braden thought of them as his caravan. Although he considered them equals, he took responsibility for their health and well-being.

They continued across the plains in silence. Skirill spent some time aloft, but most of his time was in trees or on rocks, waiting for the caravan to catch up. He hunted while he waited, catching a few ground squirrels, which he ate in single, massive Hawkoid gulps.

No one followed. No one was ahead. The Hawkoid's view of the Great Desert showed a seemingly endless waste.

They pushed on, but wouldn't make the hills until the next turn. They camped by a lone tree, old, its growth diminished by dry earth and a lack of water. Braden did not make a fire. The 'cat climbed into the tree, relaxing on a lower limb with all four legs dangling. G-War liked this position. Braden called it the lazy 'cat. Skirill stayed on the highest branch that would support his weight. Braden hobbled the horses so they could graze on their own. He reclined against the tree and ate sparingly of the smoked meat and cheese. It might have to last for weeks.

It would be good to get another deer. And maybe even harvest some of the plains grass to fill the cart. It wouldn't be heavy, but it would come in handy.

He put some water from the flasks into their cooking pot and let the horses drink. They drank three pots between them. That was three flasks worth. Braden refilled the flasks from the casks and watched as the water level dropped.

Being a trader, Braden could quickly do basic calculations in his head. At this rate, the water in the casks would last roughly two weeks. If they drank more, which he suspected they would in the dryness of the desert, then it might last as little as one week.

With Skirill, their chances of finding a water hole, an oasis, were vastly improved. When they reached the last stream in the foothills, they would discuss how best to attack the Great Desert. Braden's success counted more on his companions than him. He looked at them as they rested.

One's true measure could be found in the value of one's friends.

24 – Other Hawkoids

Another uneventful night followed by an uneventful daylight. The cart trundled on, leaving a light scar in the grasses of their wake. Braden's horse ambled continuously forward, toward a spot on the horizon that Skirill had directed them to. He sat there now, waiting, watching.

G-War stretched out his senses. He could feel nothing except for the human and the Hawkoid. The Hillcat wasn't used to such voids, and he expected that the Great Desert would be even worse. He needed to reconcile himself with the quiet or he would go crazy.

Braden was used to the relative quiet. He heard the horses crunching the dry grasses, scuffing the earth beneath. He heard their leather harnesses slapping, the creak of the cart. The grass swished in the breeze. He felt the sun on his face.

Where G-War was anxious, Braden was alive. What he felt and heard was the freedom of the open road. This was the trader's time to relax and enjoy the wonders of the caravan's journey. He looked at the 'cat and wished him peace.

He saw and felt Skirill in the distance as he took off and climbed. He flew higher and higher past the foothills and toward the Bittner Mountains. He flew hard and straight.

Braden opened his mind, but couldn't touch the Hawkoid. '*G, do you know where Skirill is going?*'

'*Yes,*' was the 'cat's short reply.

'*Where?*' Braden asked in his thought voice, ignoring the fact that the cat answered his first question without answering the real question.

'The near peaks. He has seen other Hawkoids and is flying to meet them.'

'Are the Hawkoids friendly?' Braden asked. He had never seen one up close until they met Skirill. Circumstances forced that meeting and enabled Braden to establish their friendship. He hadn't heard of other humans interacting with Hawkoids. The humans thought they were eagles. They kept to themselves, frequenting areas where humans were scarce.

'No. Hawkoids and humans are not compatible.'

"But Skirill..." Braden said out loud, now confused. Through G-War, the Hawkoid and the human had talked. Without that, surely Braden would not have attempted to work on Skirill's wounds?

'Skirill is his own Hawkoid. He breaks tradition. He will confirm shortly that he is not allowed back among his own kind. He is and always will be an outcast.'

"I didn't know. I'm not sure Skirill made a good trade. What can we do to help?"

G-War mentally shrugged. If Braden understood 'cat logic, the shrug meant that there was nothing to do. Once the choice was made, he dealt with it.

As Braden thought about it, he realized what G-War had said. "'He will confirm shortly...' you said. You can see the future, can't you?" The 'cat didn't respond.

25 – Hawkoid Disdain

Skirill had seen the Hawkoids as they circled near the cliffs far above him. He knew that his own kind barely tolerated him. Hawkoids were intelligent, but they were limited in their ambitions. He was unique and that alone made him stand apart. The others couldn't think like he thought. They didn't see the world as it could be. They only saw it as it was.

He wanted a mate, confident that their offspring would be like him. He could help the Hawkoids become more than just cliff dwellers, hunters of small game. He could help them develop a culture that rivaled that of the humans!

When he was cast out, he sought the mutie Bear to prove that he was superior or die trying. It hadn't worked. He failed and almost died because of his arrogance. He was amazed that he had survived. The Bear had frozen his mind, but only until the first slash of that massive paw, then Skirill cast off the mental reins and flew. He flew for all he was worth, but the blood streamed from his wounds and he had lost his vigor.

That was over seven turns ago. Since then, a great deal had changed. Now, he had firsthand knowledge of how the one with the long braid thought, how he worked. Braden was unique, like him. They could speak without speaking and that helped Skirill learn to talk like a human. Braden accepted him as an equal. He wanted the other Hawkoids to see this and accept him as readily.

When he saw the flock of nesties, he knew he had to go to them.

Hawkoids protected their territory, but not from other Hawkoids. They were intelligent enough to know that a war would lead to their destruction. They argued, but never fought. They would challenge each other to duels of dancing in the sky, trying to out-fly one another, weaving intricate patterns, one around the other. Sometimes accidents happened, but they generally ended with one victor, however, a good dance could result in both winning, increasing the respect they received from all who watched.

As Skirill approached this nesting ground, the parent Hawkoids took to the sky, circling between him and their young in order to establish a boundary which he was not allowed to pass. He honored their request and turned to fly perpendicular. He passed them, waving his wings and bobbing his head in greeting as he continued toward a rocky spire in a neutral area away from the nest.

The other Hawkoids bobbed their heads in greeting and followed, landing a short way off.

To a human, Hawkoid language sounded like screeches with clicks. Hawkoids were equally visual and oral. Their language wasn't just spoken. A screech could mean a number of things depending on how the head and body moved when the sound was made. The clicks covered an even broader range, far more than what humans could hear. The speed of the clicks, the range, and the coordinated head movements helped enrich the quality of the language.

"Greetings, fellow Hawkoids. My name is Skirill. Thank you for the good hunting below." Skirill clicked and screeched the ritual greeting, bowing fully at the end to show his respect and deference to their hunting grounds.

"Greetings Skirill. I am Teeleech and this is my mate, Awkar. The fertile hunting ground serves us all." He ended with a deep bow.

"Are there any others near? I have flown far seeking my life companion and have yet to be successful."

"To the north. There are no more Hawkoids to the south or the west. We have not flown beyond the peaks to the east. They are too high and we don't wish to get lost on the other side."

"Thank you, my brother. My journey will continue then. Before I go, what do you know of the Great Desert?"

"The barren land to the south? We know little. There is no hunting in the Great Desert. You fly. You get hot. You don't eat or drink. We don't go there."

"Do you know of any water holes there, no matter how far in?"

"I have personally seen trees and green, but it was far in the distance and I was already cooked. I barely made it back," Teeleech said, emphasizing his story with a series of deep bows and wide head shakes.

"Please tell me where, point me in that direction," Skirill asked, needing the information. Teeleech went into a long explanation, detailing all the markers he had seen, all the waypoints. He noted that the sands often shift and much could be different. He also begged Skirill not to try it. There was nothing in the Great Desert worth a Hawkoid's life.

"I travel with a human and a Hillcat. We have water and food to help us on our journey." Teeleech and Awkar stiffened.

"Hawkoids do not travel with humans. They do not travel with the Hellcats. We eat 'cats," Awkar said coldly.

"I've never heard of a Hawkoid traveling with a human," Teelech added diplomatically as he looked at his mate. Awkar continued to shake and bob her head.

"He saved my life after I fought a mutant Bear. He asked for nothing in return. These humans are more than I ever thought. They can be dangerous and they can be great friends. I prefer the latter and have been rewarded with his friendship."

"No, no, no. Hawkoids do not travel with humans," Awkar repeated forcefully. She was so agitated that she almost fell and finally decided to fly from her perch.

"Well, that's that then. We wish you well." Teeleech launched himself into the air using his powerful legs. He fell smoothly until the air filled his wings and he glided down and away from Skirill.

"I guess that's that then," he said in the human tongue to the empty spire. "I a' Skirill the Outcast and I will show the hu'an a way across the

Great Desert." He looked after the retreating Hawkoids, despair in his heart at the loss of his people.

26 – The Camp before the Storm

Skirill leapt from the rock and angled away from the nest. He fell into a glide, but that didn't match his mood. He wanted speed. He let his wings fold back along his body, letting his wing tips give him just enough lift. He picked up speed until the wind screamed past his head. He roared toward the foothills at a dangerous pace. Even Hawkoids had limits, and he was pushing them. His wing was mostly healed, but not completely. He risked more injury. He needed to get his frustration under control.

He extended his wings away from his body a little at a time until he leveled off, then rose gently into a long glide. His wings lifted him effortlessly. He circled once without flapping his wings, coasting in for a flawless landing on the rocks beside the stream.

The flight from the cliffs was far quicker than the flight up. Despite his side trip, Skirill was still at the stream before Braden and his caravan.

When Braden and G-War arrived with the horses, Skirill had dragged a few branches to help Braden start the fire. In the foothills of the Bittner Mountains, there was a little bit of everything--woods, plains, wildlife, water, and shelter. Each of them could find something to their taste as they rested and prepared.

Braden unhooked the cart and hobbled the horses. He set up camp, knowing that they would probably stay there for as many turns as necessary while they planned their attack on the Great Desert.

Skirill sat on a boulder nearby. His body was massive, bigger than the Hillcat's. His chest feathers were finally clean and shown a glistening white in the waning daylight. His wings and back were a dark brown, with light brown streaks. His head was covered in short, light brown feathers. On the rock, he stood with his claws spread, talons hooked and ending in needle-sharp points. They were longer than a person's middle finger. His beak was slim, yet squarish, ending in a fine point, made to penetrate soft flesh. His beak was strong enough to break thin bones, big enough to rip through Braden's neck in a single bite.

Skirill watched the human study him, finally ending with a nod in the Hawkoid's direction. Skirill nodded back. He needed someone to be proud of him. Getting shunned by his fellow Hawkoids weighed on him heavily. His body did not betray his sadness. Maybe the human and the 'cat would help him bring glory to himself and by extension, all Hawkoids. At that point, he was happy that a warrior with Braden's inner peace had accepted him into his nest.

G-War drank his fill from the stream, casually listening in on both Braden and Skirill's thoughts. The 'cat was gifted among Hillcats. Most simply linked with their human and then went about their business. G-War's mindlink was strong. He had trouble in towns where there were too many humans with their chaotic thoughts beating against him. His dalliances helped shore up his defenses and kept him calm. Even with this, he had lost control in Cameron. He hadn't meant to kill the two men in the square, but something evil hung over the town and made him fight as if he was fighting against the world's darkness, fighting for his life.

He liked the calm of this journey. There were moments of excitement, but it was usually peaceful. He understood Skirill's pain, having left the clutch of his Hillcat litter while still very young. He had run across few of his kind in the last ten cycles. He turned his head until he could see his own body, orange with black dots and one slash back towards his tail continuing down his left leg. He was sleek and long legged. His body was a little smaller than the average Hillcat's, but he was strong. This made him faster and, in his mind, more deadly.

Braden had been right. The Golden Warrior could see into the future, but no longer than it took a heart to beat fifty times. It was enough to save their lives, but not enough to change how they lived those lives. He didn't know their destiny.

Braden busied himself with getting their camp ready, setting things up and preparing for a relaxing evening, doing little, and most importantly, not doing it on a horse. He wasn't yet accustomed to long rides. He thought that he might be getting bow-legged and that he had a permanent bruise at the end of his tailbone. He didn't even have any numbweed to put on it. They needed to rectify that before they continued their journey.

When he looked up at his companions, they were both looking at each other and at him. He couldn't sense anything from either, so G-War had his mindlink closed.

"What?" Braden said, holding his hands up. "What did I do?"

27 – Bonding

G-War had so conditioned Braden that whenever he saw the 'cat looking at him, he assumed it was to highlight one of his many flaws. Skirill bobbed his head in the way that Hawkoids did when they laughed. G-War shook his head has he often did when Braden said stupid things. Pet the nice kitty, indeed.

"I missed the joke. C'mon, G, let me in." The mindlink opened. Braden could sense both G-War and Skirill.

'What are you two laughing at? Or should I say, who are you laughing at?'

'It's so sensitive,' G-War mocked. *'Nothing like that.'*

'I was thinking,' Skirill began in his edged form of human thought speech, interrupting the 'cat. *'I flew to the cliffs. I saw my Hawkoid brothers there. I asked them about the Great Desert and they showed me where an oasis might be.'*

'That's great! Will it take long to get there? Which way do we need to go?' Braden's thoughts rushed at them in a jumble. G-War looked at him sternly. *'Sorry. Go on, Skirill,'* he said, more reserved.

'Once they learned I traveled with you both, they chased me away.' Skirill looked down at his talons, not wanting to meet the eyes of his companions. *'It's not the first time I've been chased away. My nesties. My click. I wanted to kill the Bear to show them that I was better than them. That I was the best of them.'* He paused to flex his talons as he remembered the fight that wasn't a fight. It was him getting mauled and flying away.

'I showed them, didn't I? I showed that I wasn't any smarter than they were, even though I told them all that I was. I told them that we needed to develop a culture more like the humans if we were ever to realize our full potential.' Skirill shuffled back and forth. *'They weren't ready for that, and I wasn't the right Hawkoid to suggest it.'*

He hesitated and looked at Braden. *I've been shunned by my own people. I'm an outcast,'* he said with a final exasperated sigh.

'So?' replied G-War. The Hillcat saw things as much more black and white. He saw that Skirill had eaten well since joining with Braden, his terrible wounds were mending, and he was safe. Life was simpler for a Hillcat.

'What G means to say is that we are all outcasts,' Braden said matter-of-factly. *'Look at us, Skirill! Look where we are and look where we're going!'* He pointed to the south to emphasize his point. *'And you know what? I wouldn't have it any other way. Who else has been bold enough to attempt crossing the Great Desert? No one I heard of because if they tried, they died there. But we're better than that. The world's never seen a caravan like ours. A Hawkoid? A 'cat and a human with an ancient Rico Bow? I think that I've been preparing for this my whole life.'*

Braden walked as close to Skirill as he could get without climbing the rocks. *'Ski. You are my friend, and I will do what it takes to protect you. If that means helping you to prove your click wrong, then we'll do that. If it simply means surviving to see another turn, then we'll do that, too. What do you think, G? Can you help the poor human and weak Hawkoid survive for just one more turn?'* Braden laughed as he walked toward the 'cat, who was holding up his furry paw with his mock rude gesture. Braden caught the 'cat's head in both hands and rubbed behind his ears. G-War allowed this, maybe even a little longer than usual.

'Hungry,' was all the 'cat said.

28 – The Pain of the Great Desert

Braden was deliberate in his preparations to cross the Great Desert. He calculated water usage rates in order to best supply the horses first, then everyone else. They needed more water or they needed a water source in the desert. They needed numbweed just in case. They had a good supply of food, although it would never hurt to have more. Water was the most critical. Without it, food alone couldn't save them.

They also needed it to be cooler. It was the fall. If they waited a couple moons, then temperatures wouldn't be so hot, but they could find themselves at the mercy of the winter storms. Braden didn't know how these affected the desert, but he suspected they wouldn't be kind. Better warmer now without a sandstorm. They could go when they were ready, but Skirill wanted to find a source of water first and then determine the best way to get there.

In the morning on their first full turn at their campsite, Skirill ate a rabbit, then drank his fill directly from the stream. He hopped into the air and with a few powerful strokes of his wings, he gained altitude. He kept to his rhythmic beating, slow and purposeful, steadily climbing above the land. Soon he was a dot against the shimmer of the desert's heat. Then they could no longer see him. It seemed that he had already flown further than they could travel on the ground in a single turn.

Then they waited.

But waiting did not mean wasting time. Both Braden and G-War headed into the woods in search of the raw numbweed which they could process in their small pot. It would take time, but having prepared numbweed could be the difference between life and death. They found a few small patches, which Braden harvested in their entirety.

Braden also downed a young buck who didn't seem to be aware of the companions in his woods. G-War was pleased to have fresh venison. They would keep some warm for when Skirill returned.

The heat of the daylight passed, and the sun got lower and lower in the sky. The numbweed was in the pot with just a touch of water, simmering slowly. It couldn't boil and it couldn't get too dry. He had to keep adding just a little water at a time, watch it reduce, then add a little more. When it turned a certain light green color, it would be ready.

'He comes,' G-War said. As it edged toward dusk, they watched as a familiar dot reappeared in the southern sky and approached slowly.

Almost too slowly. The Hawkoid was struggling to stay aloft. He would glide for a while, then beat his wings, slightly out of rhythm, making him weave as he gained height. Then he would glide and repeat the process. It took him an agonizing amount of time to return, although that was more perception than reality.

Skirill glided the last few hundred strides and landed in the stream. He dipped his head under the water repeatedly, drinking until he threw up, then drinking again. Braden rushed into the water to help him.

"Hot... Hot," Skirill said out loud. Braden hadn't thought the Hawkoid could get sunburned. How would they survive the heat?

Skirill's legs were swollen, the stitches stretched tightly across his half-healed wound. The raw skin on his wing was dry and cracked. He dipped his body completely under the water a few times, enjoying the cool of the mountain stream.

"I need to take out those stitches before they rip your skin." The water helped soften the thread and surrounding skin, so removing the stitches wasn't difficult, but the skin had already been stretched to the extreme. Braden took his time to ensure that he didn't cause any more damage to Skirill's leg. The fire threw little light as he couldn't allow the numbweed to get too hot. It wouldn't be ready for some time yet.

G-War showed up at his side, front paws deep into the water as he chewed a mouthful of the weed. Braden knew that the 'cat's mouth and mind would both go numb from this effort. Only in an emergency would someone chew numbweed as it made the chewer weak and sleepy. Both the injured party and the rescuer would be unable to defend themselves. Chewing numbweed was the last ditch effort made by one willing to risk his life to save another's.

'Don't be so dramatic. It can watch over us for once.' G-War would never let on that he cared.

Braden put out his hands and the cat promptly spit out the gooey mess. Braden watched to make sure that G-War got out of the water before collapsing. Rubbing it in his hands to make a small patch, he put some carefully on Skirill's wing and the rest on his swollen leg wound, freshly diced by the removed stitches.

Skirill sighed audibly as his eyes rolled back in his head. Braden helped him out of the water and settled him onto a small boulder, high enough to keep his tail feathers out of the dirt, but not too high where Braden couldn't lift him up. Braden expected the Hawkoid to be far heavier than he was. Skirill weighed about half as much as the deer that Braden had killed earlier in the daylight. Their bodies were about the same size, but Skirill seemed much larger.

Braden checked the cooking numbweed and added a little water. He brought some strips of fresh deer to Skirill, who ate them without opening his eyes. Braden took a cloth and wiped G-War's front paws dry. The 'cat's tongue was hanging out of his mouth onto the ground. It was up to Braden to help restore the 'cat's dignity, which he did by putting the cloth under G-War's head as a pillow.

Then Braden returned to the fire, settling in to watch over his friends for the night.

29 – Healing Time

By morning, Braden was exhausted, but he had two full batches of numbweed pouched and ready for use. G-War had gotten up halfway through the night and staggered closer to the fire, where he curled up and promptly went back to sleep. Skirill remained on the rock, unmoving. Braden put his hand on the Hawkoid's broad chest a couple times to make sure he was still breathing.

When the time was right--that is, late morning--they both ate heartily of the remaining deer. Skirill ate so much that he was unable to fly. He apologized profusely before climbing back on his rock for another long nap. Braden cooked venison for breakfast, took a long nap, ate more for lunch, and then napped further.

About mid-daylight, he went hunting for more numbweed, but wasn't able to find any. The hunt was more of a way to stretch his legs, which he enjoyed. He also appreciated that he didn't have to ride Max this turn.

Skirill and G-War were back to themselves come dinner time. Only Braden ate, though. The other two were still digesting their rather excessive lunches.

"So, Ski, what's out there?"

"Yess, you called 'e that last night. It is 'y older 'rother's na'e."

"Your older brother is called Ski?"

"Yesss," Skirill said.

"Friends give each other nicknames. Golden Warrior of the Stone Cliffs is a little long, so I call him G-War or even just G for short. Your name is Skirill, or Ski for short."

"'ut Ski is 'y 'rother's na'e."

"What did you say? Buttski?" Braden laughed at his own joke.

The Hawkoid had lost the human's train of thought. With the 'cat's help, he switched to the mindlink. *'Ski is my brother's name. You can't call me by his name.'*

"I'm sorry, but Ass is taken too. What do you want me to call you?"

'My name is Skirill, yes?'

"Ess. I like it. Ess for the first letter of your name. Ess for yes, your name is Skirill. Ess it is."

'I used to like humans,' Skirill shot back at the speed of thought.

"How many other humans do you know?"

'I'll revise my statement. I used to like you!'

"Wow, Ess. That hurts. You and G teaming up against me." Braden smiled broadly at the Hawkoid, putting his hand on the feathered back of his large companion. "Let me check that wing of yours, Ess. We can't have you in pain." He looked the wounds over, pleased with the progress. He added a little numbweed to Skirill's leg and wing. His chest would be fine once the feathers grew back.

In a more serious tone, Braden asked, "What did you see out there, Skirill?"

30 – The Plunge

'Infinity,' was the first word that came through the mindlink. *'I never saw the other side, but I saw a garden. I cannot describe it any other way. It will take you ten turns to get there by horse.'*

"Ten turns," Braden said, thinking through the variety of calculations he'd made before. "At that point, three turns will have passed since we ran out of water. If we cut back on water, will we have the strength to cover the distance?"

'Our lives depend on getting this right,' G-War added unnecessarily. Yet, his statement was encouraging as G-War had supported Braden, in his unique 'cat way. He was deferring to Braden's judgment.

The risk was too high. He didn't know how much distance they could travel and how long it would take with any certainty. Then it came to him.

"Since we've never traveled in the desert before, we need to practice. Tomorrow, we'll head into the desert, as far as we can go in a single daylight. We'll camp, then come back here. We will do this until we have what we need, our bodies and our supplies perfectly tailored for travel across the Great Desert. No one will be able to do what we can do." Braden ended with determination.

They bedded down and tried to sleep. Braden was too excited to sleep well, and ended up getting up early.

First thing in the twilight before the dawn, Braden finished hooking up the cart and getting Max ready.

He thought about when he named his horse since he knew it was going to play a key role in their journey. He chose Max. Simple, but if Max couldn't give the maximum effort, they would be stranded where they couldn't survive. If they made it, Max was a horse to be remembered.

Turning back toward the pack horse, which he called Pack for short. He could make out G-War and Skirill in the cart. They had everything they would take with them. He wanted the trial to be as close to real as possible. What would they learn if they took shortcuts?

"With this first step, we move closer to our ultimate destination: the other side of the Great Desert! My friends, WHEN we cross, we will make history! We cannot fear the unknown. We must conquer it!" Braden said with a final flourish, head held high.

Who is it talking to?' Braden heard the 'cat say.

I have no idea,' Skirill responded.

"Let's go," Braden said, his grandstanding moment deflated.

I think it was talking to us. How odd.'

31 – Into the Great Desert

Two turns later, they made it back to the campsite by the stream in the middle of the night.

"I don't think I've ever been so hot and so tired before in my life. It was like getting cooked over a fire, without the benefit of spices or tubers." Braden almost fell from the saddle into the stream. The horses were already muzzle deep, enjoying the unlimited supply of fresh and cool water.

G-War hopped lightly from the cart, although his fur betrayed his seeming resistance to the heat. In two turns, the 'cat's sleek coat had been replaced by dry, frazzled hair sticking straight out. G-War waded into the stream, letting his paws cool and slowly lapping his fill.

Skirill had flow to the camp just before nightfall. He was already recovered, stately sitting on the rocks and watching over his worn out companions.

They traveled quickly at first, then slower and slower as the heat of the sun beat down on them. Their breaks lasted longer and longer, but were less and less restful. When they settled for the night, the desert sand radiated heat, preventing a sound sleep. The horses drank and drank, but never seemed to cool down. Over two turns, they drank half their water supply. The distance they covered on the first turn was greater than what they covered on the second turn. It took them halfway into the night to make up the time. Half the water with a precipitous drop in travel suggested that they would make it only halfway to the garden, as Skirill had called it.

They slept well into the next morning, happy to wake to the cool of the foothills.

"I don't know how we're going to make it, G. I think I'm trying to lead you on a fool's errand," Braden lamented. He sat with his head down, his face still red from the burning sun.

G-War sat upright and licked a paw which he used to groom his ears and cheeks. The 'cat was unperturbed as usual.

'Why does it insist on traveling in the sunlight?'

"So we can see where we are going, of course." Braden responded without thinking. As he looked back, he understood. The distances were so vast in the Great Desert that he could see the entire turn's track at his first glance. As a new moon waxed, they would have enough light to see any obstacles immediately in front of them. They could focus on something in the far distance to help them go straight toward the oasis.

"You're a genius G! Dig into that big brain of yours and tell me, how can we rest during the daylight?"

'It builds a shelter with a sun screen. Dig into a bank, opposite the sun, put up a roof.'

"All because I have thumbs," Braden answered with a smile. G-War never stopped grooming himself during their conversation.

"What would a shelter look like? How can we carry something big enough to cover us all, including Max and Pack? How far can we travel at night?" Although Braden asked these questions out loud, they weren't questions as much as problems that he was already working to solve. Deer hide. Light but long branches, wide forks at the end. He could tie these across the top of the cart. Yes. He could see how it would all work. Traveling at night was the key.

They spent the next two turns resting and finding the materials Braden needed to build their daylight shelter. With G-War's help, Braden was able to find three deer. He smoked the meat to build up their supply, but it was the hides they were after. Braden didn't have time to tan them properly. Even untanned, they filled the need.

It took some creativity to cut down the right branches. They were usually higher in a tree, where G-War and Skirill could see them. If they fit the description, Braden would climb up and use his knife to hack them down. It wasn't pretty work.

They settled on ten branches, cutting the leaves off and sharpening the thick ends so they could more easily be driven into the sand and ground. He wove the bark to make short ropes for tying the pieces together at final assembly. The deer hides didn't cover as much as he wanted, so he broke down the blanket pack and used the blanket as the main sun screen,. He added the deer hides to the sides, extending the shaded area.

As the third night after their previous foray into the Desert approached, they departed. They trotted until they reached the heat of the desert, then they slowed to a fast walk. As the air cooled, they picked up the pace. They only took one break, around midnight, and they drank from the casks without drinking to excess. They pushed on to the morning. As twilight revealed more of the desert around them, they looked for a place with an embankment facing northeast, to give them the least exposure to the hottest sunlight. Nothing at first, so they continued.

As the sun poked over the horizon, bathing the Great Desert in deep reds and vivid browns, Braden started to panic. He didn't want to push too far into the daylight. Their gains during the night would be quickly lost.

He settled for an embankment that was only his height, but it faced the right direction. He went to work immediately digging with a wood shovel he had fashioned for just this purpose. It wasn't near as good as a steel counterpart, but moving sand wasn't difficult, and he didn't have a steel shovel.

Braden drove the main branches into the top of the embankment at an angle to give them more space over their heads. He braced them with branches fashioned for that purpose, then put the blanket and deer hides in place. He dug out as much of the ground as he could under their shelter, letting out the stored cool of the deeper ground. It took Braden a little while to get the horses to lay down. It had been a long daylight followed by a long night. The sun was going to be brutal shortly. But they were finally settled in the shade. Braden used Max as a back rest. Skirill stood on the casks after they all had a good drink. G-War curled to the side away from the horses. He refused to get too close where he could get kicked or stepped on.

Braden splashed a little water on the horses' necks to help them calm down. He took a drink from the flask, and then was instantly asleep.

32 – Moment of Truth

Braden awoke with a start. Sweat poured from him. Max breathed heavily. The sun's heat pressed in on him. He had misjudged the sun's path and it was now shining on him and Max, although Pack, Skirill, and G-War were still in the shade and sleeping peacefully. When Braden stood up to adjust the poles of the shelter, Max stood up, too. The horse clearly understood that it needed to get out of the sun, so it turned and looked for an open space in the shade. As it completed its turn, it bumped one of the shelter supports, knocking it down. The rest of the shelter came down with it.

Pack panicked and jumped up, throwing branches around, snapping a couple. Braden waded in, grabbing his harness and stroking his nose to calm him down. Skirill was protected against the embankment where the casks were dug halfway in to prevent their accidental overturn. Braden could see his wide eyes in a gap between the deer hides. G-War was nowhere to be seen.

"G! Are you under there?"

'No.' Braden looked around, finally spotting G-War on the top of the embankment.

He lifted the branches and watched as Skirill hopped out. Braden went to the top of the embankment and resunk the poles that made up the roof. He tied a couple together that had been broken. From the bottom side, he used two support poles to lift the roofing part of the structure into place. He reseated those two poles. Although he worked quickly, the heat and sun had him hot and worn out when he finished. He corralled the two horses back into the shade, and pulled down on their harnesses until they laid back down on the ground. Braden helped G-War and Skirill drink sparingly from a flask, following with a deep drink for himself.

They settled back down, but sleep did not easily return. Everyone was restless. Eventually the daylight passed. As the sun headed for the horizon, the group ate their fill, while Braden took apart the shelter and reloaded the cart.

"Moment of truth, my friends. Do we continue on or do we head back and consider this a successful second trial run?"

Why would we waste that first night's effort? Have we not already come further than when we traveled during our daylight practice run?' Skirill said over the mindlink. Since he believed that meant the decision was made, the Hawkoid leapt into the air, circling their camp as he gained in height, then he raced toward the south. Braden knew that he was scouting the night's route ahead. He would be back shortly.

"What do you think, G?"

'I think it needs to keep the stupid horses from knocking the shelter down.'

Braden laughed heartily. He should have known where the 'cat would focus. Life or death? No. Personal comfort? Yes.

"I have some ideas. We need to find a better embankment tomorrow morning, my friend. Maybe Ess can give us some options around dawn. I don't want to fix the shelter in the middle of the daylight like that again. That was brutal."

33 – Half Way

The trip through the second night went better than the first. Braden was comfortable with how fast they could go, so he maintained a steady pace until after midnight, when he pushed harder.

In the relative cool of the night, they made good time. In the morning, he asked Skirill if he could determine how far they were away from the oasis. He wanted to make it in seven turns instead of ten, because he wanted to have water remaining in the casks when they arrived. Desperation could lead to bad decisions. He did not want to be desperate.

Skirill took to the lightening sky and swerved back and forth lazily on a general route southeast. G-War opened the mindlink and Braden saw the world spread out before him. Not far ahead, there was the remnant of a dry river bed. He knew where they needed to go and mentally thanked Ess for the view.

Skirill stopped the lazy strokes and flapped heartily on a beeline toward where he thought the oasis might be. He gained altitude quickly and disappeared into the pre-morning haze.

Max carried Braden to the embankment where they would make their camp, and he dismounted as Pack drew the cart to a slow halt. Braden looked over the area, quite pleased with this spot. He unhooked Pack from the cart and then used the cart to stand in as he worked the branches into the bank. He drove them at about a thirty-degree angle so they could hold the hides and blanket without needing a vertical support. This would ensure that G-War would not have his sleep interrupted.

Using the shovel, he dug into the hard earth. It was dry and cracked. Water hadn't run through this area in a long, long time. Braden couldn't dig too deeply, but he was able to make some progress. The first thing he prepared were the casks. They had to be protected. They were two full turns travel from the nearest water supply. They couldn't make it without a drink.

He then moved the horses in and once again fought with them until they finally laid down. He realized that once he got Max to lay down, Pack quickly followed. Max was the key to shelter bliss. G-War curled up on the ground behind the casks in a small hole that he dug out for himself. It was probably significantly cooler than on the open ground. Braden was tired, but couldn't sleep until Skirill came back. The heat of the morning had not yet arrived, but it would and soon.

Skirill contacted him well before he made it back. He sent his thought voice to G-War, who passed it to Braden. *'I have seen it and we are nearly halfway there!'* They could feel his excitement. Braden hadn't realized how much they struggled when they tried to travel during the daylight. They were making twice the progress by traveling at night.

'What's that?' Skirill suddenly asked. The sun was a couple finger-widths above the horizon by now. Braden clearly saw the branches of their shelter. Between the Hawkoid and the shelter, a light spot moved along the ground. Skirill swooped in low, flying by quickly.

Braden thought it was a tortoise, a massive sandy-colored tortoise. *'G, is he a mutie?'* Braden asked with his thought voice as he slung his Rico Bow and pulled out his knife.

'Yes,' the 'cat answered.

34 – The Tortoid

Skirill back winged to a soft landing just outside their shelter. It was getting too hot for him to keep flying.

"G! Let's go see what our visitor wants." Braden waited while G-War joined him. "Ess. Watch the fort, please. We'll be home soon." The human and the Hillcat walked purposefully away from the shelter.

As they approached the strange creature, they noted the tortoise was floating slightly above the ground. He used his legs to propel himself through the air.

"Ho there, friend!" Braden offered, holding up an empty hand. The other he kept at his side, holding the long knife. The tortoise stopped his swimming motion and hovered without moving further. Braden was surprised that he didn't glide forward.

"We are poor travelers, making our way across the Great Desert! Is there water anywhere near?" Braden asked in what he thought might be a typical conversation among desert dwellers. The tortoise remained where it was, eyes blinking slowly as it studied the two creatures before it.

Reducing his voice to a whisper, he leaned toward the 'cat. "Can he hear me?"

'Yes. Wait. It should cover its ears. NOW!'

"What?" Braden looked at G-War, taking a moment too long. As he was reaching for his ears, a thunderclap sounded beside him. He gasped in pain and dropped to his knees. The long knife fell to the ground, forgotten as Braden held his head. Blood ran freely from his nose and trickled out one ear. He used his fingers to pinch his nose shut, stemming the flow. He tipped his head back, and rolled to a sitting position.

"What the holy crap was that?" Braden stammered. He finally opened his eyes to see that G-War had gone forward and seemed to be carrying on a conversation with the tortoise. Was there any creature the 'cat couldn't talk to?

He was probably talking about how stupid his human was. He wouldn't be wrong, and it pained him to realize it.

'...*we appreciate your kind words and consideration, Master Aadi,*' the 'cat was saying in his thought voice. *'We continue to the oasis that our Hawkoid friend has shown us only two turns of the sun from here.'*

'You are far too kind, fuzzy one with the kind soul. I haven't been to the oasis in many cycles. It is a long journey for me as I don't travel as quickly as I once did.'

Fuzzy one with the kind soul? Braden would never have described G-War that way, and he had known him for ten cycles of the seasons. He had never been able to look past the words the 'cat allowed him to see. Braden had been more deeply in contact with Skirill, one he had known for less than a single moon. Maybe the tortoise's mindlink was deeper with G-War?

'He's waiting for its answer,' G-War said to Braden.

"You're talking to me?" Braden asked, although he knew the answer. He continued, "What was the question?"

'Master Aadi would like to join the caravan until we reach the oasis.'

Braden stood up a little wobbly, but with an effort, he remained on his feet. He bowed, not deeply as he didn't want to fall over. His head felt like it weighed the same as the rest of his body. "Master Aadi is welcome to join us in our journey to the oasis."

The tortoise blinked a few times in quick succession, then resumed his swimming motion. He moved forward. Braden found it an easy pace to walk by his side.

'Do you trust this Master Aadi?' he asked the 'cat using his thought voice.

'Yes.'

Since Braden trusted the 'cat, and the 'cat trusted the tortoise, Braden trusted the tortoise. Besides the thunderclap that almost shattered his brain, the tortoise seemed harmless enough.

It took no time to make it back to the shelter. Braden crawled in so he wouldn't spook the horses. The tortoise moved in under the shade, but stayed as far out as he could get. It was weird how he stopped moving the second he stopped the swimming motion with his legs. He then descended until he was on the ground. Skirill watched him closely.

G-War opened the mindlink so everyone they could talk as a group. *'I am Skirill, a Hawkoid. My click is of the Bittner Mountains, far to the north.'* He bowed his head to finish his introduction.

'I am Aadi, First Master of the Tortoise Consortium. I have never met a Hawkoid before. Or a Hillcat. Or a human for that matter. This daylight is a banner turn! And what are these magnificent creatures? When the consortium gathers three cycles from now, I shall have to tell them all about you.'

"I am Braden, Free Trader of Warren Deep. I intend to cross the Great Desert to find an Old Tech outpost from which I can obtain rare items of significant value."

'Pleased to make your acquaintance, Free Trader Braden. Thank you for taking me with you. I thought you might not after that minor episode with the focused thunderclap. Sorry about that, by the way. I don't like surprises. I'm a Tortoid, after all. We are deliberate in everything we do.'

"I am very pleased to meet you. And surprised. I didn't know that anyone lived in the Great Desert."

'Oh yes, a great number of creatures call the Desert home.'

"Are any dangerous?"

'Not to a war party such as yours.'

"We are a trade caravan, that's all. Not a war party," Braden corrected.

'Call yourself what you want, but it does not change what you are. One's fundamental nature cannot be changed. I see within you, young human. I see your soul at

peace, and I see war at your fingertips. There is no greater friend than you, and no greater enemy. I seek to be called your friend.'

"Then friend you are, Master Aadi." They continued talking well into the heat of the morning, until Braden could no longer stay awake. The Tortoid suggested that they could all benefit from a good daylight's sleep. He did a curious thing then, digging at the surface of the dirt with his clawed feet to make a hole while also covering himself with the sand and dirt. Aadi had many tricks that helped him survive more than two hundred cycles in the desert.

'I wonder what he eats and drinks?' were Braden's last thoughts as he drifted to sleep under G-War's watchful gaze.

35 – A Rough Night

They repeated their routine as evening approached. Braden broke down their camp and packed the cart.

He stopped to wipe sweat from his forehead, the others watching him curiously.

"The curse of having thumbs. Your humble servant apologizes for the short delay in this evening's activities whilst he takes a wholly undeserved drink of water." Braden bowed deeply to the assembled group. Skirill bobbed his head in amusement. Neither G-War nor Aadi showed any emotion. Braden drank less than he wanted, but as much as he needed.

Once loaded, G-War assumed his position within the cart with Skirill behind him, tail feathers hanging out the back. Aadi was to the side of the cart, floating even with the top of it.

"Skirill, you flew this yesterday. What's the best path forward?" G-War opened the mindlink and the Hawkoid showed the path as a series of pictures. Braden gently prodded Max forward and Pack followed as he always did.

Braden thought for a second, then realized that he was being disrespectful to his new friend. "Aadi, do you agree? No one knows this desert better than you. What do you suggest?"

'Very nice. Thank you for the pictures, my feathered friend.' Braden suspected the Hawkoid bowed in response. *'I've never seen the desert from this angle. It is so very interesting and disorienting. As we go along, I will rectify what I know with what Master Skirill has shown me.'*

'Not a Master,' Skirill quickly replied.

'Don't be ridiculous, Master Skirill. Who better represents the Hawkoids here in the Great Desert than you?' Braden found it hard to refute that logic. The Great Desert was vast, but tiny.

'Tell us about the oasis, Master Aadi,' Braden said.

'Yes! Yes, it is a bit of paradise. I haven't been there in years. It is dangerous at the best of times. But with this war party, we will chase any evil ones away. You make me feel safe.'

'Thanks. Not sure about that. There are only three of us, now four.'

'Correction, young human. There are six of us. Your horses are magnificent creatures! They could be two of the largest in all the Great Desert! Anyone powerful enough to tame not one but two creatures of this size will intimidate many potential enemies. They make you strong.'

'You can drop that thunder boomer of yours on them. That was pretty strong, if you ask me. My ear feels like I packed dirt in it.'

'No, no, no. Everyone here has something like that. We all live alone. We travel alone. There is never enough food or water for two, so we don't put ourselves in the position to decide who dies. We decide for ourselves. We are accountable to us. We survive or we don't. There is no one or anything else to blame. It is our way.' He hesitated. 'My. You travel a bit more quickly than I do. This is a quandary.'

'We travel as fast as we can because we need a great deal of water. I don't know how you manage, but we need those two casks and what is left in our flasks. If we take too long, we will die of thirst.'

'Ahh. That's what those are. They smelled like heaven to me. I didn't know that water could be carried.'

'When was the last time you had a drink, Master Aadi?'

'Let me think. That would be never. I tried, at the oasis, but our mouths are not made for it. We absorb moisture through our feet and through our shell. It is enough for us Tortoids.'

'We can't slow down, but maybe we can tow you.' Braden stopped the horses and waited for Aadi to catch up. He threw him a length of rope, but the

Tortoid didn't catch it. His motion to grab it in his mouth was far too slow.

"Ooh! Sorry about that, Aadi." Braden jumped down and picked up the rope, handing it to Aadi. He made to grasp it in his beak-like mouth. "Hang on. Here, have a drink from my flask." Braden readily pulled out his flask, opened it, and made ready to squirt some warm water into the Tortoid's mouth.

'I don't know about this, Master Braden. I've never done anything like it.'

"Relax. You'll like it." Aadi reluctantly opened his mouth, and Braden squirted barely more than a mouthful to the back of his throat. Aadi blinked rapidly, choked and coughed, but kept the water down. He clamped his mouth shut.

'That's quite enough, Master Braden. Cactus and Fireweed! I feel funny.'

"It's water. I have no doubt you'll feel better than ever before. Here." Braden offered the rope, which Aadi took and clamped his beak-like mouth on it.

They departed anew, picking up the pace a little.

'Woohooo!' Aadi howled through the mindlink. He floated above the cart, over Pack, then back. His feet were tucked in as he flew through the air, back and forth, up and down.

'What's wrong with him?' Braden asked G-War.

'Why did it give the Master water?'

'It's water. What's the problem?' Braden responded.

'Water is different for the Master. Remember when it drank that flask of firewater?'

'Oh. I see. That was a bad night.'

'And this will be a bad night for Master Aadi.'

'Why didn't you stop me, G? I didn't know. It's just water!'

'The Master's mind is well disciplined. He knows many things. He has lived a long

time and is wise beyond that. We would do best to listen to him. It needs not think or speak. Just do as the Master asks.' The mindlink slammed shut. G-War's usual beratings were much shorter, as in, the human is stupid. This was a diatribe for the 'cat, but the basic message was the same. They could have avoided it all with a simple, 'don't give Aadi water.'

36 - No More Water For You

Toward morning, Aadi's wild gyrations stopped and he drooped lower and lower toward the ground. Braden pulled the rope closer to him until he could balance the hung-over Tortoid on one leg. Aadi was the largest tortoise he had ever seen. Beak to short tail, he was almost as tall as Skirill, half Braden's height. He was half as wide as he was tall, but his shell arched high. He was shaped more like a box than the flat round tortoises Braden had seen before.

It was awkward trying to balance him, but Braden felt horrible. He was responsible for this. He hoped to talk with his friends to make the time go more quickly and learn something. Instead, no one wanted to talk with the stupid human. It made the night drag on endlessly.

Towing a drunk Tortoid through the dark of the desert's night hadn't been what Braden had in mind when they started the evening before. He had to admit the oldster was agile. Well, just until his post water crash. Now, he could barely keep himself afloat.

Finally the morning twilight revealed the world around them. Skirill took to the sky, flying slowly, looking for a place to make their camp. He kept going, further and further, finally circling a spot in the distance.

'Nothing closer, but this is a good place,' Skirill said to them all.

'Wait there. We're coming.' Braden kicked Max into a trot and reluctantly, Pack started trotting too. This made the cart bounce, which elicited an unhappy snarl from G-War. Braden wanted to beat the morning heat. They would be able to cool down before the heat came, but if they got hot and it was hot outside, everyone would be miserable for the daylight.

They hurried on. The horses breathed easily while trotting in the cooler night air. The coolest temperature of the night was just before sunrise.

That's the time when the sun heats the upper air, driving the cooler air down, until it was replaced by the heat of the daylight.

Braden did all he could to hang on to Aadi while also keeping Max on track.

The sun was up and balanced on the horizon as they ran the final paces to the place Skirill selected for their camp. They halted, breathing hard from their efforts. G-War immediately jumped off the cart, walking past Braden, giving him a furled-brow glare.

"Sorry. Master Aadi! Can you let yourself down to the ground?"

No answer, but Braden was having difficulty holding him. The rope fell from the Tortoid's beaked mouth. Braden leaned as far down as he could while still holding Aadi upright. Then he started to slip. Aadi was headed toward the ground with Braden headfirst after him.

Mere finger widths from the ground, the Tortoid came to abrupt stop. Braden hit the top of Aadi's shell with his face, sliding down, bouncing once, and landing flat on his back on the ground.

"Holy crap, that hurt," he said out loud.

'Huh, what? Sorry. I fell asleep,' Aadi stammered. *'Wow. I feel great! These old muscles are lubricated like they've never been. I never thought it could be this good. Give us another drink, just a little sip, my friend.'*

'G! What the hell is going on?'

'No water for the Master!'

"Sorry, A-Dog, no water for you. Haven't you had enough?"

'Ah yes, you are right. A-Dog! I like it. What's a dog?' Aadi asked.

'It's a pathetic creature with no wit. Humans adore them because dogs look at them with their big eyes and their wagging tails,' the 'cat replied before Braden could muster a response.

"Those are lessons someone in this group could learn, someone fuzzier than the rest of us." The 'cat lifted one paw toward to Braden, gesturing deliberately. Braden got to his knees and started brushing himself off.

'Bravo! My apologies for last evening. I don't seem to remember much of it, but I feel great! Is there any way I could get a small drink? Water would taste so good right now.'

"I have to build the shelter." Braden got up all the way, then leaned down close to Aadi's head. "Two things, Master Aadi. Please don't blast my head with that thunderclap of yours, ever again, and I can't give you any more water. It makes you weird and gets me yelled at. So, please, to keep my soul at peace, as you suggest, no more water for you."

37 – Tonight's the Night

Skirill took to the sky as the sun was setting. He flew high into the air, sharing his view with his companions. The Oasis was clearly visible on the horizon. The shimmering of the heat on the sand and dirt made it appear bigger than it actually was. Skirill returned shortly after suggesting a way forward that Aadi agreed with.

Master Aadi suggested they would reach the oasis toward morning, maybe even earlier. If danger was there, Braden wanted to address it in the daylight. He counted on Aadi to let them know when they were getting close. He didn't want to surprise something that would attack them in the dark. There were creatures that could see much better at night than Braden and the companions.

He envisioned G-War sneaking in on a flank, and Braden armed with his Rico Bow, ready to take on all comers. He wore a covering over his head in case Aadi let loose with his focused thunderclap. Skirill flew overhead and showed them everything.

But they needed daylight to get the most from each of their gifts. They had to arrive at dawn.

One water cask was empty while the other was mostly full, and all the flasks but one were empty. It was better than Braden had hoped. They could make it all the way back north out of the desert if they had to. If they found the oasis to be too dangerous. According to Aadi, though, the threat wasn't as great as Braden had feared it might be. It always lurked in the back of his mind that any and every creature in the desert would be at the oasis, carving out some kind of niche for themselves.

They would know soon enough. Tonight was the night they reached it.

38 – Preparing for the Oasis

Aadi urged them to stop when twilight was still a ways off. Braden watered the horses. They ate smoked pork and venison, cheese and dried greens. Aadi was curious about the meat, but Braden staunchly refused until G-War told him it was okay.

Braden gave a tiny strip to the Tortoid, who chewed it cautiously. They all watched him, even G-War, who knew that nothing was going to happen.

'Interesting flavor and texture. Not as rich as a good nest of cactus weevils, mind you, but palatable. It'll do. Thank you. Very refreshing,' Aadi told them.

'You said there were dangerous creatures here, but they would be intimidated by us. So, what can we expect to see?'

'There were Seeders there ten cycles ago. If they are still there, then that could be a problem. There was a Mirror Beast. Let's see, a Sand Crawler, some very nasty, and tasty if I may add, beetles, and oh yeah, don't forget about the Gila Monster.'

"What? How do we fight all that?" Braden asked in a surprised voice, then put his finger over his mouth as he realized his outburst. Sound carried in the desert.

'The Seeders are easy. They shoot seeds out of an obvious pod near their flower. They can't penetrate my shell and they only have one shot. If I can get them to attack me, you can pass with impunity.

'The Mirror Beast reflects attacks made upon him. He feeds on your mental energy. I tried my focused thunderclap on him all those years ago and I was lucky to survive the encounter! He stays in one place.

'The Sand Crawler is long and thin, one mouth, two fangs, and no legs. It crawls on the ground by twisting its body. It is colored like sand and hides well. If you can see it,

then you can defeat it.

'The beetles will take a lot of bites out of the soft flesh you have. They'll swarm over you if you get too close. So don't let them get close.

'The Gila Monster is the most dangerous. She lures you in by making you feel that you aren't afraid. Her bite is poisonous. Her skin is thick. She is slow, but that doesn't matter. She gets in your mind and you become slower than her. Since there are four of us, we should be able to protect each other.

'The source of the water is a strange creature. It never moves. It exists to spew water out of its mouth, maintaining the small lake in the oasis. It welcomes all equally. I remember floating over it and feeling unafraid. When are we going in? I'd like to visit that creature again.'

"Skirill. When it's light, can you fly over the oasis and find if any of these creatures are still there? If we know where they are, I can kill them with my Rico Bow before they realize there are more of us than just you."

'What? You're just going to kill them?' Master Aadi was confused.

"Of course. It's us or them, right?"

'Of course not,' the Tortoid responded firmly. Braden took a deep breath. He expected that his eyes would be opened to some hidden wisdom that he wasn't in the mood for.

'We make peace with the Gila Monster by offering her smoked meat. She will probably accept it and leave us be. The Mirror Beast cannot be defeated as far as I know. I suggest we don't attack it. No attack, nothing to reflect. He feeds on your mental energy, but it just tickles. He doesn't take anything that you can't do without. The Sand Crawler, well, okay, if you can kill the Crawler then do so. They are rather creepy. I'll take care of the Seeder myself. Once it attacks me, it is done. There are no seeds for another cycle.'

'You are wise, Master Aadi. You saved me from making a huge mistake. You saved us from a battle we didn't need to fight.'

'Your soul is at peace, even as you readied for war. Be wary of the flames of battle. Be ready, but battle last.' Braden nodded in understanding.

'What about the beetles?' Braden asked.

'Very tasty, but only if they aren't trying to eat you at the same time.'

'Now that is wisdom I can wrap my head around!' Braden held his hands high in the universal hallelujah sign.

39 – Just a Scratch

At first light, Skirill took off. Within seconds, the oasis was in full view. They had stopped only a couple hundred strides shy of the outer foliage while Skirill quickly circled the area. His eyes were second to none, but he couldn't see through the heavy shadows of the undergrowth. He saw trees unlike any he'd seen before, with straight, tall trunks with few huge leaves at the top. He saw green bushes and plants. A lake stood at the center of the oasis. At the very middle of the lake, he saw the creature that Aadi had described. It continued to belch water, rippling and foaming the area around it. The water looked a deep black where the sun had not yet touched it.

He circled a couple more times, then dove in quickly over the lake. There! To the side, they all saw the Seeders at the same time. Three of them stood serenely, huge purple and white flowers topping their heavy green stalks and the seed pods prominent between the stalk and flower. The Mirror Beast stood among the Seeders, unmoving and glistening as the first rays of the sun reflected brightly from a squat, shiny body.

Movement. In the underbrush. There. The Gila Monster. *'She's no threat. So sweet.'* Skirill's thoughts came through the mindlink. *'I should go down and talk with her.'*

'STOP!' G-War's 'cat voice roared.

'What was that for?' the Hawkoid asked.

'She was in your mind. Fight those thoughts! If you don't, she'll end up eating you.' Skirill made a few strong strokes and climbed quickly away from the lake.

'I didn't see anything else.'

'Good enough, Ess. I think we can make this work. G, can you go first? Make sure

there are no surprises. Master Aadi with me. Skirill overhead.' Braden had Max's lead in his hand. Pack followed, pulling the cart behind him.

They walked over the top of the low hill. Braden smiled as he saw the oasis in front of him. After nearly five turns in the desert, as Aadi had described it, it did indeed look like heaven.

G-War walked in front of the others as if strolling through an open meadow. Braden watched the 'cat's head and neck to give him an idea of the 'cat's mood. If his ears were back, a fight was brewing. Fur ruffled around the neck, something unknown lurked. Whiskers back? He usually saved that for the lady cats or a good meal. Right now, he showed no signs that Braden could read. His mindlink was open, connecting all the companions.

G-War angled slightly from their original path to head toward an opening between two small bushes. Although he could have entered anywhere since he was an agile Hillcat, he was being mindful of the horses. The cart was another matter. Braden wanted to go as far as they could into the oasis before unhooking it. With water so near, their greatest treasure was the smoked meat. He didn't want to put too much distance between him and their food.

The cart caught up on that first bush, so that's where it had to stay. Braden quickly unhooked it while the others waited. The 'cat sat upright in a small open area, casually watching everything. Master Aadi floated in place, eyes unblinking.

They continued several strides into the area toward the largest of the trees, when suddenly G-War jumped straight up. His claws came out and he twisted sideways. Braden began pulling out his long knife, but the 'cat's actions were so quick, the blade hadn't made it free of his belt before the 'cat struck.

A Sand Crawler appeared from under a bush. It struck at G-War's leg, narrowly missing. G-War's jump brought him back down on top of the Crawler, where the 'cat had the best leverage to drive claws from both front paws into the head and body of the snake. The thing twisted furiously and flipped from under the 'cat, who jumped straight into the air a second time, its eyes never leaving its enemy.

Braden's long knife finally appeared in his hand as he let go Max's reins. The horse bucked and jumped, trying to get away from the snake that was flopping and twisting on the ground between the 'cat and the human. With a quick slash, Braden cut the snake neatly in two. The 'cat landed on the snake's head a second time and, with well-practiced motions, shredded it.

Braden watched as G-War limped away from the fight.

"G! What's wrong? Let me see." Braden ran the few steps forward and dropped next to the 'cat.

'Not as fast as I used to be. I never felt it. I barely saw it. Something is different here and I don't like it,' the 'cat told Braden as he looked at a thin cut across the 'cat's back leg. He pulled some numbweed from the pouch at his waist and applied it liberally on the wound.

"Just a scratch, G. Enough for some of the poison to get you, although it doesn't look like the fang penetrated the muscle. You're one lucky 'cat. That's seven lives left for you." Braden didn't know where he heard that 'cats started with nine lives, but he'd seen G-War in grim places and walk away without a scratch. Besides the turn Braden saved him from drowning, this was the closest anything had ever gotten to hurting him.

"If you can't sense them, how do we protect ourselves if another Sand Crawler is around?" Braden asked.

'We talk with the Gila. She will tell us if there are more. She should know. Tie the horses behind the cart. Bring meat,' Master Aadi told them.

Tying the horses wasn't as easy as that. They were spooked by the snake, the whites of their eyes showing with their fright. They danced wildly, trampling bushes and bouncing off trees. Once Braden had a tight hold on Max's reins, he was able to pull the horse down to calm him. With Max under control, Pack quickly followed. He tied them to the back of the cart, giving them some dried grass that they had brought with them. The snake was soon forgotten.

G-War limped forward, head slung low as he looked under each bush, in each patch of grass before he passed. The going was slow, but the distance wasn't far. The oasis wasn't large, about a hundred strides out from the central lake, creating a circle of life in the waste of the Great Desert.

40 – The Oasis Pacified

As they approached the lake, they heard the pleasant tones of the Gila Monster's siren song. She sang to them to come closer. Braden started to fade, a beautiful woman projected in his mind. *It's Ava. She is so nice waiting here for me.* Then sparks as something smashed into his head, knocking him off his feet.

"What the hell?" He looked up, rubbing his temple. Master Aadi floated there, looking down at him.

'Get a grip on yourself. Your Ava is not here. She pulled the image from your mind and you were falling for it. You are naïve, Free Trader Braden. If something is unbelievable, don't believe it. I have much work to do with you.' With that, the Tortoid swam forward, leading the way toward the Gila. *'Don't forget the meat,'* he said as he passed.

The three of them continued toward the Gila Monster, avoiding the Seeders by moving in a wide arc. Skirill circled overhead, getting lower and lower as the heat of the daylight built. Finally, he gave up trying to fly and landed in the top of the highest tree. The branches weren't anything like what he was used to. They were prickly, but not like a cactus. It was better than getting roasted, so he repositioned to a better perch. The oasis felt much cooler. He let out a Hawkoid sigh, returning his attention to his companions as they approached the Gila Monster.

'Master of the Gila Monsters, we bid you good tidings and bring you a gift from the foot of the mountains far to the north,' Master Aadi said in his stately and deliberate way. The Gila Monster bobbed her head one time. Aadi looked at Braden, motioning slowly with his head. The human walked forward cautiously and dropped a substantial pile of smoked pork on the ground before the Gila Monster.

Her tongue darted out, barely missing Braden's outstretched hand. He withdrew quickly until he was slightly behind the Tortoid. The Gila Monster's tongue touched the strips of meat, then she moved forward in one very slow motion. With one bite, she had half the pile in her mouth. She let it sit there before throwing her head back and swallowing it. Then she ate the rest.

'Welcome to the oasis, Master Aadi. Yes. I remember you from when you were last here.' A new voice entered their mindlink.

'I am honored that you remember me although ten cycles have passed.'

'One turn, ten cycles. It is all the same to me. You've brought an army with you. Why?'

Braden stepped forward, bowing deeply to the Gila Monster. "I am Free Trader Braden," he said, flicking his head and sending his braid behind him with a flourish. "We are but travelers on our way south. We have joined together in our quest for Old Tech. We found that we share gifts and are better as friends. Is it possible to include you as a friend?"

'I am Tiskanay. Welcome to the oasis.' She bobbed her head slightly. *'I've never tasted flesh as you have provided me. This pleases me. I would be happy to join your army for the time you are here.'*

Braden bowed deeply again. "I thank you for your kindness and look forward to sharing with you more about ourselves, as well as learning about your oasis." Tiskanay had taken a step back and rested on the ground. It appeared that she was going to sleep. "One last question, if you don't mind. We had a misfortunate encounter with a Sand Crawler. How many more can we expect to see?"

'There has been only one. There will be only one.' Her thought voice trailed off as she mentally retreated to the calmness of sleep.

"Shall we?" Braden asked the 'cat and the Tortoid, gesturing toward the lake. "I believe the stage is yours, Master Aadi."

'What's a stage?' the Tortoid asked.

"That's where the actors are during a play." Thinking better of it, he added, "According to the plan, you will defang the Seeders?"

'Ah yes. Wait here.' With his strange swimming motion, he moved forward toward the Seeders. He drifted at various heights as he passed, doing his best to look like a target. They watched as leaves over the pods slowly parted, exposing dart-like seeds. Turning carefully and keeping the heavy part of his boxy shell toward them, he drifted back in front of the pods. The first one erupted in a puff of dust, the seeds bouncing harmlessly from Aadi's shell. He floated back and forth in front of the other two Seeders until they shot their seeds at him.

'Master Skirill. If you would be so kind as to use those incredible eyes of yours to see if the pods have any seeds remaining, I would greatly appreciate it.'

The Hawkoid jumped from his perch and glided over the lake, looking beneath the large purple flowers. One. Two. Three. No seeds left in any of the pods.

Braden headed toward the lake after getting the all-clear from his companions. He kneeled down, watching the water carefully and checking the water beast at the center, while getting his mind tickled by the Mirror Beast. He scooped a small handful of water, smelling it before letting it wash over his tongue. It was sweet and clean. He would wait and give it time. He didn't expect there would be any poison as life seemed plentiful.

He looked toward the creature standing among the Seeders. It stood an arm-span high and the same wide, rounded on the top, square at the bottom. The sun reflected from its shiny surface. It was called a Mirror Beast, which Braden had assumed was based on its ability to reflect attacks. He hadn't expected its surface to be that of a mirror.

He walked to the side opposite the sun, watching the Seeders carefully. He couldn't imagine a fate worse than having a plant grow inside him.

From the back side of the Mirror Beast, he could see a seam. Was that a rivet? The Beast was built of metal. He assumed by man. In the past couple moons, he had seen more curiosities than in all his previous life. Maybe the Mirror Beast was underneath and the metal was only a shell to protect it. Braden leaned down, trying to look underneath it. He saw wheels and a base plate. If there was a living creature, it was sealed inside. He got close enough to reach out. As he approached the surface, something invisible pushed back against him. The harder he pushed his hand toward the surface, the harder it pushed back.

'Force is the enemy of wisdom, my friend,' Master Aadi said quietly.

Braden closed his eyes and calmed himself. He focused on the muscles in his arm, relaxing them until his hand dropped of its own volition. It fell onto the surface of the Mirror Beast. He let his hand drag across the hot metal.

"Is anyone in there?" he asked to no one in particular, lifting his hand away from the creature's surface. He felt a much stronger tickling in his mind.

'The creature is attempting to talk with it,' G-War told him.

"How can I make contact? I don't know what to do," Braden responded aloud. Then he changed to his thought voice.

'Good morning, kind sir! I am Free Trader Braden…' When his standard greeting was complete, he waited for something from the beast. The tickling became more intense. He focused on it, wrapping his mind around it. He saw something that looked like leaves blowing in the wind. They assembled themselves in order. It was letters and numbers, like the words in one long sentence from a book's page.

'X 7 W K K L Y 8 V 4 W N J E T 4 P X 1 9 5 7 …'

'I don't know what you're trying to tell me.' Braden continued trying to talk with the Mirror Beast, but he only received strings of numbers and letters. At least he knew how to write, but that didn't seem to help him here. His head started to hurt as the stream grew more insistent. Braden staggered away, breaking the link. His head instantly felt better.

'I must not be smart enough to figure out what it's saying,' he told his companions over their mindlink. *'I don't think it's a creature at all. Odd, but I think it's a machine. A thinking machine!'*

They committed to trying to communicate with the Mirror Beast again, but later. They had horses who would appreciate fresh water. Skirill landed on the beach and waded into the water after letting everyone know that he could see all the way to the bottom of the lake. There were no creatures in it. The water was pure and clean. He ducked his head under, then did it again and again, shaking off the water after each dip.

"Where were you when the cold-water croc was trying to make me his dinner?" Braden asked from his knees as he plunged his face deep into the coolish water of the desert oasis lake.

'I was contemplating the remainder of my life as a Bear's meal,' Skirill responded with a mental smile. Braden agreed. That deserved a smile.

Braden watched G-War wade into the water, sitting down so that it covered his leg where the Crawler's poisoned fang had grazed him. Cleaning out the wound would help, followed by another application of numbweed. The 'cat would be fine and he now had a scar to show that he was mortal. Braden wondered, after seeing so many death-defying feats from his furry friend.

Master Aadi floated gracefully above them all, watching and enjoying the cool of the oasis. He contemplated a long nap in the shade of a short tree. He watched Braden head out to bring the horses and the cart to the shore of the lake. With that, he nodded off. The horses drank heartily and grazed on the oasis grasses. Braden hobbled them to keep them away from the Gila Monster. Having just fed, she would probably leave them alone. He would remain aware, with Master Aadi's help.

Braden pulled his trusty telescope out, wrapping the hard hide around the special glass. He looked at the so-called water beast at the center of the lake. It was a man-made pipe from which the water gushed. He had never heard of such a use of the precious steel. He looked at his long knife. There was no reason why steel couldn't be shaped to carry water. He shared this revelation with his friends.

With numbweed freshly applied to G-War's wound, he assumed the watch while the others fell into a restful, deep sleep.

41 – It Sucks

After resting most of the daylight, Braden and the others decided to explore the oasis. Not knowing what to expect, Braden slung his Rico Bow and carried his long knife in his hand. G-War was already walking without a limp. Skirill made many low passes over the trees, showing them more of the same throughout the oasis.

Master Aadi seemed perfectly content floating waist high above the ground and swimming along peacefully. Braden chose a path that took them from the lake straight to the edge of the desert. They turned and tracked along just inside the oasis. They made one trip around the oasis, then moved closer to the lake and circled again. Braden was surprised the remains of the Crawler they had killed were nowhere to be found.

"Be aware! We're not alone!" The 'cat harrumphed and the Tortoid bobbed his head as the Hawkoid did. In the real world, one was either a hunter or prey. G-War strolled to the side and sat down next to a mark on the ground. Braden looked closer and guessed those were Gila Monster tracks. Tiskanay had gone for a walk.

'Is she a threat?' Braden asked himself.

'No,' G-War's thought voice came through without any judgment. *'She has fed better this turn than in many cycles. There is nothing to fear from her. Show her the respect of her station as Master Aadi has advised and we will be forever welcome.'*

Turning to Aadi, Braden asked, "Why am I so ready to look for danger, so ready to fight?"

'Being ready for war is not the same as making war, or liking it, young human. Make war as a last resort.'

"Thanks, Master Aadi. Aren't there supposed to be some flesh eating beetles around here some?"

'Over the cycles, Tiskanay has eaten them all.'

"Like you said, Master Aadi. Tasty as long as they aren't eating you." Braden put his long knife into his belt and spent the rest of the exploration enjoying the strange trees. There were nuts the size of his head that grew near their leafy tops. He smashed one against a rock to find that it had a sweet pulp inside. He ate his fill. It was like nothing he'd ever tasted before.

They found a bush bearing a red fruit that Skirill found particularly tasty. The juice ran down his beak and over his white chest feathers. When Braden tried to wipe away the juice, he couldn't. It was sticky and hardened quickly. "Damn! You're a mess." The Hawkoid stared at Braden, unblinking, until Braden felt uncomfortable. "But you are still one scary Hawkoid! Creatures large and small flee before you!"

Finally, Skirill blinked and bobbed his head. He didn't try to fly to the lake, but ran as a bird runs, across the beach and into the water. *'Something doesn't feel right,'* Skirill told them over the mindlink.

"I'll be right there, Ess." Braden ran the short distance to the lake. He jumped in the water and helped the Hawkoid ashore. The juices on the Hawkoid's chest had hardened. "Well, now. What are we going to do about this? Any suggestions? Anyone?"

'Did you have any problem when you ate some of the fruit?' Aadi asked Braden.

"No. It was pretty good, but I feel fine. How about you, Skirill?"

'Fine. My chest hurts because my feathers can't breathe.'

'Your mouth juices will soften the fruit and help you remove it from Master Skirill's feathers.'

"What? You want me to spit on Skirill?"

'No. You must suck on the hardened juice until it softens. Then I expect it can be removed without harming our friend.'

"You cannot be serious," Braden said in disbelief.

'*Our friend is in pain. Get to it,*' Master Aadi said with finality. He turned and swam toward the shade of a tree with oversized leaves. G-War moved to a position on top of a fallen log and sat, watching.

Braden sat down in front of the Hawkoid and leaned toward him. Skirill moved closer, and Braden took in a mouthful of juice-hardened feathers. It was sweet, like a candy, and it softened quickly. When he could feel it loosen, he let go and worked the softened juice with his fingers. A few heartbeats after that, a mouth-sized gob of the juice came free.

Braden took a deep drink from the lake, then started on a new spot.

The 'cat opened the mindlink just so Braden could hear him giggling. Skirill tried to step in and let Braden know that he was already feeling better and looked forward to being done with the whole affair.

Using his thought voice, since his mouth was most ingloriously occupied, Braden said, '*Why don't you come over here and help?*'

'*It has gifts besides its thumbs. No one sucks like it does.*' The 'cat seemed to be taking great delight in the entire situation.

'*Ass,*' Braden thought while continuing to work on Skirill's chest feathers.

'*Sometimes he is such an ass,*' Skirill added. '*Maybe we could make a pillow from his stuffed hide. It would be so comfortable. We could pet it and snuggle with it.*'

'*Please excuse me,*' the Tortoid interrupted. '*I have never seen such friends. There is nothing you won't do for each other. And there seems to be no limit to what you'll do to each other. I have so much to learn from you. If you would be so kind, I would like to accompany you wherever you go from here.*'

'*See, G! That's how you talk to people.*'

'*I also have to admit, from my humble Tortoid point of view, you really do suck well.*'

'*By all that's holy! Will it never end?*' Braden started to laugh, but choked on a mouth full of feathers.

'*Right there! Yes, right there. That feels so good,*' the Hawkoid purred.

42 – The Lake

The red fruits and the large brown nuts were rather good and supplemented their meat supply nicely. After the unfortunate incident with Skirill's feathers, Braden cut the fruit into bite size chunks for them all to enjoy. Everyone except G-War, who was already getting tired of his smoked meat diet. He wanted something fresh.

Which meant they needed to leave the oasis.

For Braden, the goal had always been to find Old Tech. He'd found it, but it wasn't what he expected. He thought it would be salvage--find it on the ground and pick it up. The oasis changed how he thought about it. He knew the oasis was a product of still functioning Old Tech. Who else besides the ancients could have built the lake? Who built the Mirror Beast? He wanted to study these more and he needed help.

'Master Aadi, can you swim to the bottom of the lake and tell me what you see?'

'I most certainly cannot, young human,' Master Aadi responded.

"Wait. You're a turtle and turtles swim," Braden said aloud.

'I most certainly am not a turtle, and Tortoids do not swim.' To emphasize his point, Aadi floated higher and waved his thick legs about. Although he used them to swim through the air, Braden realized that was part of his ability to float and not anything to do with swimming.

"Sorry, my friend. I think I can do it, but if you would all be so kind as to make sure that nothing eats me, I would appreciate it." Braden waved at Skirill and G-War.

'I'm not going in the water,' G-War said simply, with a look of complete indifference on his 'cat face.

'I'm afraid I can't do more than skim the surface,' Skirill told the group over their mindlink.

"Fine. I see how you are. If I don't make it back, have fun trying to hook up the horses," Braden said, staving off further conversation with a dismissive wave of his hand. He stripped naked and waded into the soothing, cool water. As he got deeper, the sand changed to something smooth, like a processed metal.

He dipped under the water to get a closer look, but he was buoyant. He had to kick his legs out of the water to hold his head close to the bottom. It looked like glass with a regular pattern underneath. This was undoubtedly Old Tech, but what did it do?

Much of it was covered with sand. Standing upright, he slowly dragged his feet toward the shore. He wanted to expose as much of the bottom as possible, without clouding the water. He moved deliberately around the lake. One pass, two passes, three passes as he got closer to the shore. G-War lost interest three passes ago and was taking a nap. Both Skirill and Aadi looked on stoically. Then again, Braden believed each of them could sleep with their eyes open.

Without seeing it happen, he realized that the fountain had gained in strength. It was now throwing water a full arm-span above the lake, where before it was only a hand-span. The level of the lake rose slightly, climbing up the shore into the long-dry sand.

"Master Aadi. Have you ever seen anything like that?"

The Tortoid shook himself, then bobbed his head in thought before finally answering. *'As trees can block the wind and rocks can block a stream, maybe the sand blocks the spring?'*

"You have a point, Master Aadi, although I can't see how clearing sand from a smooth bottom has opened anything up. But it must have." Braden looked over the lake for a couple heartbeats, then waded back in until he could no longer keep his head out of the water. With a deep breath, he submerged and dove for the bottom.

Once there, he swam with broad strokes toward the middle of the lake.

He wasn't sure what to expect, but his expectations were more than what he found. At the middle of the lake, the pipe simply disappeared below the strange bottom material. Small vents surrounded it. And that was it. When he put his hand by the vents, he could feel water flow into them, as if draining from the lake.

He put his hand on the pipe. It was smooth and cool. It vibrated slightly as the water raced skyward. He planted his feet on the bottom and pushed toward the surface. He broke the water beneath the fountain and took a deep breath as the arc of fresh water splashed into the lake around him.

He looked closely at the fountain's mouth. The end of the pipe had been shaped to spray the water in a pattern. If the artisans and smiths back in Warren Deep got together to build something like this, how great would the world be? A never-ending supply of water. Who wouldn't benefit from such a thing?

He couldn't see how it all worked, only that it did. After appreciating the quality of the metalwork for a while longer, he slowly swam back to shore.

43 – Development Unit

Once ashore and dried off, Braden decided to take a closer look at the Mirror Beast. Just like he knew the fountain at the middle of the oasis was Old Tech, he knew the Mirror Beast was a most complex example of Old Tech. In fact, it was different from the Old Tech that existed anywhere in Warren Deep.

If he could only talk to it, maybe it could tell him what it was.

He slowed as he got closer to the thing, opening his mind to the tickling of the Beast.

'*84js9r9sy6432nbwevs002...*' The sound of its thought voice was loud in his head. He didn't know what the letters and numbers meant. He pinched his eyes shut and held his hands over his ears, trying to soften the litany of letters and numbers that bore down on him.

'*Listen to me. Answer my questions. What are you?*' Braden tried to think of what an even more basic question would be. If he was asked that same question, he knew that he wouldn't be able to easily answer it. He tried something different.

'*Where are you from?*' His answer was the endless stream, delivered in a monotone. He continued to move forward, stumbling as his foot caught under the roots of a nearby bush. '*Crap! My boot,*' he thought before he could stop himself.

The numbers and letters stopped and a clear voice emerged. '*Does the user request a reboot?*'

Braden didn't know what that meant, so he asked. '*What's a reboot?*'

'*Does the user request a reboot?*' it asked without hesitation.

'Careful, young master,' Aadi's voice cautioned.

Not knowing what else to do, but wanting something besides the current stalemate, he took the only course of action he thought available. *'Yes,'* he said.

The Mirror Beast voice disappeared and after a few heartbeats, the shimmering around the creature stopped. It seemed to settle into the sand, before coming back to life. It rose slightly, exposing the wheels beneath. The shimmer returned.

And the voice.

'Reboot complete. Phase 3 of desert oasis project zero three is complete. Commencing Phase 4.'

"Stop!" Braden commanded in a loud voice.

'Does the user wish to cancel Phase 4 implementation?'

"What is Phase 4? What are you going to do?" Braden asked in his normal voice. His companions were alert. G-War's whiskers arced forward as they did before he joined a fight. Skirill took to the sky and started circling higher and higher above the lake. Aadi swam backwards, putting more distance between himself and the Mirror Beast.

'Phase 4 is the construction of fields and the subsequent establishment of viable soy plants.'

"Why would you do that?"

'It is the next phase of development,' the Mirror Beast answered without emotion.

"Why would you develop this place?"

'As part of the surface transportation network to establish contact with the northern colonies. Oasis zero three is the third of six oases needed to cross Devaney's Barren.'

"Is that what you call the Great Desert?"

'There is no reference in my database to a location called the Great Desert.' Braden

couldn't follow how the Mirror Beast thought. How could it not know about the Great Desert? He took a deep breath and put himself into his best trader frame of mind.

"I am Free Trader Braden. What are you called, good sir?"

'I am Development Unit 67C.'

"A very long name, but elegant. I shall call you C. Is that okay?"

'I will add that to my programming.'

"Where are you from?"

'I was manufactured at the Higgins Bot Construction Facility.'

"And where is that?"

'Higgins Bot Construction Facility is located outside Sanctuary within grid zero zero.'

"And where is that?"

'It is grid zero zero.'

"You're not helping. Is it south of here? How many turns?"

'Grid zero zero is one thousand, seven hundred, eleven kilometers southwest of this location.'

"What's a kilometer?"

'A kilometer is one thousand meters.'

"Again. Not helpful. Are you looking at me? Here. This is one stride. How many strides is a kilometer?" Braden stepped purposefully forward with his left foot, then held that position, indicating by pointing that his is what he meant by a stride.

'Your stride is zero point eight seven meters. By your measure, you are one million, nine hundred sixty-seven thousand, four-hundred ninety nine strides from grid zero zero.' C didn't seem phased when spewing out long numbers.

"That's a long way, C. You said that this was oasis zero three. Does that mean there is a zero two and a zero one? And where would those be, in direction and strides, from here?"

'Oasis zero two is eighty-six thousand, two hundred six point nine strides to the south-southwest from here.'

"Well, that's not far, but still sounds like a long way. Skirill! Have you been listening?" Braden asked.

'Raptly,' came the Hawkoid's response.

"Great. If you can fly that direction for a dozen or so heartbeats, maybe we can find out how long it would take you to fly there and check things out." Braden turned back to Development Unit 67C.

'C. Watch my Hawkoid friend flying above us. How long would it take for him to fly to oasis zero two if he maintained his current pace?'

'This unit cannot make the calculation. As a surface development unit, only ground measurements are possible.'

"My friends and I need to talk about some things. Go ahead and begin your Phase Four, whatever that means, but don't go too far. I'm sure that I will have more questions." Without another word, the Development Unit scooted out from the brush and across the beach, heading directly out of the oasis. Soon the unit was in the desert, digging into the sand with invisible hands.

44 – Distance Check

"What do you make of that, G?"

'I cannot feel this Beast. I hear its words, but it is empty to me. I do not like it or trust it.'

"That's odd, G, because it didn't give me the impression it was capable of telling anything other than the literal truth. What'd you think, Master Aadi?"

'It is an interesting creature. Why does it shimmer like that? How can it reflect attacks upon it?'

"I think those are questions for the next time I talk to it. I wish it could tell us how far we've come. Is eighty-six thousand strides further than what we've already traveled? I need to walk it to get my mind wrapped around it. Skirill, keep your eyes on me. I'll take a few flasks." He held his hands up and waved at the Hawkoid. "Care to head out into the heat, Master Aadi? G-War, how about you?"

'Yes, Master Braden. That sounds pleasant. It is so cold in here. I shall enjoy getting out.' The Tortoid took their departure as imminent since he started air swimming toward the beach.

'Surely it jests?' was the simple response from the 'cat.

"Let me grab a couple flasks and then let's head toward the next oasis. G, if you would be so kind, keep track of time for us." Braden slung his Rico Bow over his back along with three flasks. He shifted his long knife until it was comfortable in his belt. With a small cloth wrapped around his head, they set off.

Braden diligently kept count of his steps as they walked. It took little time to reach one thousand paces. He thought it would take longer.

He was getting hot beneath the desert sun, even for this brief time he was exposed, but knew the oasis waited not far off. He drank one full flask before turning around and pointing his toes back the way they had come. Aadi swam through a small arc and joined up at Braden's side as they started their return trip, the daylight's mission complete.

This is quite pleasant, Master Human. I only know how far we came since we met. I believe the oases are not too far apart.'

"I had the same thought. I think we should be able to get there in three nights of traveling, or somewhere there about." Braden ran the calculations through his head. He was confident that they could find the next oasis without any great stress. Skirill had the eyes of a Hawkoid and would show them the way.

"What lies beyond oasis zero one?" Clearly another question he would have to ask the Mirror Beast when they returned.

The oasis readily welcomed them. Skirill and G-War hadn't moved. The horses were eating grass which grew spartanly between the bushes. Even the Gila Monster hadn't changed positions. It was good to see that their truce held, despite Braden and Aadi's absence.

The Mirror Beast threw up clouds of dust as it plowed purposefully through the sands just beyond the outer trees of the oasis. It was making significant progress. Braden was impressed with how much work it could do. He wondered if he could command it to help them?

"C! Can you hear me?" He changed positions and yelled a second time. Then a third, before finally giving up.

"Master Aadi, any ideas on how I can talk to it?"

I suspect, my human friend, that it is singularly focused on the task at hand. You may have to wait until it completes that task before it is open for further conversation.'

"Well, that's just a cloud of dog breath! Who knows how long this Phase Four is going to take?" Braden waded into the lake for a refreshing swim, then waited.

And waited.

Still waiting.

45 – Moving On

Three turns passed and there was still no contact with the Development Unit. It went diligently about its work, both daylight and night, oblivious to the presence of the companions. Braden even tried standing in front of the Beast as it dug and plowed, but it deftly moved in a tight circle and neatly avoided the human obstruction.

Their supply of smoked meat was getting low. They needed to leave.

Braden expected to find another Mirror Beast at the next oasis. He would talk to that one.

He manhandled the cart to the south side of the oasis and prepared it. Come twilight, he would saddle Max, harness Pack, and they would depart.

He encouraged everyone to rest, although Braden was the one who needed it most. The horses would probably perk up when they got to stretch their legs.

Skirill took the time to fly south-southeast for a good while. He flew the distance he figured they would travel on the ground that night. He saw nothing different from what they traveled before. He did not fly far enough to see another oasis, and told Braden that he would do this daily until he saw their destination.

G-War remained unperturbed as usual.

They departed in the early evening, as the sun was setting, having drunk their fill of water. Braden thought he sloshed as he walked. He knew that drinking to excess was a fleeting thing to do, but it was what they decided. The extra water would be meaningless if they became stranded under the desert sun.

They angled south-southwest, moving quickly at first but intending to slow gradually through the evening. Temperatures seemed cooler than their previous trip. As winter approached, Braden's caravan benefitted. They maintained their pace through the early morning hours, only slowing when Skirill flew before them, looking for a place to rest for the daylight.

He found nothing.

He circled wider and flew further. Still nothing.

G-War knew before the rest of them that Skirill could not find a place to make camp. He told Braden and they stopped where they were. Braden needed the extra time to dig a shelter. He was already tired before taking the first shovel full of sand and dirt. He kept digging past the sunrise and well into the morning. He planted the branches in the ground, angled away from the sun to create a shaded area over the pit. It was cool in the back, at the lowest point, but toward the front, it received the least amount of shade and was the shallowest.

They left the cart in the sun, while bringing their meager amount of smoked meat and both casks into their shelter. It was a tight squeeze for all of them to get in, especially after the horses laid down. In the end, Braden got the least sleep as he was half in the sun most of the time. He drank a little more than his self-limited allotment of water to compensate, and he didn't feel bad about that. Hopefully tomorrow would bring them to a better shelter.

46 – Oasis Zero Two

The second night of travel ended on a better note. Skirill found a place quickly, not far off the track they were following. They set up in an elbow of a dried riverbed, protected from the sun on three sides before Braden put up their awning-like contraption. They slept well that turn.

It was cooler earlier in the evening, so they left before nightfall. They again traveled quickly. Braden felt that the horses were surging ahead each night as they sensed fodder at the end of their journey. With their limited rations, the horses were starting to lose weight.

Aadi took to bracing himself against the cart as they traveled. He floated and the cart carried him along effortlessly. Skirill wedged himself between the tree branches tied across the top of the cart. G-War was inside the cart somewhere. Braden suspected the 'cat relaxed on a soft blanket. Then again, despite the Golden Warrior's calm exterior, he was ill-suited for life in the desert. He was probably the most miserable of them all. Braden was surprised he hadn't heard any complaints.

On cue, *'Crossing the Great Desert was our journey to a better future. We all agreed it needed done. There is no sense in crying about it now. For its information, I am hungry. I have been hungry for the past seven turns. I will continue to be hungry until I can eat a fresh kill. Looking around, I don't think that will be any time soon.'* The 'cat snorted in derision.

'Sorry I brought it up, G. I will get you to fertile lands in the south,' Braden answered in his thought voice.

'Why did it not ask about the lands to the south when it was talking to it?' G-War was not pleased. He was convinced the Mirror Beast had much more information to share. He didn't trust the Beast as it was not forthcoming. By that, the 'cat meant that he was unable to look directly into the thing's mind and see what he wanted to know, like he did with Braden. His fur was

dry and he was hungry. He was hot.

Braden could now feel the 'cat's discomfort. All it took was to ask. He hoped that by sharing, the 'cat could free himself from some of the burden. They called people who removed pain like that empaths; they were the healers.

Braden wasn't one, but he and the 'cat shared a bond. He knew that G-War reduced his pain, and Braden wanted to reciprocate. In the end, he settled for the simple act of listening to the 'cat's complaints, sharing the experience.

Master Aadi was unaffected by the dry, the dust, and the heat. He was the only one native to the desert.

After the third night of travel, Skirill flew off believing that he would find the next oasis. He was surprised when he saw it due east of where they were. Braden watched as the Hawkoid started south and abruptly changed course to the east, beating his wings hard against the cool of the morning air. Braden closed his eyes and opened his mind. He linked and could see what Skirill saw. It looked like the sands of the desert had won the battle against the green of the oasis.

Long dead trees peeked out from the sand. In a few more cycles, no one would ever know there had been an oasis here. It had fought the battle against the desert, winning long enough for the trees to grow tall and strong, but in the end, lost the fight.

Braden turned Max's head toward the oasis and laid into the horse with his heels. Pack sensed the urgency and trotted along behind, losing ground but keeping Max in sight as they fled into the morning dawn.

The darkness of dead trees rose before him as Braden arrived. He fell from the saddle, grasping the strange and long dead leaves of the trees unique to the oases. They were sharp and he cut his hand. He hung his head in despair, never having thought about an oasis that wasn't.

He walked around the open area between the dead trees, assuming the lake was somewhere below him. After Pack arrived, Braden dug out his shovel and quickly found the metal fountainhead. He hit it a few times with the shovel to encourage water to spew forth, but it defied him.

He found the shore and dug into the sands until he found the strange material that made up the bottom of the oasis lakes. He cleared it, and then worked to expand the patch. Last time he cleared the materials, water surged from the fountain.

He continued clearing the area closest to the beach; it was the shallowest. As the sun climbed slowly into the sky, he realized that he best build the shelter. Despite being in the oasis, there was no water and the sun would beat down on them mercilessly if they didn't have shelter.

He used the existing trunks to rig a wide awning. It would be hot as they were in the open, but they wouldn't be in the direct sunlight. He made quick work of the shelter and went back to digging the sand away from the shore of the lake. His back ached as he continued to dig, until he finally gave up and joined the panting animals in the shelter. He fell into a fitful sleep.

47 - Restored

When Braden awoke in the middle of the afternoon, he heard the noise but couldn't figure out what it was. He walked from under their shelter and was immediately blinded by the relentless sun. He covered his eyes with his hand and pressed ahead, walking over the hard surface of the small area he had cleared from the lake bottom until he reached the fountain. It was gurgling, but no water was coming out.

It was confirmed. The lake bottom powered the fountain.

With a new energy and despite the sun, he dug into the sand, throwing it where the beach should have been. He cleared the entire shore for a few arm-spans, then began moving into the deeper sand. The lake bottom was a dark glass over top of a fine pattern of intricate metalwork.

If the ancients could make something like this, why could they not save themselves? These creations were like magic.

Humans had lost the ability to do this. What a shame.

Old Tech called him. Maybe it was in his blood to find it and restore that which had been lost.

From the cleared shore, he started digging a path directly to the fountain. The sand walls collapsed as he dug into them, so he cleared a wide path, getting wider as he got closer to the middle of the lake. It was hard work and he was wearing down from the heat. He drank often, to keep his energy up.

Once at the fountainhead, he cleared the strange vents he had seen in the other oasis. He exposed the smooth metal of the pipe buried in the ground and dug out around it. And dug. And threw sand. And dug some more.

It was twilight when he finally cleared the vents enough that sand stopped falling back into them.

With a great sigh, air rushed into the vents, dust in the air and grains of sand disappeared into the darkness. Heavy vibrations shook the pipe until it turned cool as water surged through it. The water bubbled out and quickly filled the area around the bottom of the pipe. The vents covered with water and the level rose. Surrounding sand was washed away into the vents. He let it go. He couldn't dig any more. Let the water do the work.

He knew that all he needed was to keep the glass exposed to the sun and the oasis would work.

It filled the trench he had cut to the center pipe. It didn't make it to the shore area he had cleared. There wasn't enough water, enough energy driving it from the pipe.

He sat in the cool water as it swirled around him. When he looked up, he saw that he had company.

The 'cat sat at the edge of the water, enjoying the coolness it brought to the air. Skirill waded in next to him and stood majestically leg deep in the resurging lake, while Master Aadi floated over the fountain, taking in the moisture through his feet, as was his way.

Even the horses were making their way to the water. They waded in, kicking up clouds of sand dust as they drank heartily.

48 - Hope

"I think we need to leave tonight," Braden said, even though he was already exhausted. He knew that he would fall asleep in the saddle, but there was no food here. The horses needed to eat. Everyone needed to eat.

No one suggested anything different, so after they drank their fill and loaded up, they were off to the south-southwest. Skirill had not scouted the area before it got too dark, but they figured the risk of traveling into the unknown was better than the alternative of starvation.

It had to be more of the same. If the next oasis was like this one, Braden would shovel it out. They would drink and move on. So what if they were hungry. At this rate, they could be out of the Great Desert in six turns.

What waited for them on the other side? This started to bother him. When traveling the roads of Warren Deep, very little was unknown to him. This was completely different. There were no stories told in pubs about what lay south of the Great Desert. No one alive knew anything. By not asking the Mirror Beast before letting it go back to work, he had squandered their chance to know.

He hoped that his mistake had not led the caravan to certain death.

For now, they had their routine. Through the darkness of night they traveled. The morning brought a quick flight, a frenzied run to cover, building the same shelter, over and over, and then sleep in the heat of the shade.

They traveled more slowly with each passing turn.

As twilight ended the third night after their departure from Oasis Zero Two, Skirill took flight, looking for the next oasis, hoping for a green oasis and not one in the throes of its own demise.

He flew in circles around the group. If their direction was off, the oasis could be anywhere. He found nothing. He proceeded south making a wide swerving S, creating a cone of travel. Skirill expected to see another oasis that lost its battle to the desert.

But that wasn't it at all. Far to the south-southwest, he saw a complete settlement: trees, fields, buildings, and the wondrous sparkling blue of a lake.

'Is this right?' Skirill asked. *'Is this the oasis or have we made it through the Great Desert?'*

'We shall see after a good sleep. We shall see,' Braden said, feeling far more hope than he had felt since they saw the last ghost of an oasis.

49 – Oasis Zero One

They traveled in the darkness, the cart creaking loudly and the horses' harnesses slapping and jingling. They didn't hurry as they wanted to enter the village in the light.

'Buildings. Who lives out here?' Braden thought. *'Maybe we can trade. I still have one vial of saffrimander, platinum, silver, and gold. Do they know what any of that is?'*

'Fields.' Braden thought about the horses. *'They are going to love those. I already love those and I don't even know what's growing.'*

"G-War, can you feel anything from that village?" Braden asked aloud, not bothering to turn around. He would not have been able to see the 'cat. He was barely able to make out Pack's large form.

'Nothing,' came the 'cat's reply.

Maybe they weren't close enough yet.

Braden called a stop while the moon was still high overhead. They ate a little of their remaining stores and drank heartily. Braden sat on the ground, looking south, and waited.

Twilight found Braden still sitting, but with his head between his knees as he was sound asleep. Aadi floated by, bumping him gently.

He awoke to the oasis' outline in the distance. They remounted quickly and got underway. Skirill was already airborne, flying circles around the oasis, carefully looking for any creatures. He saw movement among the bushes, but couldn't see anything specific.

He continued to circle, going lower as the sun broke the horizon and flooded the oasis with light.

The others looked through the Hawkoid's eyes, seeing a well-maintained series of one-story buildings standing along the shore of the lake. Small shapes swam in the water. Skirill swooped down for a closer look. Fish, not cold-water crocs. No monsters.

He headed away from the lake, passing over the fields, plants heavy with beans and grains. He banked as the desert approached and winged gently back toward the oasis.

Movement, coming from one of the small buildings on the end. He back winged to a hover, focusing on the creatures now moving about. They looked like Mirror Beasts, only smaller, with many arms, which were shaped more like snakes and tree branches than a human's arms.

They moved with purpose, each going to a separate part of the oasis. It looked like they were working. One was trimming plants. Two were now in the fields, working with the dirt, then the plants. One looked to be feeding the fish. The shapes in the water surged together, breaking the surface as the mini Beast dropped bits of something from a box on a small dock.

In the underbrush, he finally got a clear view of what looked to be a small, wild boar. It was misshapen, though. It walked with a jerk as its legs were different sizes. A fifth leg protruded uselessly from its side. The Hawkoid at first thought that he'd like some pork, but that creature didn't look appetizing. The fish, however, were a completely different matter.

50 – Dinner Awaits

"Master Aadi. You had the plan last time. What do you suggest we do?"

'I suggest we not get killed! I've never seen the like of what awaits us.'

"And you still don't feel anything?" Braden asked G-War.

'The small boars, yes. They are barely functioning animals. I suspect they will taste good.'

"I think Aadi and I will lead the way, G. You bring up the rear. Skirill, can you find a place to perch without being seen so you can watch us?"

'Yes,' was Skirill's simple answer. That was all Braden needed. His trust in his companions was implicit. If they needed help, the Hawkoid would be there. G-War made sure that they were all connected via mindlink, so communication between the companions was instantaneous.

"Thanks, Ess. We'll tie the horses to the first tree we come to and then bring them when the way is clear. Master Aadi, shall we?" Braden crooked his arm as if offering to take a lady dancing. The Tortoid looked at it briefly, blinked twice, and swam forward.

They entered the oasis without being challenged by any of the mini Mirror Beasts or the boar pack. With the horses secured behind them, they moved forward. Braden had his hand on the hilt of his long knife still in his belt, and the Rico Bow rested easily across his back. The Tortoid floated at Braden's shoulder, swimming slowly, keeping pace with the wary human. The 'cat padded effortlessly behind them by a few strides, staying to the shadows and the cover the bushes provided.

The small boars, which Braden recognized as wild javelina, ran around them, but never too close. They seemed disinterested in the companions.

Many of the javelina were malformed; all of them were smaller than those from Warren Deep. He realized two things about them. They had no fear of him and they were vegetarians.

'Let's check the buildings first to see if there are any people,' Braden told his companions with his thought voice.

As Aadi and Braden walked from the cover of the trees to the open area in front, a mini Mirror Beast popped out from the underbrush at their side and came straight for them. The Tortoid instantly unleashed his focused thunderclap. Braden was happy not to be the target this time, but it still took him unaware. Too late, he clasped his hands over his ears as he made to jump aside.

He expected the blast would be reflected and that he'd be hit a second time, but this creature did not have the abilities of his larger brother. It popped its seams, two of its four arms were ripped off, and it toppled sideways to the ground.

All of this in less than a heartbeat. Braden was still trying to get his hands over his ears when the attack was finished.

Braden shook his head to clear it. "Master Aadi, I'm not sure that thing has any weapons."

'My apologies, young human. It surprised me.' He floated down close to the wreckage on the ground. *'My, my. Isn't that strange. It seems to be made of material like your knife.'*

Braden looked to see if any other attackers lurked nearby, but there wasn't anything or anyone besides the javelina, playing and eating in the underbrush.

Braden examined the pieces of the mini Mirror Beast without touching any of it. Using his knife, he levered the thing's body until it flipped over. It was roughly the shape of a small tree trunk. Round. Flat on the top and bottom. The bottom plate had fallen off. Inside was a great number of small metal parts, a black and waxy box, some thin green pieces, and many, many thin, colored strings. These were bundled as they connected one thing to another, their tendrils ending in gold and touching everything inside.

He reached into it and touched the various parts and pieces. "This is all man-made! These strings are gold, silver, and copper with a thin layer of something to protect them. This is amazing!" His voice changed to a whisper. "Old Tech." With this, Braden had now seen more Old Tech than any other human in Warren Deep. He was the only one to see functioning Old Tech.

But they had accidentally killed it. He continued his inspection of the detail within. He knew there was no way he could put it back together and make it function again.

'Master Human…' prompted the Tortoid. Braden looked up and saw another one of the creatures, this one boxy, shorter, with four arms. It was standing right next to him. Braden fell over and scooted away, holding his knife in front of him and pointing at the newcomer.

This mini Mirror Beast was only interested in its companion. Using its arms with various devices attached at the ends, it collected up the entirety of the broken Beast. With a final brush of the dirt, it rolled away, its friend piled into a cart behind it. They disappeared into a shed-like structure near the end of a long building.

Braden had never encountered a facility like this. He needed to take better stock of his surroundings before they took another step into it. These man-made creatures scared him because he didn't understand them. He hadn't tried to talk with them, but he needed to. They needed information that they could only learn by getting answers to their many questions.

"Next time, we talk first and blast second."

'Hungry,' popped into Braden's mind. He looked back to see the 'cat crouched, ready to pounce.

"G! Not now, by all that's holy! We already killed one creature. How many more before they all turn on us? I'm not sure we can win that fight, my friend," Braden said firmly.

'Let's go, then. Dinner awaits,' the 'cat responded without humor.

51 – Repair Shed

Braden decided to follow the boxy beast to the shed. As he approached, the door opened by sliding upwards into the roof. He jumped aside, expecting someone or something to emerge. The door promptly slid back down.

He stepped from his cover toward the door. It opened again. He jumped aside. It closed.

'This is rather fun, don't you think?' the Tortoid offered.

Braden hung his head and laughed silently to himself. How did he get here? He not only had a 'cat that constantly questioned his intelligence, he now had a Tortoid giving him grief. He looked at Aadi and shook his head. The Tortoid blinked once, floating serenely to the side.

"Be my guest, Master Tortoid," Braden said. Aadi swam toward the door, but it remained closed. He floated left and right in front of it. No change.

'Sorry. It seems to like you better.'

'There's no accounting for taste,' the 'cat chimed in. *'Like one of these tasty morsels running around. Can it stop goofing around, please? Hungry.'*

Braden stood before the door. It opened and stayed open as he stood there. It seemed dark inside, but his eyes quickly adjusted. It was a work area, but nothing like he'd ever seen before. The bench was low and in the middle of the room. On it, all the parts of the blasted beast were arranged. A mechanical device was overhead, working itself along a beam. Other smaller devices were arranged around and on the table. They appeared to be working to put the mini Mirror Beast back together. Sparks flew here and there, but Braden couldn't see a forge of any sort.

Along the inside walls were bits and pieces of various metals, bands of the coated copper, silver, and gold, and a wide variety of parts and pieces. It was an Old Tech repair shop. The tech repaired other tech. *And that's why the ancients aren't here anymore,* he thought. If he had nothing to do, he would wither and die. The ancients built these magnificent creatures and then the humans themselves no longer mattered.

That's what Braden supposed anyway. Maybe he would find out some turn, but not if he couldn't talk with these things.

He went inside the room, filled to bursting with Old Tech. "Oh wondrous creatures from the before time, incredible Old Tech creations, I am Braden, Free Trader of Warren Deep." He bowed as he finished, watching for any sign that the metal creatures had heard and would talk with him.

Nothing.

The door finally closed as Braden moved to look more closely at the materials along the sides. Aadi was still outside. Braden started to panic and rushed back at the door.

It promptly opened. Aadi looked at him with his expressionless face. *'Yes?'*

"Nothing," he quickly replied. "I'm not sure they can talk with me. C'mon in, Master Aadi, and see for yourself."

'Thank you, but no. I'm perfectly fine right here. I shall await your return.'

Braden looked at him. A single blink as the Tortoid hovered motionless outside the door. Braden went back inside, the door slid down behind him. He looked around to make sure that nothing had changed, that nothing was coming after him now that he was alone.

Nothing did.

While digging in a box, he found a small round device with two arrows. The numbers one through twelve were inscribed on the outside. It had a metal band shaped for a person's wrist. He put this in his belt pouch. He looked up to see if anything cared. The small Bots continued repairing the mini Beast.

"What are you?" he asked, knowing he would get no reply.

He went back outside, walking briskly past the Tortoid. "Let's check out the building. There's no one in here."

52 – A Venison Meat Pie, Please

Braden pushed on the first door they came to, but it was closed. There was no handle, only a small panel to the right of the door frame. It looked to be shaped for his hand, so he put his hand on it. It flashed red. The door remained closed. He tried it again with the same result. He tried the remaining five doors in the building and received the same result. Each panel flashed the color red beneath his hand.

He tried looking in through the windows between each of the doors. Although the windows were large, he couldn't see inside. They were glass, but black and opaque. Even with his nose against them and his hands cupped around his eyes, he couldn't see in. He expected that he could break the glass, but he didn't want to do that yet.

He thought no one cared that they had damaged one of the Old Tech devices, but he didn't want to push his luck. It wasn't his intent to destroy the oasis. First and foremost, he wanted his party to be safe. They hadn't found anything so far that was a threat. He wanted answers from these Old Tech creatures.

Another small building stood beyond the building with the dark windows and closed doors. This had a single door, of a type like the shed, with larger, clear windows taking up much of the wall space. He looked in to see various overstuffed chairs, a strange desk area, and a table with Old Tech devices on it.

He boldly walked up to the door, and it promptly opened. Cool air welcomed him, like a gentle breeze coming off the mountains. He hadn't felt air this cool since before they entered the Great Desert, and it felt good against his face. Aadi blinked rapidly and backed away from the cold air.

Braden went inside. He ran his hand over the materials of the chairs and the couch. He looked around the room. It reminded him of the hotels in the bigger cities where he had often traded, but this was an Old Tech version. He looked around in awe. At the table, a flat pane of glass was held upright by a clever black metal stand. He had no idea what it did.

He continued to a high desk, enclosed in a U shape facing toward him. When he stood in the middle, the desk was chest high on three sides.

Suddenly, a figure appeared before him. It looked like a reflection in a pool of water. He knew it wasn't flesh and blood like him, but it was still real. And it talked.

"Welcome to Oasis Zero One," a pleasant female voice sounded from what seemed like all around him. "We do not have you in our records, for some reason, but if you would like, we will add you and then you can be checked in and given your room. Would you like to be added to our records at this time?"

Braden was wary. Last time he had simply agreed to one of the Old Tech creations' requests, he lost the ability to learn from it.

"What lies to the south of here?" he asked.

"The desertscape of Devaney's Barren covers the next seventy-five kilometers to the south. Does that answer your question?"

From his conversation with the Mirror Beast, he knew that this was about eighty-six thousand strides, two to three turns of travel with fresh horses, or only part of one daylight's flight for the Hawkoid.

"What's beyond the desertscape?"

"The Plains of Propiscius lie beyond the desertscape," the pleasant voice responded.

"How far from there to where we can find an outpost of the ancients?"

"I don't understand your question. Do you wish to be added to our records?"

Braden felt the 'cat's impatience in his mind. Aadi floated outside. He was on edge. The Tortoid was uncomfortable around the Old Tech.

"Are the javelina outside pets or creatures that you take care of?"

"Javelina. The small pig-like creatures. Wait, please." The lady's reflected face smiled at Braden. "Those creatures are new additions since Oasis Zero One was built. Would you like us to clear them away for you?"

"No need..." Before Braden could finish his sentence, the image of G-War's claws digging into the neck of a javelina flashed into his mind. A brief struggle and then the Golden Warrior purred his delight as he feasted heartily on his fresh kill. "Where were we? Oh yes, we are looking for Old Tech, but it appears like we've found it. I am willing to trade for Old Tech that we can take with us. Are there any weapons here?"

"I'm sorry. There is no trade here. Oasis Zero One is a rest stop as people travel through Devaney's Barren. We provide food, water, and a place to rest, before travelers continue on their journey. We have no weapons here. Would you like to be added to our records now?"

"Yes, yes, go ahead. No, wait!" Braden forgot himself.

"You are now added to our records as Caretaker Braden. You have been assigned Room A, the first door on your right. It is coded to your handprint. Thank you and please enjoy your stay." The reflection vanished.

"Crap!" Braden shouted. He stepped out of the area in front of the desk. Then stepped back in.

"How may I help you Caretaker Braden?" The woman's reflection returned with a welcoming smile.

"Thank the 'cats in heaven! I'm so glad you returned. I thought I'd lost you. You can call me just Braden." He didn't know why the Old Tech had given him the title of Caretaker, but there were too many other questions to bother with this one.

"I am here twenty-fours a day and my purpose is to ensure you have a pleasant stay. I will always answer when you call. How may I be of service?" She was so pleasant, and Braden felt relieved. He expected that he would spend a great deal of time asking questions.

In his mind, he saw Skirill's view of a small Javelina running across an opening. The Hawkoid dove on it with a vengeance, snapping the thing's neck as he hit it and then lifting it into the air as he flew away toward his perch.

"You said that food and water were available. Can you tell me where, please?"

"Yes, it is my pleasure. A fabricator is in your room. It will respond to your voice commands."

"A fabricator. Sounds great. What is it and how does it work?"

"It converts provided base nutritional packs, both solid and liquid, into food and drink items of your choice. The menu is rather substantial as this is a fully functioning rest area."

"Thank you. I expect that I'll return shortly. I have more questions." Braden headed outside, where it seemed much warmer than before. How did they keep that building cool?

Aadi swam along beside him as he approached the first door of the long building. He put his hand on the panel and it flashed green. The door slid open. He looked inside. There was a bed the likes of which only the richest people in Warren Deep enjoyed. He saw a table with chairs, a couch, and another large panel of glass. He'd have to ask the reflection at the desk what the panels were for. There was a box above a small counter. There was a metal sink with a metal pipe above it. A door led to a small room at the side. It had a white throne like you'd find in an outhouse. There was more, all shiny white, like the finest pottery. He wasn't sure where to start, but he had to start somewhere.

"Oh fabricator, I would like some water please." He looked around to see what would respond.

The box above the counter hummed and there was a beep. He could see a glass inside, but he could not see a handle. "How do I get you out of there?" He ran his hands around the box, down the sides and across the front. A depression moved slightly as he brushed it. He pushed in and the box popped open. The front of it was the door.

He reached in and took out the glass with the cool water. He tasted it tentatively. It was water. It tasted good. He felt like a rich man drinking water out of the glass.

"Oh fabricator, I would like a fire-roasted venison meat pie, please."

"Your request is not a menu option. Please select again."

"Who doesn't know about venison meat pies? One of the finest delicacies anywhere! Tell me, Mr. Fabricator, what kind of meat do you have?"

"I have a wide variety of beef, chicken, pork, and fish dishes. May I recommend a beef pot pie?"

"Sure. I'll take that."

A few heartbeats of humming later and the ding signaled that the food was ready. He looked at a steaming creation in a decorative bowl. He pushed in the depression, opened the door, and took out his lunch.

Braden needed his spoon, which was back in a blanket pack. He hadn't needed it for weeks. The horses. He needed to turn them loose to drink and eat. He left his lunch on the counter and raced outside. He and Aadi left to find the rest of their party. They needed to set up for a short stay, and he needed to discuss things with Aadi, Skirill, and G-War.

And get a spoon. The beef pot pie smelled good.

53 – Masters of Water

Braden found the 'cat not far from the main trail. Hillcats were like other cats in that they could eat once a week, but at that feeding, they ate up to one third their body weight. It meant that they were no good for hunting while they digested their massive meals.

The Golden Warrior was in a food coma. Braden could feel his contentment radiating from the furry body; he left him where he found him beneath the bush.

Skirill sat majestically on a tall tree. Watching all that was happening.

Or he was sleeping. From this distance Braden couldn't be sure, but figured the latter more likely.

The journey across the Great Desert had been tough on the Hawkoid and the 'cat, especially the 'cat. They deserved to eat well. Braden hoped that the loss of a couple small javelina would not cause any grief. The loss of the mini Beast didn't seem to bother anyone. Then again, there was no one to bother. He needed to put together all the questions he wanted to ask, and for that, he needed G-War, Skirill, and Aadi.

The questions would have to wait.

He brought the horses to the lake, removed harness and saddle, then hobbled them. The mini Mirror Beasts were no threat. The horses might be afraid of them, but they would have to get over that.

The horses drank deeply from the lake water, then ambled into the bushes in search of grass and weeds.

Braden picked up the 'cat on the way back to the room. He was distinctly heavier than usual, and Braden wondered where the javelina carcass was. He wanted to see how big a kill G-War had made, but he couldn't find it. The sand had been brushed clean. A mini Mirror Beast had removed the carcass and cleaned the area.

All questions to ask the pleasant woman's reflection. He would ask about her, too. Who was she?

He didn't ponder that too long as he arrived at the room. Aadi preferred the outdoors where it was respectably warm. The frigid temperatures of the room were painful for him.

Braden put the cat on the over-stuffed chair and covered him with a towel he found in the side room. Then he dug into his beef pot pie. It tasted funny. The beef didn't taste like beef at all. The pie crust, gravy, and vegetables hit the spot, though. He ate it all, and even licked the dish clean. There wasn't anything else to do with it, so he put the dish back in the fabricator. Once the door closed, it disappeared.

He was continually impressed by what the ancients had built. What would his world look like if he didn't have to hunt or cook?

He went to the side room. He understood that it was a room for relief and bathing. He didn't like the idea of leaving his waste in the bowl of water on the ceramic throne. That made no sense to him, so he determined not to use it. He shut the lid and left it alone. The tub, like so many things at this oasis, looked unlike anything he'd seen before. The pipes from the wall looked similar to those from the fountain in the lake.

The ancients were masters of water. He should have figured that from the last two oases. Even here, in this room, he could control the water. He knew what he had to do. He turned one of two knobs above the lower fountainhead and water began to flow. It was cool at first, then hot, too hot to touch. He turned the other knob. The water cooled to an even lukewarm temperature. He turned it back a little and the water warmed pleasantly. He stripped and lowered himself into the tub as the water swirled around him.

He played with the knobs as the water splashed around his legs. He pulled on a small protrusion on the fountainhead itself and the water stopped. He couldn't push it down easily. Then water burst from the pipe that was higher than his head when standing. He pushed the protrusion down and the water reappeared from the lower fountainhead.

He liked it. On a small counter in the corner were various packets. Dripping as he exited the tub, he looked at them. They were clearly labeled soap and shampoo. He knew about soap, but the liquid shampoo baffled him. Conditioner. No clue.

He returned to the tub, pulling the protrusion so water splashed over his head and down his body. He used the soap and cleaned himself, finally rinsing while standing under the water for a decadent amount of time.

Even though the ancients provided the water in what seemed like an unlimited supply, he was raised to conserve. He turned the knobs and shut the water off.

He dried himself with a towel, then hung it over the rack so it would be ready the next time. He was a modern man, who appreciated the finer things in life. He had never had them, but he often dreamed of what it would be like. A successful trader retired to a life of ease, but few were that successful.

He wanted to be one of them and that's why he was going to continue south, continue to a place where he could find a supply of Old Tech that people wanted. Then he would know the value of wealth.

54 - Feeding

Once cleaned and refreshed, he decided to give the fabricator another go.

"Oh Mr. Fabricator, what do you suggest I should eat now?"

"Many travelers enjoy a lime sherbet with orange slices for a mid-afternoon snack."

Braden had eaten oranges when he visited the far west region of Warren Deep. He'd even carried some for trade, but they didn't last long enough to make it where their trade value would have been higher. They were only good for a few turns before they had to be traded.

"Yes. That sounds perfect for one of my station, Mr. Fabricator. Please work your magic and deliver unto me the lime sherbet and orange slices. By the way, what does this cost?"

"There is no cost. The fabricator is provided as a standard rest area service." The familiar humming returned, followed by the ding. Braden felt his mouth begin watering at the sound. He thought that was an odd response, although his mouth watered while watching a rabbit turning on a spit, too.

He pulled out the dish that looked remarkably similar to that which had held his beef pot pie, but this time, there was one large light green snow/ice ball with orange slices arranged around it. He tried an orange slice. It was as he remembered. He savored the flavor and the little bite on his tongue. With his spoon, he tried some of the ice ball, which he figured was the lime sherbet. Tart, but good. He took a big bite. The cold stung his teeth. He swallowed without chewing and it felt like a spear had poked directly into his brain. He threw the dish away from him.

The 'cat was immediately standing and ready to attack, even though his body may not have fully cooperated. He couldn't tell if Braden was under attack or not. He sensed nothing in the room except for himself and the human.

"What kind of poison is this?"

"If the guest is displeased with the selection, I will happily provide a replacement. Please return the dish and unconsumed portion to the fabricator for recycling. This unit has determined that the guest would prefer dessert that is not chilled. How about a chocolate brownie?"

The pain in his head quickly went away, while the enticing flavors of the lime and orange remained in his mouth. Maybe the cold was too much. G-War changed positions on the chair, pointing one furry paw toward Braden in his mockery of the one finger wave before lying down to go back to sleep.

"Not sure about the dish. I'll give you what's left." He set the orange slices on the counter as he put the broken pieces of the dish and puddle of lime sherbet into the fabricator. He licked his fingers clean and wiped them dry on his clothes.

The ding. The mouthwatering. He opened the door eagerly to find a small dark brown square. It looked like an odd cake. He tasted a small bite.

It was like a little slice of heaven. He quickly devoured it, then ordered five more. After those, he felt sick to his stomach.

55 – Get Up

Braden laid down on the bed for just a few heartbeats. The bed embraced him like his mother's arms.

When he awoke, it was dark and Skirill was calling his name in a loud squawk. He opened his sleep-fogged mind. "What is it? What happened?"

Braden! Master Aadi said that you were within the building, but I couldn't see you. I couldn't feel you. I was worried. Are you okay?'

'Yes, yes. I'm fine. More tired than I thought I was.' He sat up in bed. He couldn't remember the last time he slept that well. *'What about you? Are you okay?'*

'I feel refreshed after a good meal and a long sleep. I am hungry again, though. The little javelina are more energetic about avoiding me now. They are making it interesting. I will watch them for a while.'

'I'll meet you in front of my room in just a few heartbeats. I have something for you.' He stood up, stretched, and ordered a beef pot pie.

The Hawkoid was hesitant to land on the ground, as he did not trust the mini Mirror Beasts. He balanced precariously on the wayward branch of a small tree. Braden held the dish up to him. Skirill sniffed it cautiously.

"Go ahead, try it. It's called a beef pot pie. I want to know what you think."

Skirill jabbed his curved beak into the dish, and Braden almost lost his grip on it. He repositioned to hold it better as the Hawkoid jabbed again and again, his beak dripping with gravy while he threw down the bread-like crust and concoction within.

"Hmmm. It isss good. There is no 'eat in it," Skirill hissed aloud.

"No meat? I thought it tasted funny. I'll have to ask about that. Hey! You missed it. There's this reflection of a woman that appears when I stand in a certain spot in that small building over there. She answers any questions I have. I was going to talk to her for a bit. Is there anything you'd like to know?"

"'irror 'easts. Are they sa'e?"

"Are the mini Mirror Beasts safe, huh? That's a good question. I expect she can tell me all about them. Hang on, I'll be right back." Braden returned the dish to the fabricator. He considered asking G-War to go with him, but thought better of it. 'Ass,' he whispered as he left the room.

56 – Puke

Braden stood in front of the desk and on cue, the reflected image of the smiling lady appeared.

"Good evening. How may I help you, Braden?"

"Good evening to you, too. I have to say that your bed is the most comfortable I've ever slept in. By the way, how much will this cost? I have platinum, gold, silver, and saffrimander I can trade."

"There is no cost for the use of the Rest Area. All travelers are welcome."

"When's the last time you had a traveler?" Braden asked without thinking.

"You are our first traveler since this station came online two hundred seventy-four years, six months, and two days ago."

"What's a year?" Braden suspected he knew what the measures of time were.

"A year is the time it takes for the Planet Cygnus VII to make one complete rotation around the sun Cygnus Prime."

"A cycle of the seasons. You call it a year. Summer to summer. And a month? A day?"

"There are twelve months in one year. A day is the time it takes for planet Cygnus VII to complete one full rotation."

"A day. Where the sun sleeps each night. We call it a turn of the sun, or just turn. Thank you, but you talked about Cygnus, what, seven? Cygnus Prime? Are you talking about Vii?" Braden asked, his curiosity piqued.

164

"We are on planet Cygnus Seven, written Vee Eye Eye, which is a pre-space numbering system to designate the number seven. Cygnus Prime is the star around which the planets rotate."

"Planet Vii. I got it. There are other planets?"

"There are eight planets in this solar system, two of which are capable of supporting life," the pleasant voice answered.

"We aren't alone? I thought the only people on Vii lived in Warren Deep."

"The latest census data I have is nearly four hundred years old. At that time, there were more than one hundred thousand people on Cygnus VII, or Vii as you call it. There were two thousand people living on Cygnus VI. Cygnus Six, that is."

"Wow. I didn't know. No one knows that. Are they still there? Are there people on Cygnus Six?"

"I am afraid that my data is nearly four hundred years old. I cannot confirm their continued existence, reduction or growth in population," the reflection said with a slight hint of sadness.

'*Ask about the Mirror Beasts,*' Skirill interjected as Braden was thinking about the enormity of it all.

"I was lost there for a second. Are these mini Mirror Beasts dangerous? What do they do?"

"I don't understand the question. What are the mini-Mirror Beasts?"

"Those metal things moving around. They look like they are man-made."

"Those are the standard complement of Maintenance Bots. They maintain this facility. They are not dangerous. Each has a number of tasks that it performs to ensure that the rest area is always in peak operating condition. As a matter of fact, right now, a Service Bot is making your bed and cleaning your room."

"My room? Oh no! G-War." Braden bolted from the office. The battle cry of a Hillcat pierced the dark of the evening. Soft lights from hidden torches showed the area, but Braden didn't think about that. He was focused on keeping his friend from getting hurt.

The door to the room stood open, and Braden rushed through it. He was greeted by the screeching sound of claws on steel. "G! They're safe. It's safe. It's not attacking." Without thinking, Braden grabbed two handfuls of the 'cat and pulled him from the top of the Server Bot.

The 'cat turned in a flash, eyes wide, claws out, ready to rake across the human's face and throat. Braden froze.

"G. It's okay. Look at me. It's okay," Braden reassured the 'cat. G-War stopped struggling.

'Put me down,' he said, anger boiling just beneath the surface.

"I didn't know they were coming in, G," Braden said as he put the 'cat gently on the floor. "This one is a Server Bot, and the other ones are Maintenance Bots. The ancients built them to maintain the oasis. They aren't dangerous."

'Fine. Hold on.' The 'cat started heaving and puked the remainder of his javelina onto the floor. Licking his 'cat lips after finishing, he added, *'Have that cleaned up before I return.'*

Braden looked at the Server Bot, which had returned to its work making the bed. Two long tendril-like arms deftly pulled the sheets and blanket tight, fluffing the pillow before moving toward the counter area. The 'cat walked slowly, head and tail high as he left the room.

The Tortoid had joined them, watching all of it from the safety of the outdoors.

Braden started laughing, taking care not to step in the steaming mound of 'cat puke as he left the room to the Server Bot.

57 - Endless Questions

Once learning the functions of the beings in Oasis Zero One, peace descended on Braden and his party. He was amazed at how lazy they all grew when their whims were readily indulged.

Braden spent a great deal of time with the reflection, learning as much as he could about the world of the ancients. Humans settled on Vii from another planet, a long ways away. The original landing site was called Sanctuary in the south.

What was it like? How far? Can you show me a map of the land? Where are the ancients' cities?

Only one city, many outposts, manufacturing facilities, and more. The original settlers had the task of building the infrastructure to support a follow-on civilization. James Warren was the first to settle the area known as Warren Deep. They built a road network to support farming and ranching. Warren Deep was established for the purpose of supplying food for all inhabitants of Cygnus VII. James Warren was a bioengineer, his strength was in creating and modifying animals to make the transition to a human-based world more smooth.

William Devaney named Devaney's Barren, the wasteland between the southern and northern continents. It was bracketed on the east and west coasts by mountains rising from two vast oceans that covered most of the planet.

The reflection, a hologram she called herself, instructed Braden on how to use the desktop interface in the office to access a map of the area. Braden looked at the pictures, then looked behind the monitor to see where the paper was. He didn't understand how it worked, but he appreciated what it provided. He asked the hologram for a regular map that he could take with him.

"The map will be downloaded to your neural implant, so it can be recalled and personalized at any time."

"I'm not sure what any of that means. I would like a map on paper that I can add to my rudder."

"I'm having problems accessing your implant. Has it been damaged in some way?"

"I don't think I have one of those. I'm the son of Traders Derek and Agnes. I grew up in my parents' caravan as they traveled the roads of Warren Deep. My companions are a Hillcat named the Golden Warrior of the Stone Cliffs, a Hawkoid called Skirill, and Aadi, First Master of the Tortoise Consortium."

"Welcome. All travelers are welcome to Oasis Zero One, rest area for those traveling between the north and the south continents."

"And that travel would be so much easier with a map."

"Once we can access your implant, then we will download all you desire."

"Sounds like I'm drawing some maps," Braden said to himself as he walked out of the office. He returned with his rudder, pencils, and chalks. He sat down at the monitor, recalled the maps as the hologram had showed him, then began to draw.

58 - Maps

Braden was having a hard time focusing, when he realized the sun was about to rise. He'd been up all night drawing maps of the world. There were so many place names. He had dutifully captured them, but they didn't mean anything to him besides the big ones: Warren Deep, Devaney's Barren, Plains of Propiscius, the Eastern and Western Oceans, and most importantly, the capital city of Sanctuary.

Sanctuary. It sounded like a safe place to trade for Old Tech.

The ancients' life was not for him. He needed to hunt. He needed to trade. He needed to do something with himself. The ancients didn't have animal companions as the hologram confirmed. None of the doors would open for any of his friends, even after he told the hologram that's what he wanted. The Maintenance Bots would serve, but only humans.

Braden couldn't accept that.

Time to leave.

First, they needed to restock. Braden had the fabricator working overtime as he questioned it regarding meals that would last for a few turns. It made granola bars, energy cookies, dried fruits, and a variety of sandwiches on a hard tack. He bundled it all into towels.

They also went on a killing spree, cleaning out a good part of the javelina population. Braden had a difficult time smoking the meat as every time he started a fire, a Maintenance Bot showed up to put it out. He finally settled for building a fire in the desert, a place where the Bots would not go. He smoked as much meat as possible, but it didn't amount to much.

Skirill and Aadi found the granola and dried fruits to be palatable, but both preferred javelina, so Braden committed to eating the fabricator-produced meals, leaving real pork for his companions. Aadi most preferred bugs, but he couldn't find any. Braden expected the Maintenance Bots eliminated any infestations, although those same Bots completely ignored the javelinas.

Braden also learned that the Mirror Beast was similar to the Maintenance Bots, but as a Development Unit, it had an energy screen that helped it manage its work in land development and heavy construction. It reflected anything that came at it so it wouldn't be damaged as it displaced earth, rock, and trees.

Braden's brain hurt. He had never been bombarded by so much new information. Every other word from the hologram required an explanation. The planet Vii, pronounced Vee would always be Vii not Cygnus VII. And all those other places he had on his map? The Great Desert was what it was called. He would think about whether to share the map with others.

Probably not.

He found out that the small device he acquired in the repair shop was called a watch and a bracelet. It kept the time. He had no use for it, but it was small and the right person might trade a great deal for it.

While Braden viewed the maps, he shared their images with his companions over the mindlink. The Hawkoid was able to match the pictures with what he had seen in his life. He felt that he could guide the group south on the best track. The maps showed a Hawkoid's view from above. Braden shook his head at the ancients' technology.

G-War remained aloof for the entire time they were at the oasis. Braden expected it was because he could not feel any of the ancients' creations. His attack upon the Server Bot was brushed off by the metal creature. Maybe G-War finally learned what it was like to be afraid.

Master Aadi said very little during their stay, but he constantly demonstrated that wisdom is gained in listening, not speaking. He heard every word that the hologram said. He saw every image that Braden shared. He would not forget any of it. During their time crossing the remainder of Devaney's Barren, he would contemplate all he had learned. After that, he would discuss his perceptions with the young human.

59 – Feeling Bad

They left at dusk, traveling as they had arrived. Max led Pack, who pulled the cart, and everyone else came along for the ride.

Night came, then the moon shone, then the moon set, and daylight returned.

Braden mechanically built their camp in the location that Skirill selected. No one talked. They prepared to sleep, each claiming a spot under their foliage and blanket awning. Their spirit waned. Was it that hard to leave the life of comfort? Was it that hard for G-War to accept that man created these Bots as servants? No one was happy.

He wasn't even that tired. He felt like he was in a fog.

He pulled out his Rico Bow and cleaned it. He looked over its curves, how the string attached. He was good with the bow. He nocked an arrow and picking a spot fifty strides away, he let loose. The arrow hit home, a finger's width to the right of his target.

"G. Are you sleeping?"

'No,' the 'cat answered.

"Is anyone sleeping?" The other two shook their heads as they locked eyes on the human. "Why do we feel so bad?"

'We've learned that we are but one grain of sand in the Great Desert. We've learned that people had power over the very universe, but they are no more. I wonder what happened to them,' Aadi offered.

'They didn't recognize us. Only you could open doors,' Skirill added.

"And they are lesser for it. Maybe their knowledge disappeared because they didn't recognize the intelligence that exists in our world, on Vii. The oasis isn't how we want to live! Is that what they did with their knowledge? They made it so they no longer mattered. Their existence no longer mattered." Braden dug the toe of his boot into the dirt as he thought of what he wanted to say next.

"So, my friends, what would we do differently? If this so called technology was available to us, what would we do with it?"

'Not that,' G-War said definitively.

"I have to say, G, you left some pretty righteous scratches down the side of that Server Bot. I'm sure it will wear its scars with pride. Then it cleaned up after you, too. You put it in its place." Braden scratched behind the 'cat's ears. G-War purred reluctantly, then settled down and finally batted the human's hand away.

The friends passed the time discussing what they liked and what they didn't. They talked about how they thought the world could be better. It had little to do with things and everything to do with relationships. None of Braden's companions liked the last oasis. They all liked the first oasis. Provide water and make food available, then leave the rest to them.

The concept of too much of a good thing was real. As Skirill had found out when he ate too much of the juicy red fruit, as G-War found out when he gorged on the javelina, as Braden learned when he ate all those chocolate brownies.

Only Aadi had restrained himself. "How did you do it?" Braden asked for the group.

'Simple, Master Braden. In all my years, one thing I like less than starving is eating too much. I haven't run across the opportunity often, but when I did, I suffered greatly. I'm too old to go through that again. You youngsters will learn one of these turns.'

60 – Leaving the Great Desert Behind

One more night of travel found Braden's caravan leaving the sands of the desert behind. As the morning sun shone, they entered plains where short trees and grasses grew. Gentle, forested, rolling hills filled the horizon. Heavy foliage here and there showed where springs might be present. The Plains of Propiscius were expansive rolling grasslands, fertile and probably teeming with life.

Braden smiled broadly, before jumping off Max and kissing the ground. They had done it. They'd crossed the Great Desert.

Skirill was airborne, flying in circles around the party, seeing all there was. He looked for a pond or a stream. They'd rest there for a full turn before starting the next leg of their journey. They no longer needed to travel at night. It was hot at the edge of the Plains, but not desert hot. There was moisture in the air. Master Aadi found it very pleasant.

"Do you sense anything G?"

'Yes,' the 'cat said as he looked south while sniffing the air. *'Deer are that way. Boars. Wild dogs.'* He coughed in disgust. Braden snorted at that. *'And a human.'*

"What? Where?" Instantly alert, Braden didn't know what to think. Even though the hologram confirmed there were humans in the south, he assumed they had disappeared. It had been nearly four hundred cycles and none made it beyond the Plains of Propiscius.

'That way. Not far.' G-War indicated the direction with a nod.

'Do you see anything, Skirill?' Braden watched as the Hawkoid circled lazily, finally focusing on a stand of trees wrapped around a small lake. Through their mindlink, the companions saw Skirill's clear view of a person who

appeared to be fishing. When he looked up and locked eyes with the Hawkoid, he threw his pole down and started scrambling for something under a tree.

"Get out of there!" Braden shouted out loud, although Skirill only heard him through the mindlink. The Hawkoid dove to increase speed and put a tree between him and the unknown person. He beat his wings hard back to the companions.

"It looks like we know which way we're going." Braden said as he pointed Max's nose toward the lake. He loosened his Rico Bow at the same time and held it across his lap at the ready. Venison sounded good, just in case something appeared before they arrived. And it didn't hurt to be ready in case the human was unfriendly.

Braden set a brisk pace. The cart bounced along as Pack trotted behind Max. G-War expressed a certain amount of dismay, which Aadi found entertaining. The Tortoid floated along behind the cart, a rope grasped tightly in his beak-like mouth.

Strange thoughts raced through the young human's mind as he contemplated his first meeting with an ancient.

61 – She's Hungry

Braden's caravan approached the trees and the lake. "Is he still here?" he asked the 'cat.

'Yes, she is.'

"Interesting. That changes things," he responded.

'How, young human?' Master Aadi asked.

"Well, she could… She might… She is, well, different." The Tortoid blinked rapidly in response and managed a cough, too. G-War jumped from the cart and silently disappeared into the shadows.

'Threat?' Braden asked.

'Yes, if we are not careful. She will protect herself, but she will not attack first,' G-War answered.

Braden knew what he had to do. Assuming his well-practiced role as a trader, he climbed down from the horse and walked ahead with his hands up.

"Hello! I am Free Trader Braden. I am no threat to you. I simply want to talk, possibly trade, and maybe you can provide us with directions to Sanctuary."

"Stop right there or I'll blow you away!" came a harsh bark from a young voice. Braden looked in her direction, seeing that she held a complex Old Tech item in front of her. She stood with a tree at her back. Her accent was odd to him. He understood her words clearly enough, but not the meaning.

"Are you an ancient? Do you command the wind?"

"What? What wind? Where did you come from? You said 'us.' Where are the others?" She rapidly spit out the series of questions.

"I'm sorry, maybe I didn't understand. Let me start again. I am Free Trader Braden, on my way in search of Old Tech that I can take north of the Great Desert, I mean Devaney's Barren, back to my homeland of Warren Deep. The others are my companions.

"The Tortoid is called Master Aadi. You saw the Hawkoid Skirill earlier while you were fishing. And I am bonded with a Hillcat named Golden Warrior of the Stone Cliffs." The Hillcat stepped onto a tree branch not far from her and sat down, wrapping his tail around him as he looked at her.

"Your companions are animals?" she asked without lowering the device she held in front of her.

"Yes," Braden began. "But they are the most trustworthy and faithful friends I've ever had." He held his head high, nodding to Master Aadi, who swam forward and floated at his side. "Is that a weapon? I would appreciate it if you stopped pointing it at me so we can converse peacefully."

"I don't trust you. I don't trust your creatures. You need to go."

"We've come a long way. We need water and rest. We would very much like to stay at this lake. We have smoked pork and other food items if you are hungry." He watched as she licked her lips. He expected food was the hook to get her to relax. He didn't need to mention that some of his food had been produced by the fabricator at Oasis Zero One.

"Show me what you have…" the young woman said, finally lowering her weapon.

62 - Micah

They sat together on the shore of the small lake, around a fire pit the young woman had made to cook the fish she had not yet caught.

"I am Micah. I'm from the village Trent, on the coast east of here." She talked in between bites of granola, smoked javelina, and dried fruits. She ate like one starved. Braden's instincts told him that to gain her trust, he needed to let her talk. His job was to listen.

"I've never met anyone from north of the Barren. What's it like?"

"Very green. Big mountains in the east. Towns and villages. People. Animals, both dangerous and friendly, both intelligent and dumb.

"I'm a trader. We have blacksmiths, weavers, carpenters, paper makers, artisans, farmers, ranchers, butchers, and more. What about you? How did you get here? What about that Old Tech of yours? What does it do?"

The young woman looked apprehensively at Braden. She was short and sturdy, without any fat. She also had braids, but hers were chestnut and multi-colored. She shook her head, before focusing on a point in the distance.

"I ran away from my village some moons ago. My father wanted me to marry into another village, further down the coast, so he could make peace with them. He arranged a meeting between our families. He and my mother came, along with my brothers and sisters. We all showed up at a place on the beach, halfway between the villages. The son I was to marry was evil, as was his father. They both wanted me and were determined to have me. I am not to be treated like that. I broke the old man's arm and killed the son. I took the old man's blaster and ran. I ran to avoid my father's anger and the vengeance that would come from the other village.

"I didn't live my life to be offered as a sacrifice. I didn't learn to fish, hunt, fight, and weave, just to be used like a piece of meat. I couldn't, even though I knew it meant war. My father should have known better." Braden watched her, mouth set in grim determination, taking full responsibility for her actions.

"Sorry about the blaster. It's a gun, but the energy module needs recharging." Braden made the tell-me-more sign. "It's from the ancients. We have little of their tech left. The ancients' war was too long ago, beyond anyone's memory. We only know the words because of the stories our elders tell around the fires at night. Just like I'll be expected to tell them when I get old."

"I don't know what a gun does or what an energy module is, but I understand that it is an ancient's weapon. It must be powerful, like my Rico Bow." Braden unslung his bow and showed it to her. Trust had to be earned. He wanted to get a closer look at the blaster, as she called it, but knew she wouldn't just hand it over.

She looked at the bow with great interest. "Yes. This is very nice work, light carbon-fiber. Durable. Smooth curves. I've only seen one other recurve bow like this." She handed the bow back to him.

"Recurve bow, you called it?" he asked.

"Yes. These curves improve the strength of the pull, and help it to be more accurate." Braden laughed. He had assumed the inventor's name was Rico. His easy laugh and smile seemed to put her at ease.

What do you think, G, can we trust her?' Braden asked in his thought voice.

'Yes.'

'I thought so, too,' he answered via the mindlink before talking aloud so Micah could hear.

"Micah. If you would like to talk with my companions, I think G-War can arrange that."

"Really? What could an animal say that I want to hear?"

Braden was surprised by her attitude. "They think as we do. They talk as we do, or better, if you're Master Aadi." He nodded to the Tortoid, who blinked a couple times in response. "Look at me, Micah. Now listen, with your mind."

Her eyes narrowed as she watched Braden, then popped wide open as she heard the others' thought voices.

'And now it can hear us all. I am a Hillcat. I can speak with all creatures,' G-War said.

'I am Skirill, a Hawkoid from the Cliffs of the Bittner Mountains. I can speak the language of the humans and with Golden Warrior's help, I can also speak to you through our mindlink.'

'I am Master Aadi, young human. How are you feeling this daylight?'

"I don't know how I feel. I'd always been taught that animals were less than humans. They were to be used, eaten, anything we needed from them because humans are superior."

'Not so much, human,' G-War said coldly. *'I never considered Braden to be enlightened, until I listened to your thoughts.'*

"Hey! You called me by my name," Braden exclaimed. The 'cat sighed and let his legs dangle as he sprawled on a thick branch. It was going to be a long turn.

Braden nodded to Micah, who was still reeling from the revelation of intelligent animals. "Once you get to know him, you'll realize that he can be quite an ass. Master Aadi, on the other hand, will let you know before you go too far down the wrong road. He is the wisest one I've ever met. I would encourage you to listen closely when he speaks."

Micah laughed to herself as she looked at the 'cat in the tree. "So he can be an ass, huh?"

63 – Dinner Tales

The daylight passed quickly as they talked. Late after midday, Braden's attention waned as he was falling asleep while sitting. Micah returned to her fishing, promising to get something good for dinner. Braden roused a sleeping G-War to help him find a deer or a wild boar to add to their food stocks.

Micah had taken a liking to Master Aadi and Skirill. They both feasted on the fish that she brought to the surface. Skirill impressed her by catching the fish that she threw high into the air. He also talked to her with his squawking, high-pitched Hawkoid voice. He showed her where the fish were, improving the effectiveness of her line tosses.

Aadi ate fish from her hand. He found her fishing technique to be interesting, so he hovered close by. Braden asked her not to let him get into the water or drink directly from the lake. She didn't ask for a further explanation, understanding that everyone had a vice or two, no matter their age.

By evening, they were both successful. Braden returned with a spike buck carried across his shoulders, cleaned but not butchered. The 'cat ate his fill from the organs at the kill site and almost had to be carried back. He waddled under his own power, barely able to keep up with the burdened human.

A number of small, round fish cooked slowly over a small fire. What they lacked in size, they made up for in quantity. Braden soon added fresh venison to the spit.

While their meal cooked, Braden cut branches for a field smoker. He then started butchering the buck to strip out the meat for smoking. Micah joined him with a curious curved blade. They made quick work of the deer.

With the meal cooked and a large stock of venison smoking, they ate. This time, Micah ate more slowly, enjoying the mix of fish and venison. Braden enjoyed the evening. It had been a long time since he sat and talked with another human. She was a link to the south. For her, he was a link to the rebels of the north.

The biggest revelation came when she told him that he was the offspring of the ancients. All humans were. For some reason, he always thought of the ancients differently. They were no different, she assured him. The ancients fought among themselves, but with terrible weapons. Those who lived lost the ancients' knowledge as they struggled to simply survive.

We're all descendants from the ancients, he thought. Why had he never understood that? Because that's not how it was taught. The ancients were mystical creatures, to be revered, not emulated. Braden thought back to the oases and the amazing things the ancients had built, but they couldn't overcome the human tendency toward conflict. He recognized the irony as he felt his long knife at his side, his recurve bow on the ground next to him. He thought about their run from the men who followed them out of Whitehorse, of those G-War had killed so he could escape Cameron, of the man being hung in Binghamton.

"We never change," Braden said as he settled in to tell Micah the story of his recent travels as a Free Trader, telling her everything until the moment they saw her at the lake.

64 – The New Caravan

The morning found Braden and his companions preparing to leave. From Micah, he learned a great deal about the world of the ancients. The people who survived in the south embraced the passing of knowledge about the ancients and their history, while the people in the north, his people, had forgotten all there was to know from the before time.

Micah looked uncomfortable as Braden finished loading the cart. Master Aadi was the first to speak.

'Micah, if I may be so bold. Traveling in a group, we are safer. Braden seeks items to take north to trade. On the way, we learn, broadening our knowledge. In my two hundred cycles, I have never learned more than what I've gathered in the short time traveling with Braden and his companions. I, for one, would like you to join us. Teach us and learn from us,' the Tortoid ended with a hopeful tone in his thought voice.

Braden thought it would be natural for her to join them, but didn't want to ask. He didn't know if it was his male pride, or suspicion of other humans. She seemed trustworthy. He was a good trader, which meant that he could read people well, understand them. What he believed was that people always put themselves first. No one was truly selfless. It bothered him that he felt this way. He trusted his companions fully, but couldn't find that same level of trust in any human besides his parents.

"That's so odd, hearing you in my head," Micah said aloud. She didn't seem to let it bother her, though, and adapted quickly. "Thank you for the offer, Master Aadi." She let that linger as she looked at Braden without moving. It seemed like she wanted confirmation that he supported her joining the companions.

'I like her,' said the 'cat. Micah smiled. G-War was talking to all of them.

"By all that's holy! Ten cycles, you don't tell me anything. One turn and you like her?"

"I'm beginning to see who the ass is," Micah offered, laughing.

Braden shook his head and then offered his hand. "Welcome to the caravan, if you'll have this pack of misfits."

She shook his hand heartily and hurried to get her small pack of things ready to go.

"Ten cycles, G! C'mon, Ess, you like me, don't you?"

"You healed 'e when I was in need, young hu'an, and 'or that, I will always 'e grate'ul," Skirill said out loud.

"That's not much, but it looks like that's what I'm going to get. So that's how it's going to be, huh? Four to one, now. I think I need a dog…" A chorus of laughter answered him over their mindlink.

When they were ready, Micah joined Braden on Max. Skirill flew ahead. There were plenty of trees for him to sit in and watch as Braden's caravan slowly made its way south.

Braden was happy to have Micah join the caravan. She could help guide them in this part of the world, help him to understand Old Tech should they find any. And the 'cat liked her, which was all he really needed in order to give her his trust.

"I've never seen creatures like these. You've tamed them. What are they?" she asked as she carefully stroked the softness of Max's neck.

Braden started to feel funny with Micah riding in front of him.

"I think you should ride Pack. He wears a harness, but it's a saddle, too. That way we don't wear poor Max down. We don't want that, do we, Max?" Braden stroked the horse's neck as he helped Micah down and watched her awkwardly climb into Pack's saddle.

"How's that feel?" he asked.

"Fine. Just fine." She looked at him oddly. He felt the color rise in his face. What was wrong with him?

65 – Everyone Adds Strength

Braden had forgotten what it was like to travel with another human. He was used to making the decisions--where to go, how far, when to stop. His companions were indifferent to those issues. Micah was far more engaged.

Braden carried the burden of leadership with him, even though it often felt like the others knew his arguments before he made them. They nudged him in one direction or another, yet he was the one who made the final decisions. The journey through the Great Desert was his decision and the others followed. Preparing them to survive the trip was his job, and he did it. They all had a role in keeping each other alive, but Braden carried the full weight of their lives on his shoulders.

And now he was responsible for one more. Still, nothing changed. There would be one more voice in the conversation. In the end, they had to count on each other to stay safe.

"If we get into trouble, you need to know what we can do. G-War is known as a Hellcat by those who aren't bonded. He is fearless in battle and quicker than a snake, as we saw in the Great Desert." Braden nodded back toward the 'cat, who looked into the distance seemingly indifferent to the human's conversation.

"Skirill is a Hawkoid and can see like you can't imagine. He is our scout and he also is hell on our enemies. When we were attacked by wild boars, you should have seen him wheel and dance, just over their backs, raking them with his claws. We want him on our side. You should see him eat this big red fruit that we found in the oasis. We'll talk about that at a different time. As a matter of fact, that's probably more embarrassing for me than him." Skirill must have been listening in as he swooped over their heads and let out his Hawkoid screech.

Micah watched as he glided upward, losing speed until he flapped his powerful wings to quickly gain more altitude. He circled the area before them, diving and frolicking. She felt at ease with his keen eyes watching over them.

How long had she traveled alone? Maybe a couple moons? She was constantly afraid of being found by people from the other village, even by her own family. She didn't want to go back, under any circumstance. It was too much.

Maybe she found a new home as a member of this caravan. The companions' voices sounded pleasant in her mind, reaching her at a level she didn't know possible. The caress of their thought voices was soothing. The courage of their convictions was comforting. She felt protected, a rare feeling in this part of the world.

Braden kept turning in the saddle to look at her while they talked. He had seen that she was thinking, so he let her go. Once her eyes focused back on him, he continued. "Now Master Aadi has a special gift. He makes a sound like a thunder clap. It explodes right in your head. I got a glancing blow of it when we first met him, and I thought my head had bust open. I expected to see my brains all over the ground. He exploded a Maintenance Bot back at the oasis." The Tortoid blinked rapidly. Was that embarrassment?

"You've seen functioning Bots?"

"Yes. Oasis Zero One is completely functional. The Bots keep everything clean. They feed the fish. They tend the fields. They even recovered the Bot that Aadi destroyed, and they put it back together! I saw it the next daylight going about its business. I think it intentionally avoided Master Aadi after that. Oh yeah, almost forgot about the Development Unit at Oasis Zero Three. Another Bot, but this one was big and it was still building the oasis. I wonder what we'll find when we go back."

"I've seen Bots, but none of them worked."

"Then that's where we want to go, unless you have a different idea of where we can find Old Tech? That's our goal. Then we take it back north to trade."

"I think you need to see the capital city of Sanctuary," she offered.

"Exactly. If anyone lives there, we will work with them and see what we can do. That is where we were headed when we had the fortune of finding you." Why had he said that?

"Uh huh. You have to see it. That will tell you everything you need to know. Then maybe we can look at what else we can do, where we can go."

Braden didn't dig into that statement. He knew she was being secretive, but not malicious. He wanted to see what she wanted to show him.

He resumed the conversation he started earlier.

"I'm pretty good with my Rico Bow, I mean, my recurve bow. I can hold my own with the long knife, but we try not to let things get that close." He waited, but Micah wasn't forthcoming. He needed to know. They all needed to know. "So what do you do? What are you good at?"

Micah hesitated before answering. "I can weave and I can fish, all different kinds of fishing. I make my own gear." She was holding back.

"And?" Braden encouraged. "How were you able to break the old man's arm and kill his son?"

"I can wrestle. I broke the slime dog's neck. The old man had more warning, so I was only able to get hold of one of his arms."

"I never heard of a girl who could wrestle," Braden started saying. Micah jumped down from her horse and walked over to Braden. She waved him down. As he started to dismount, an arm wrapped around his head and twisted until he was thrown on the ground. Micah followed him down, where he was tangled in his bow and long knife. As she reached for him, he rolled away, leaving his bow behind.

He came to his feet, facing Micah with his arms wide and ready. She circled slowly, low to the ground. She was shorter than Braden and he saw that if he went toe to toe, she would have better leverage. He had the better reach, but that would only work if she couldn't grab his arm. If he overextended, then she would have him.

They circled. He feinted a couple times, throwing short punches toward her to gauge her reaction. She twisted, staying compact, minimizing Braden's target.

He threw his knife to the ground by his bow and started to jog in a circle, then ran around Micah. She looked at him oddly, but followed his movements. She kept her feet active so she didn't cross them. Braden didn't see an opening at first. He would wear down quickly if something didn't happen soon. He watched, and she offered him the side of her head for a moment as he kept running. With a short left hook, he took a swing, counting on his momentum to give it strength.

She caught his fist, pushing it so it passed harmlessly in front of her face. Then she rotated his arm, letting his momentum continue to twist it. He went face first into the dirt. She landed on top of him with his arm pulled behind his back. He breathed heavily and thought about trying to buck her off, but she was low, parallel with him. If he tried to kick, his arm might be forfeit.

He couldn't afford to get hurt. They had too far to travel.

"I give. I give. You win!" He panted. "I stand humbled by your mastery of the art." She let him up, where he bowed deeply to her. She was far stronger than he suspected.

"I'm sorry, Braden. It seemed like you wouldn't believe me. It was quickest just to show you."

"I guess it's the same as how you felt about the animals. It was easiest to show you. And I'm the one who's sorry. I don't know why I would question your abilities, just because you're a woman. In the north, men do the hard work, but it doesn't have to be that way. It would probably be easier on everyone if they shared." Braden massaged his sore arm, then picked up his weapons.

He offered his hand to Micah. "What do you say? Partner?"

She shook his hand heartily. "I can't say that I've ever felt more welcome."

"Too bad I got my ass beat first, but it's good to know what you can do. Have you ever fought with a knife? Our fight with the boars…we had to kill them to save the horses."

"I have a small knife for cleaning fish. Do you have a better one I could use? Or, if we can find a charging station, then you will see what a blaster can do. I'm afraid without a charge, even a bad knife is better."

"Besides my long knife, I have a small skinner, probably no bigger than yours. If we run across others, maybe we can work a trade."

"If we run across others, that's when I'll need it the most," she replied.

"Is it that bad down here? How many people are around and what do they do?"

"Villages support themselves. There are no people like you who go from village to village. Usually, everyone has their own territory to hunt, to cultivate, to fish. Sometimes we have to trade, coastal village with a mountain village, trading fish and oils for hides and precious stones. But we all go together to make the trade. There is no trust between the villages. Everyone here does what they need to survive."

Braden thought about it. He would call the north civilized compared to what she described. In the south, they knew about Old Tech and seemed to have more of it, but they lived isolated lives. Maybe his destiny was to start a Caravan Guild here, establish routine trade, and help these people out of their dark ages. "Is there a road system here? In the north, the ancients' road system is the backbone of the traders. Without it, I don't know where we'd be."

"You'd probably be more like us," Micah suggested. "There are roads, but people avoid them. If someone knows where you'll be, you are easier to attack." Braden shook his head. He was a Free Trader. It was incomprehensible that people would be such savages. Trade brought the people together. In the north, every town had a market square where trading took place. It was the foundation of civilization.

Braden couldn't fathom this new world where they had no free trade. He didn't like it.

66 – You Really Should Have Talked

The Plains of Propiscius, or as Braden liked to think of them, the Plains with the Ridiculous Name, were extensive. They traveled for turns through sparse trees and limited brush. Eventually, the trees got thicker, becoming a full forest, as the humidity grew just as thick and the heat oppressive. Micah said they were approaching a rainforest. It even had a name: the Amazon.

To continue, they needed to find an ancients' road. Braden expected it to be grown over. The Hawkoid said that he couldn't find anything, no matter how far he flew in either direction. Micah had never approached the city from this direction, so she couldn't advise him. If they traveled east toward territory she was familiar with, they risked running into hunting parties from villages she wished to avoid.

They decided to turn west, skirting the Amazon rainforest until they crossed the road that Braden knew must be there. Micah thought she remembered roads leaving Sanctuary, heading in all directions. She would not discuss anything else about Sanctuary, no matter how hard Braden pressed her, even asking the 'cat to dig for information.

G-War politely refused since he didn't care what they found. He was eating well and they were safe, so his needs were met. Braden suspected the Golden Warrior was soft on the human female. While sitting around a campfire at night, she would absently pet the 'cat while they talked. G-War never let Braden do anything so demeaning. Maybe G-War was working her to add to his stable of servants. That sounded more like the 'cat. He would watch to see how things played out, but he expected she would soon turn into a willing servant.

Braden looked at the 'cat riding comfortably in the cart. G-War watched back, expressionless, lids heavy over his eyes. *I know you're plotting something, my friend. And I wouldn't have it any other way,'* Braden said in his thought voice, nodding, then returned his gaze to the land in front of them.

"The road may not be obvious when we cross it. In the north, roads through wooded areas are overgrown, not visible. Many trees grow along the sides; their roots break apart the road surface. Grass grows readily in the dirt lying on top of the ancients' roads. Trees don't grow in the road itself. The trees will grow high over it and create shade, but they won't grow in the road. This is what we're looking for." Although Braden was talking for Micah's benefit, he was also talking to himself. He hoped that they hadn't already passed the road south.

He was getting distracted from his main goal of returning north with a cart full of Old Tech to trade. With the new information and the new members of the caravan, it seemed like his original goal was small, maybe even shortsighted.

There was a big world out there. The ancients had plans for it, but those fell apart when they resorted to war.

Was he the one to change it from what it was now to what it was meant to be? No. He wasn't sure he liked what it had become; the ancients destroyed themselves and their world. They forced people like Braden to make a whole new start.

No. That wasn't his goal. He wanted to find some Old Tech and then take it back north to trade, although he wasn't sure what waited for him there. His thoughts turned dark.

'They come!' the Hawkoid's thought voice shouted into their minds in unison with the 'cat's voice.

"Show us," Braden said softly, not knowing how close and who 'they' were. The view from the Hawkoid's perspective appeared behind their eyes. They saw five men running directly at them from ahead. No, six men. One lagged behind, running with a limp, barely able to keep up.

"Off the horse. They'll be here momentarily. Master Aadi, with me, in front. Micah, to the far side. G-War, the other side. Skirill, be ready to come at them from behind," Braden ordered. There was no time to discuss things.

Everyone started moving to their positions, although Micah hesitated, giving Braden an angry look. "Look. From the side, it's more likely that you'll be able to fight one person at a time. You are on your own over there. Make the best of it."

Once assured that he wasn't trying to protect her, she ran to the side and found cover behind a tree.

Braden calmly nocked an arrow to his recurve bow and drew it back as the men ran into view before him. "Hold!" he shouted with all the volume he could muster.

The man at the front held up his hand and slowed to a walk, then stopped about twenty strides before Braden and Aadi. He wore smart woven clothing that hung loosely on him, yet maintained his shape. Pants, belted. A tunic vest over a long-sleeved shirt of some thin material. His shock of dark hair suggested the man was younger. His face was clean shaven. As Braden looked from one to the other, they were all similar in dress and appearance. They carried spears and long-bladed swords.

Finally, the last member of their party limped up to the man in front, as he stopped before putting his hands on his knees and breathing heavily.

Braden had engaged men like this hundreds of times. His introduction was well practiced.

"I am Free Trader Braden, recently from Warren Deep, in search of items to take back north in trade. Maybe we can trade?"

"Trader? Warren Deep? I think you're a little far from home, son," the man in the front said. The man who was bent over put a calming hand on the other's leg.

"Who may I have the honor of addressing? And then if we may have a polite conversation regarding the viability of trade, it would be my pleasure."

"I am McCullough of clan McCullough. This is our territory. No one passes here without our permission, which you do not have." The man's hostile gaze locked on the Tortoid.

"Please accept our sincere apologies. If we cannot come to terms, we'll turn around and leave your territory without further issue. We wish to cause no problems," Braden said as soothingly as he could.

The men started spreading out, loosening their weapons as they casually gave themselves space to fight.

"That's a mutie, and we kill muties," one of them said.

"His name is Aadi, First Master of the Tortoise Consortium. If you got to know him, you would realize that he is quite knowledgeable as well as very friendly."

In his thought voice, he added, *I'll take the one talking and the next one behind him and to his left. Skirill, you take the one at the back and to his right. G, you got the one closest to you, and Micah, if you can hear me, the one closest to you is yours. Aadi, if you could assist with that one, we would appreciate it. We'll leave the old man so we can talk with him. Get ready.'*

"Hold, my warriors," rasped the old man's voice as he straightened himself. "I am Elder McCullough and I think we can discuss things like gentlemen." He smiled, but it wasn't friendly. His dark eyes glistened as he took in the horses, the cart, Aadi, and finally Braden.

"Elder!" the man to Braden's far left shouted. "There's another one over here. A woman."

Micah stepped out from behind the tree. To the men, she appeared to have no weapon. The man who saw her started to laugh and smoothly drew his sword. It was long and straight, with a great cross bar above the grip. Braden never wanted to start a fight, but he was more than willing to end one, even if it meant running away. That wasn't a choice here.

Now, Skirill.' He glanced up to see the Hawkoid start his high speed dive. Braden quickly pulled back and sent an arrow at the young McCullough's chest. It hit hard, knocking the man backward, but did not penetrate the strange material of the tunic. Braden nocked another arrow in less than a heartbeat and loosed it at the younger man's exposed neck.

It hit home, tearing out his throat. The young man gurgled as he fell dying.

Aadi's mouth opened slightly as he sent his focused thunderclap toward the men. Being beside him, Braden heard the sound build as it passed in front of him, but it didn't hurt his ears. It looked like the Tortoid attacked the remaining five men at the same time, which weakened the sound's power. All of them stopped, two dropped their swords, but they looked to be recovering quickly.

Which gave Braden time to fire an arrow through another man's eye.

Skirill crashed into his target from behind, latching onto the man's head with his powerful claws as the man stumbled forward. The Hawkoid tried to twist the neck, but couldn't get enough leverage. His claws dug deeply into the man's flesh, raking the bones of his skull as Skirill lost his grip while beating his wings to get back into the air.

The coordinated attacks galvanized the other men into action. The man closest to Micah charged her, sword raised. The man closest to G-War pulled his sword and charged straight at Braden. He never noticed the 'cat streaking in from behind to launch itself onto his back. With a well-practiced slash, the 'cat's claws dug deeply into the man's neck. He fell to his knees as blood spurted from the open wound.

Braden took aim at the man rushing Micah, but he couldn't shoot as the gap between the man and Micah disappeared. Micah stepped back as the man raised his sword for a death blow. She shot forward and hit him with her shoulder square in his mid-section. He hammered the pommel of his sword one time onto her back as he went over. She went to her knees, then crawled forward quickly until she rolled back to her feet, twisting to face her attacker.

He swung his sword in short arcs from side to side, keeping Micah away from him and on her heels. Skirill swooped low over the man's head to distract him, and he poked his sword at the fleeting figure of the Hawkoid. Micah raced in and grabbed his wrist with both hands, pulling it and the sword closer to her body. She rotated her torso, bending the man's elbow in a direction it wasn't meant to go. The tendons strained and the man shrieked in pain. The sword fell from his numb fingers. She smoothly ducked, rolling up the man's back until she got his neck and head in her strong grip. She braced her feet on the ground as he struggled. She dropped and twisted, using the man's body weight against him. His neck cracked. He hit the ground a corpse.

Micah pushed him away from her, then picked up the sword, examining its edge.

G-War crouched behind the Elder, ensuring that he didn't make any unwanted moves as Micah easily dispatched the final one of his warriors.

Fire burned behind his eyes as he glared at the upstart youth who had killed his son. The old man picked up the sword from the ground by his dead son's body. He looked at the arrow wound, hatred burning his soul.

He turned to look at Braden, then made a couple purposeful steps forward.

Braden immediately launched an arrow that bounced off the tunic covering the old man's chest. The impact staggered him and he stopped moving.

"You and I both know that you'll be dead if you try it." The old man dropped his sword arm, glaring at Braden. "Are you willing to talk now?"

"We may have been hasty in not talking with you at first. Go. Leave me. Let me mourn my clan in peace." Braden felt sorry for the old man. By threatening Micah and refusing to talk, they forced Braden's hand. They misjudged him, and they died for it. In Warren Deep, that was the penalty for bringing an unprovoked war.

'It plans revenge,' G-War said calmly over their mindlink.

'Of course he does. Does he have the means to attack us again?' Braden asked.

'Ask it and then I will know.'

"How many more warriors are in your village? Where is your village? How many people are there?" Braden asked quickly so the man would think of his answers without thinking.

'It is a small village, one turn distant in the direction we go. There are two men left and a number of women and children.'

"Thanks, G," Braden said aloud. "Two warriors at your village and you still plan to attack us?"

The old man's eyes went wide. "Stay out of my head, you damn muties!" He rushed forward, raising his sword as Braden pulled back his arrow. Master Aadi stopped him with a bump and dropped the old man with the full force of a focused thunderclap.

The old man flopped on the ground, whimpering like a small child as blood dripped from his ears. His hands, now empty, held his head in a futile attempt to soften the pain.

"A shame. All I wanted to do was talk," Braden told the man.

67 – He's a Pig

Braden tied the man up and lashed him to the cart. G-War sat nearby, looking like little more than a house cat as he watched the man closely.

Master Aadi was spent. Braden didn't realize the toll the use of his weapon took on the Tortoid. He could barely float, so Braden helped him into the cart where he rested on the blankets and their supplies.

Micah and Braden searched the bodies of the men. The tunics they wore were woven from a stiff material that moved as the body moved, but didn't allow anything to pierce it. Braden found one close to his size and put it on. He liked it. It made him feel more powerful.

The smallest of the tunics was still too large for Micah, but she swore that she could tailor it down to her size. It was easy to remove threads. Adding threads? That would have been a challenge. Maybe they could take the extra material to provide a little protection for the horses' flanks? They took all the tunics and piled them in the cart, along with the men's weapons. The men carried nothing else of value. They were traveling light.

Which meant they weren't a scouting party, because they'd need supplies for an extended stay in the wilderness. Unless they had supplies staged at various locations within their territory. Braden wanted to know.

"What were you doing out here?" Braden asked once the man was in less pain.

"None of your farging business, toad!" the man rasped as renewed pain contorted his face.

This was a raiding party. They were to attack another village, not far from here, alongside the rainforest.'

'Another village? G, can you sense any other humans nearby? Are they a threat?'

'Very far away. Not a threat, but no help either. They stay away from other people.'

"So what should we do with you? I'm not one for killing people in cold blood, but letting you go will come back to haunt us. Unless your village is willing to trade for you?"

"They will trade well for me! Take me to my village!"

'He thinks he will be able to overwhelm us with his people once the trade is complete.'

'Of course he does,' answered Braden in his thought voice.

'Maybe I can talk with him,' Micah answered over the mindlink. Braden looked for her, seeing her standing at the base of a tree with Skirill overhead, looking fearsomely protective.

"My friend Micah has a few questions for you, Elder McCullough. Be kind. Please don't make me hack your limbs off one by one. That would make me feel bad and I'm sure you wouldn't like it either." The Elder glared at him in response.

Micah strolled to the cart, taking her time. She sized up the man with her arms crossed. Then she leaned close to him, looking into his eyes. He struggled against his bindings, lunging toward the young woman. With a quick rotation at her waist, she drove her elbow into the man's face, breaking his nose, splattering blood onto the side of the cart.

"He's a pig. We should kill him now," she said as she stood up and walked away.

"I would have thought 'questioning him' would actually have included questions. I guess I'm old fashioned like that," Braden said with a smile. He thought as she did about the man. Evil seemed to ooze from him.

'If I may, Master Human,' Aadi said slowly in a tired thought voice. *'I suspect that if this man is as Micah suggests, then the women of the village will probably be happy to have him back, so that they may deal with him themselves. We could use some allies. If we have to fight the whole way south, then this will grow tiresome very quickly.'* The Tortoid ended his speech as he faded back into sleep.

"Micah, what do you think of turning this man over to the women of his village? I think the appearance that he was bested by a woman would help the others. I suspect that they are little more than slaves. What do you say we give them a taste of freedom?"

"I like it. He'll get his. I know what these women are going through. I know their pain. What about the other two warriors?" she asked.

"Between the rest of us, we'll put them in their place so you have the time to do what you need to do. I will do everything I can not to kill them. As Master Aadi suggested, we need allies."

The old man listened intently, then struggled even harder at his bonds. Every movement resulted in more blood streaming down his face from his shattered nose.

"I'll kill you. I'll kill you all!" he screamed hysterically. Braden felt even better about their plan. The old man seemed afraid of being handed over to the women.

A fitting end to this piece of crap, Braden thought.

'Hear, hear,' seconded the 'cat in an uncharacteristic use of a human saying.

68 – Freedom's Taste

One full turn later, they had not yet made it to the old man's village. They stopped often to tighten the old man's bonds, beating him on occasion as he struggled like a wild man to break free.

Aadi recovered after a full night's sleep. He floated behind Braden, the cord in his beak as he was pulled along.

G-War rode with the flailing man. His legs were tied to the cart, so he was more of a hazard to himself, but the 'cat was ready to slash him if needed. Skirill flew ahead where G-War directed him until he found the village. Braden pointed Max's nose in that direction.

He picked a stand of trees to dismount where people from the village wouldn't see them. Leaving Micah and Aadi with the man, Braden and G-War circled around the village to find the men and disarm them when they were distracted by Micah's entrance with the Elder.

Micah waited with the horses as Braden and G-War padded away through the trees. Master Aadi kept a close watch on the old man, who shied away from the Tortoid as if his nearness was toxic.

Micah waited until G-War told her they were in place. She mounted Max and urged him forward. She was a bit reluctant, being new to riding. She didn't realize that it wasn't easy. Max was less than cooperative, so she gave him a hard kick in the ribs. He surged forward, and the rope tied to Pack was pulled free. She rode ahead, picking up speed as Max galloped onward.

She pulled back hard on the reins. The horse skidded to a halt, his nostrils flaring. Max was angry.

Pack meandered forward. Micah was glad she wouldn't have to chase after him. She slowly climbed off Max, petting his neck and then his nose, which quickly calmed him. When Pack caught up, she took both their leads and walked with them. She needed Braden to teach her to ride. It was not intuitive.

Braden watched the madness from their hiding spot behind a small hovel at the edge of the village. G-War assured him that no one was nearby. He berated himself for assuming Micah could ride, even though she had told him there are no horses in the south. He thought she figured it out in the time that they'd been riding together, but then again, he never let her take the reins. He would fix that as soon as they were out of this mess.

Braden was pleased to see Micah walking the horses. It wasn't as intimidating as riding in, but it would work because she was back in control of herself, the horses, and most importantly, Elder McCullough.

"Ho, Villagers!" Micah shouted. She continued leading the horses until she was even with the outermost buildings, little more than thatch huts. "Hello! I bring you the Elder McCullough, trussed as the piece of meat he is," she bellowed with vigor and emotion.

Faces appeared in doorways from cautious village women. Nothing like this had ever happened before. They wanted to believe, but weren't sure. They tentatively gathered, dirty children clinging to many of them, and approached Micah. She held up a hand to keep them from coming too close. She went to the cart, kicking the old man viciously before untying the rope that held his legs. Grabbing an arm, she leveraged herself and pulled him out. He fell unceremoniously to the ground. With a firm grip on his collar, she dragged him into the open area in front of the horses. She dropped him, then rolled him over by kicking him in the side.

The two warriors approached from behind the women, watching warily before drawing their swords. They pushed the women in the back out of the way, while the others cowered away from them. The men stood, threatening.

Micah wondered if they expected her to simply submit because they had swords. She reached behind her and pulled her new sword from her back, testing its weight in her hand before slashing it through the air in front of her. *Where in the hell are Braden and G-War,* she thought.

At that moment, an arrow hit one of the two men at the base of his skull, neatly separating his spinal column from his skull. The man dropped like a sack of potatoes. The second man looked at his partner, who lay dead on the ground. He looked back in disbelief to see Braden coming toward him, an arrow nocked and pointed directly at his face.

He looked back at the woman standing over the Elder. The eyes of the village women grew hard and they edged closer toward him. They were no longer afraid.

He dropped his sword and fell to his knees. "Please! Have mercy!" he begged in a simpering voice.

G-War ran past Braden and jumped on the man, knocking him to the ground. The 'cat stood on the man's chest, his claws raised, ready to strike. The man peed himself, then closed his eyes tightly, preparing to die.

'I love that part,' G-War said as he retracted his claws and hopped off the man's chest. *'Hungry,'* he said over the mindlink to no one in particular.

Micah started laughing, easy at first, then with a full throated howl. The other women began to laugh and cheer. They hadn't heard the 'cat, but they saw it all and realized that they were free. Braden took the sword away from the soiled warrior and dragged him by the back of his collar to throw him on the ground at the feet of the Elder.

Braden looked at Micah, bowing. He looked at the women of the village, who eyed him suspiciously. He pointed back to Micah and started clapping and cheering. He backed away a step, giving way to Micah.

"I am Micah, recently of the village Trent on the Eastern Ocean." A couple women nodded, most others just watched, waiting. "I am a Free Trader Apprentice." She nodded to Braden. He bowed to her again.

"This man and five of his warriors attacked us without provocation, trying to steal our goods and kill me and our friends. We left him alive so you could deal with him as you desire."

One of the older women stepped forward. She looked well-weathered, sporting a black eye and bruises on her arms. She kicked the Elder in the teeth, hurting her foot as she did so, but she limped away with a smile on her face. Other women shouldered their way close, kicking the old man. He tried to cover his head with his arms, pleading for them to stop and listen to him.

Many heartbeats later, he was no longer breathing. The women were avenged, but they wore expressions showing pain and sorrow. Taking another's life was not an easy thing, even if the person was the Elder McCullough. Even though their lives had become easier with his death, killing cost a person part of their soul.

Braden leaned close to the remaining warrior. "Just stay down if you wish to live," he hissed. The man nodded almost imperceptibly, trying his best not to be seen by the women. But their hatred was spent. For the time being anyway.

"We are traveling through the area, looking for trading partners," Micah started, picking up the narrative that Braden had shared with her all those turns ago. "Trade is how we will return to being civilized. Trade, like it happens in the north, in Warren Deep."

Master Aadi swam to her side from his position above the cart. The women again shied away.

"Muties," a couple of them whispered.

"They are our friends. Treat them as you would treat me." Micah held out her hand to the woman who led the parade against the Elder. The older woman grasped Micah's hand, desperately and with surprising strength.

"Thank you," she said. "I am Mel-Ash. I guess I'm the Elder now." She looked around her. No one disputed her assumption of the title.

"Do you need an Elder?" Braden asked.

"I don't know. It's how we've always been. The Elder guides the village. The Elder keeps us safe." She trailed off as she thought about the safety of the village. "We have no one left to defend us. We are free. And doomed."

Micah returned from the cart with the swords and spears liberated from the war party. She handed them over. "Take these. Learn to use them. You can fight as well as any man. Know that you can and you will." The villagers looked at her. Micah stood proudly, trying to look strong. The tunic was too big and hung on her, making her look like a child, but they watched her drag the Elder from the cart and seen how he whimpered in her presence. "Can you teach us how to make these?" she asked as she pulled on the overly large tunic.

Mel-Ash nodded and smiled. "Yes. There are some tricks to getting the weave correct, but after that, the rest is easy." Taking Micah by the arm, she introduced her to the rest of the women of the village.

A couple of the younger women angled toward Braden, smiling. "We've never seen a man defer to a woman before. Is she your leader?" one of them asked him.

Braden started to laugh, but quickly thought better of it. "No. We are partners. All of us, equally sharing in our journey."

The shorter of the two women frowned. "She is your partner then?"

"What? No, no, not like that. We are partners in trade," he quickly corrected. He felt defensive, but didn't know why. He was uncomfortable as the women worked on him. He had been proud to have a woman in every town, but he felt differently now. He didn't want Micah to get a bad impression of him. He wasn't like other men, was he?

They took him by the arm, leading him away from the others. As he thought about it, he didn't know anything about this village. What if they took over as the new tyrants?

'G. A little help.' He knew the 'cat was not bothered by Braden's lady friends.

'The females of this village are no threat to us. Relax and take it like a man.' The 'cat chuckled over their mindlink.

'Do you two have to talk like this? I'm embarrassed enough for all of us right now. Just get over here. There's work to do.' Micah ended with a harsh tone. Braden

wondered how she managed to get so good with her thought voice that she could convey disgust. He better not push it.

"I'm sorry, ladies, if you'll excuse me. I believe we have some work to do to help protect your village. If you'll join me?" With one young woman on each arm, Braden swaggered to the hut where Micah and Mel-Ash were talking.

He entered, but the two young women quickly disappeared after a dismissive wave from their new Elder.

One other woman from the village sat beside Mel-Ash. She also was bruised, and this sobered Braden immediately. He was instantly sorry for his earlier reverie. When they solved the problem of the Elder McCullough, new problems popped up.

How would they protect themselves from raiders? Who would hunt? How could they take care of themselves?

They hadn't been allowed to think independently, but Micah and Braden were confident that once they had a taste of freedom, they would not give it up again. They only needed to survive until they learned what it meant to take care of themselves.

69 – Helping the Village

With Braden's encouragement and a sound arm-twisting from Micah, the lone remaining man in the village agreed to teach six volunteers how to use the weapons. He was only given a piece of wood himself, but he agreed wholeheartedly with his role as servant to the new Elder. G-War believed he was sincere and that was good enough for Braden and Micah.

Their training started immediately.

The next issue was food. They maintained a couple small fields, while also picking wild from a large area to the south of the village. The men fixed snares on numerous game trails, rotating them to keep the wild animals guessing. Braden agreed to show them how to make their own bows and arrows, so they could hunt and better protect their village. Sword battles were ugly and generally favored the stronger opponent. With bows, the village could keep enemies away.

In the interim, Braden, G-War, and Skirill would hunt to put meat on their tables.

Braden took his leave of the meeting, heading outside with the intention of going hunting.

Micah chased him down before he made it to the horses.

"I'm sorry about earlier," she said, head down, not looking at him. "You did a great thing for this village. I wouldn't have thought of it. I would have killed the men and run away."

"It's what *we* did for this village. We. As in all of us. There's plenty to do if we want this village to be a good trading partner. Whatever we're able to kill during our hunt, we'll trade. Maybe they can tailor a tunic for you. That would be worth a couple deer, at least."

She smiled at him, then reared back and punched him in the chest. His new tunic absorbed much of the blow, but he still staggered from the force of it. "Hey! What the crap was that for?"

She waved him away as she turned. Speaking over her shoulder as she walked toward the hut, she said, "And leave those two children alone. They don't need you to fill any void because the other men are gone."

"G! Do you know what that was about?"

'Yes and no,' the 'cat answered cryptically, not explaining further.

Braden climbed on Max's back, stroking the horse's neck vigorously. With one powerful leap, G-War was in his lap. The horse wheeled and they trotted out of the village in the direction where G-War said they'd find game.

Skirill took to the sky and looked ahead, excited about the prospect of fresh meat.

They didn't have to go far to find what they were looking for. Rabbits were plentiful. The deer grazed in a large herd. And a village full of women waited for him to return with venison as a prize. He wasn't sure it could get any better than this.

70 – Introducing a Friend

Micah and Elder Mel-Ash led the chorus of cheers as Braden returned with three deer. All clean kills, no wasted meat. They were field dressed, but needed more attention to prepare the venison to eat. A couple of the women took charge and a group went to work skinning and de-boning.

G-War had eaten the choice parts from a couple rabbits, while Skirill made his own kill of a particularly large rabbit. They were both quite satisfied. Master Aadi, on the other hand, seemed put out. He floated near the cart, well away from any villagers.

Braden went to him and stroked his neck, which he stretched out so the human hands could reach those places that Aadi himself could not.

"What's going on, A-Dog?" Braden asked softly.

'I fear that they are all afraid of me. You were the first human I've met. You accepted me and treated me with respect. I give that back to you in equal portion. You are a good man, Master Braden. These women do not accept me. Mutie they called me and mutie is what they think when they look at me.' He blinked rapidly, as he did when he was upset.

"If they knew how downright mean and nasty I am, they'd be afraid." Braden looked closely at Aadi to see if he got the jibe.

'Mean? Nasty? I think you are confusing yourself with someone else, young human.' Braden screwed up his face and made growling noises. *'Ha! I get it. Well, not really, but I understand what you are trying to do, and I appreciate it.'*

"C'mon, Master Aadi. I don't know what this village is called or what they have to trade besides these tunics. I would like to see this place as a main trade center. Let's see, where could we put the market square…" Braden rested his hand on the Tortoid's shell as they walked, side by side, into the village.

The two young women saw Braden and made a beeline toward him, giggling to each other as they approached. When they saw he was with the Tortoid, they stopped and grimaced.

"Hey! I don't even know your names. Come on over here. I want to show you something," Braden said in his best come-hither voice.

The young women started retreating, facing Braden and the Tortoid, but walking backwards.

"Come here!" he yelled with a snarl. If they had anything to fear, it was him when he was angry.

They reluctantly approached.

"Let me introduce you to Aadi, First Master of the Tortoise Consortium. He is my mentor. He is the wisest creature I've ever met, and that includes humans. Most importantly, he is my friend. This morning you wanted to be my friend. Nothing has changed between then and now. Come closer." Braden stroked the Tortoid's neck. He remained unblinking, making himself into a floating statue.

"He likes this. Here. Pet his neck, gently." The first woman complied mechanically at first, then tenderly as she felt Aadi's neck, the rough but living skin teasing her sense of touch.

"How do you talk with it?"

"Him. I talk with him. I am bonded with Golden Warrior of the Stone Cliffs, the Hillcat, over..." Braden looked for G-War, but couldn't find him. "Here's here somewhere. The 'cat connects us all. I hear Master Aadi's voice in my head."

The girls giggled again, looking at each other. "One of the oldest women here was hearing voices, too. No one else heard them so she was driven away." They let that linger with Braden. Would he be driven away? No, because Micah could hear them, too.

"Micah talks with my friends, too. You believe her, don't you?" He could tell by the look on their faces that they didn't like Micah. Maybe they saw her as competition, maybe even an interloper, changing their world and not for the better. '*G. Can you arrange a demonstration for the unbelievers?*' Braden asked using his thought voice.

'*No. I don't do tricks to impress stupid girls.*'

'*You're right, G. These two need to grow up a bit before they will realize how special it all is. Micah isn't very much older than them, is she?*'

'*It bores me with its inane drivel.*'

'*I know that I haven't told you this turn yet, G, but you are a good friend. And an ass. Wherever you are, here's one for you.*' The young women watched as Braden held his middle finger in the air and waved it in all directions. They looked concerned and backed away.

Braden laughed as they ran off.

'*See, Master Aadi? Mean and nasty. I don't think they're afraid of you anymore. It seems that they have something new to be afraid of.*'

'*Yes, Master Human. I think you've made your point. I'm sorry you won't achieve the physical coupling you desired, but I doubt it would have been as satisfying as you wished.*'

'*Whoa. Stop right there! We don't talk about those things, especially where Micah can hear.*'

'*That's what you're concerned about? Of all things…*' Micah's thought voice carried a sharp edge.

"I guess this is my life now, huh, A-Dog?" Braden said to Aadi with a friendly pat on his head. Master Aadi looked at him with unblinking eyes, then shook his head, slowly, as Tortoids were wont to do.

71 – Villagers Prepare

The next two dozen turns were a flurry of activity. They made bows and arrows, learned to shoot, then improved their bows. Hardwood for the bow, deer intestines for strings, straight wood for arrows, bird feathers for vanes, tied on with snake skin, and flat stone for broad heads.

By the third set of bows, the selected wood and bowstrings were delivering a nice impact. The women started hitting the trees with some regularity and then they drove the arrows deeper as they got more comfortable pulling the full draw. With continued practice, they would have the confidence to use them in battle.

They found a good patch of ash to make the bows and other hardwoods to make the arrows. Braden filled his quiver as he showed the women how to make arrows for themselves.

For those selected to use the swords and spears, their training was going far more slowly. They were building arm strength and that took time. They were learning basic slash and defense. Braden hoped that his new archers would keep potential enemies away. If they had to fight sword to sword, the women would probably all die.

Micah excelled with the sword. Within the first ten turns, she was already besting the young man who sought to train them. Then Braden taught her what he knew, especially in the area of movement and parrying. He was good with his long knife, but that was limited to thrusting after an opponent offered an opening. Micah's advantage was in her strength. She didn't look overly thick, but her muscles gave more than any man who was her size. He watched her carefully, trying to learn where her power came from.

He saw it in her trunk. She rotated her upper body using her core muscles. He practiced his own movements and saw where he did not use his body as much as he could. He counted on his own arm strength. He tried twisting at his waist and immediately saw the power. To match the arm swing with the twist wasn't as easy as it looked. He needed to practice, but he wouldn't take a sword away from the villagers. He needed to find a sword for himself.

That would be later. If things turned out as intended, he would be able to trade for a sword.

Braden helped build the first trader stall in what he envisioned as the village's market square. The village, which he found out was unsurprisingly called Village McCullough after its original founder, already produced a great deal, which they shared openly.

He showed them what they could trade. Everyone learned their own individual value. Even the children got into trading, which eventually led to fighting as they learned the dangers of envy. This got them a good cuffing, which returned them to just being children.

Braden's first trade earned him a tunic with sleeves that would fit Micah, including special breeches with the material woven around the most vulnerable parts of the leg. After seeing to Micah's protection, he tried to work a deal for the same kind of covering for himself, but the price more than doubled for him.

He could only shake his head. After all, he was the deputy to the savior of Village McCullough, as the women saw him.

The shift in the villagers' attitudes about becoming self-sufficient wasn't as profound as the complete change in their acceptance of the Tortoid, the Hillcat, and the Hawkoid. At Micah's urging, Mel-Ash took the time to get to know their companions. G-War wouldn't allow any of the others to share the mindlink, so Micah told them what each was saying. As they got to know Master Aadi, they welcomed him in the best way. He was a dinner guest with someone different every evening. He ate well. Braden suspected too well, but how can anyone tell if a Tortoid was getting fat?

G-War was a favorite of the children. Braden thought he enjoyed the attention, despite his constant protests. If they ignored him for too long, he would make an appearance, strolling regally in front of them, which always led to a game of chase the 'cat. He seemed to like the young girls the best. They were the only ones he would let pet him. Even then, it would only be for a number of heartbeats before he moved on.

Skirill assumed the role of master watchman for the village. He began each morning with a flight around the village and the local area to make sure that no one was near. He kept track of the deer herd so they never went without fresh venison.

He sat in the highest branches of the largest tree overlooking the village and during the daylight, he watched everything. As the villagers passed him, they waved. He ruffled his wings back at them, to the people's delight. The children gathered beneath the tree and endlessly watched him. One enterprising young boy wanted to see him move, so he threw a rock at Skirill. The Hawkoid caught it in his claw and launched himself at the boy. The children scattered in a panic. The Hawkoid landed astraddle the boy's head. Gently, using his beak, he put the rock on the boy's forehead, then shook his feathered head. It was clear to all the children that throwing rocks at the Hawkoid was unacceptable.

The fact that the boy left bawling made Skirill's parenting lesson legendary.

When he resumed his position in the tree, he held his head higher.

In the evenings. Skirill made one last flight, looking for any movement from potential enemies.

Although the villagers fully welcomed Braden's caravan, he and his companions grew restless. Mel-Ash shared with them the location of the road south. Skirill confirmed it, flying the route a number of times to help Braden and Micah visualize it and plan for the trip.

They couldn't take the cart as it was too rough. It would stay behind, waiting for their return.

One morning, they saddled Pack and Max and said their goodbyes.

72 – The Road

Braden would have missed the road south if they'd had to blindly search for it, for nothing gave it away when they crossed it. It was covered by brush and even trees. The ground here was wetter than in the north. The Amazon Rainforest was reclaiming the land.

Skirill guided them to a point where the Mel-Ash told them the roadway cut through the thick trees and the heavy foliage. Once they were on the road, they could tell it apart from the encroaching rainforest. It was hot and wet. The jungle grew heavy on all sides, including overhead. It created a roof of green that let little light through.

They picked their way carefully forward. It was hard for the horses to get through, and it was challenging for Skirill to fly beneath the canopy, between the trees and vines.

G-War sat in Braden's lap on Max. Micah rode Pack, because the horse was used to following Max. He simply ambled along behind. Micah did not have to do anything. Aadi floated along behind Pack, seemingly enjoying himself. He was probably getting excess water.

"I see movement everywhere I look, but can't quite see anything, if you know what I mean. Do you sense anything, G?"

'Yes. So many different creatures. Large. Small. Dangerous. Safe. I am overwhelmed by all their minds. It is worse than being in Jefferson City.'

"Jefferson City is the largest city in Warren Deep. It's where the Caravan Guild is based. It is where the Council sits and where all the important decisions are made," Braden said for Micah's benefit. She mumbled something in response, but Braden didn't hear her words. He watched in front of him, then to the sides. Movement, just far enough away from his line of sight that he couldn't see what it was. He jerked his head back and forth, trying to catch the creatures as they toyed with him.

"Micah, you've been there before. How did you get through all this?"

"We came from the east. The road in that direction is much better, or it was when we traveled it. It skirts the southern edge of the rainforest. We didn't travel through this."

"You know what we're going to find, so let me ask. Is this going to be worth it?" Braden asked.

"It is something you need to see for yourself. Then you can judge the value."

The first daylight went by. They made camp, but half of them watched while the other half tried to sleep. The fire burned with a great deal of smoke. The wood they found wasn't dry. It might never dry in this environment.

Then it started to rain.

And it kept raining as they broke camp. It rained as they traveled further south. They lost the ability to judge how far they'd traveled. Everything looked the same in the steady downpour.

Night came. The rain continued. G-War was at his most miserable. He was soaked and in a foul mood. Worse than that, he smelled like a wet dog.

Skirill stopped trying to fly and resigned himself to riding awkwardly in Micah's lap as a miserable Pack mindlessly put one hoof in front of the other.

Aadi was indifferent to it all. *'Water off a Tortoid's shell and all that,'* he said with annoying frequency.

They plodded south, sleep after sleep, growing more tired and hungry as they went. They snapped at each other constantly, so they stopped talking.

Finally the rain stopped as they approached the southern edge of the rainforest. The canopy above thinned, the ground dry in areas where the sun shone through.

With a more welcoming world in front of them, their spirits lifted.

Until they saw the man with the spear standing in the road.

73 – The Lizard Men

As they got closer, they saw that the man wasn't a man at all. His skin was green and textured, similar to the skin on Aadi's neck and legs. His eyes were large and bulged out of his head. His three fingers and three toes were separated by small flaps of skin. As Braden sat in the saddle, the creature's head was even with his.

Braden stopped Max. The green creature seemed unable to take his eyes off the horse.

"I am Free Trader Braden from the far north of Warren Deep." He bowed his head as he remained in the saddle. The creature didn't acknowledge that Braden had spoken.

"So where do we go from here?" he asked no one in particular. Micah shrugged, fear creeping into her expression the longer they sat.

The Tortoid used his swimming motion to go around the horses, stopping when he was directly in front of the creature. *When you're two hundred cycles old, you aren't afraid of anything,* Braden thought.

Master Aadi floated higher until he was eye to eye with the creature. They stayed that way for what seemed like forever, although it was probably only a dozen heartbeats.

The creature bowed deeply to Master Aadi, then waved his arm in a circle. Braden watched as numerous green creatures appeared from the trees and jungle. The creatures surrounded the caravan. Many had spears. Others had coils of vine. Others carried limbs that looked like clubs.

"Master Aadi, if you would be so kind as to explain, I would appreciate it. If this isn't your doing, then I fear we are farged," Braden said.

'Yes, yes. No problem. These are, shall we call them Lizard Men? Yes. They are the Lizard Men of Akhtior. I suspect that's their word for the Amazon. No matter. They live here and we have crossed their territory, but I have smoothed things over. They initially asked for one of our horses to share in a feast, but I know that you wouldn't be able to part with either of them. So I offered our smoked venison instead.'

"Really. Then what are we supposed to eat?"

'A moot point, Master Human, as the Lizard Men were going to eat something, if not the horses or the venison, then I fear you were their next choice. I assumed you wouldn't agree to that.'

"Venison it is! Are we allowed to pass?"

'Oh no, not yet. First, we must attend their celebration. It appears that Tortoids are somewhat revered in their culture. I am to be honored at tonight's feast. You and Micah will attend.'

"Of course you are. They never considered eating you, did they? Don't answer that. I know."

'It's funny. They call you two the pinkies.'

"Do they know about Skirill or G-War?"

'We didn't discuss them specifically. Why do you ask?'

"I figure wherever we're going, we won't be able to take the horses. Someone will have to protect them. I'm sorry, G. I would much rather have you at my side. We don't know what we'll run across in there. We don't know if it's a ploy to separate us so they can eat us all. Protect the horses if you can, but save yourselves first."

Braden and Micah got down off their horses and joined Aadi with the one they assumed was the leader of the Lizard Men. He led the way into the trees with Master Aadi at his side, the humans behind them, followed closely by a number of the larger Lizard Men. The rest drifted away, disappearing into the heavy undergrowth.

Braden and Micah's boots were not made for walking through the swamp. The tangled growth beneath the mud caught their feet often, tripping them and filling their boots with water. Braden could feel his skin getting rubbed off as he continued to march forward. The expression on Micah's face suggested she was losing the skin battle, too.

The leader called a halt, sniffing at the air. He used his spear to point to the right around a small pond. Before he took two steps, a croc surged out of the water. The Lizard Man drove his spear downward, but it skipped off the outer shell of the croc. Braden thought this looked like a supersized version of the cold-water croc that wanted to eat him so long ago. But this time, he had his weapons with him.

In a smooth motion, he pulled his bow in front of him, nocking an arrow in nearly the same instant. He drew back as the croc renewed its efforts to get at the Lizard Man, who was trying in vain to pull his spear from the mud. Braden's arrow embedded itself in the beast's left eye. The croc stopped instantly and slowly slid backwards into the dark water.

A second croc broke the water, then a third. With a powerful swish of their tails, they came at the leader, who now stood, brandishing his freed spear. He waited, ready for the attack. With a fearsome jab, he drove the spear point through one croc's snout, pinning the creature in the mud.

Braden had a second arrow ready, but Micah stepped in front of him, her sword held high. With all the power she could muster, she swung her sword into the head of the third croc. The sword buried itself between the thing's eyes. It froze where it was. Micah used her foot for leverage to pull her sword out, while the second croc thrashed about trying to free itself from the Lizard Man's spear. Her croc was dead, its brains oozing out around the split in its skull.

Once her sword was free, she leaned into another swing. Braden didn't think it possible, but she turned even faster, driving the sword's blade even deeper into the second croc's neck, nearly severing it. The sword readily slid out of the massive wound.

Before it could slide back into the water, the Lizard Man grabbed it and pulled it from the water. The carcass of the first one that Micah had dispatched was also saved. The Lizard Men bobbed their necks and their heads, eyes rapidly blinking.

'Well done, young humans!' Master Aadi cheered with his thought voice. *These creatures are quite a delicacy and will take the place of the smoked venison at tonight's feast. Zalastar is quite impressed with your strength and courage. You will have places of honor next to me. I am very pleased. You should be proud of yourselves. By the way, the Lizard Men are secretive people. They avoid contact with humans.'*

"Thanks, Master Aadi. If they avoid humans, then why did they reveal themselves to us?"

'Me, my good man. Me, and they had never seen horses before. To the Lizard Men, the horses smelled like a tasty meal.'

How quickly they went from being the meal to being honored at the meal. Braden still wasn't sure they'd leave the horses alone. He asked Aadi to get that assurance from Zalastar, but he was waved off as if it was a trivial thing. He and Micah would wait, but not long before they had to escape and get back to their friends.

74 – A Celebration Like No Other

As the celebration was being prepared and darkness fell, Master Aadi, Braden, and Micah were given a place to sit in the middle of an open area, a glade. Water stood throughout, and they couldn't move without being knee-deep in muck. There was no need for cook fires; the Lizard Men ate their food raw.

The humans expected nothing different. They'd watched Aadi eat in the past. It was nature against nature. The Tortoid avoided smoked meat and the fabricator-prepared foods as much as possible. He said that they didn't sit well in his stomach. Aadi would readily eat a bug or a fresh caught fish and be happy.

There were far more Lizard Men than they expected. A hundred or more filled the area, half squatting in the water. Braden and Micah tried to tell them apart, but couldn't. They assumed the small ones were the children. Otherwise, they all looked alike. They realized that there may not be a difference between Lizard males and females. They all wore harnesses of some sort and they all carried weapons.

The Amazon was a more dangerous place than the humans realized. Maybe the Lizard Men had escorted them the entire way, ensuring their safe passage, but only because of Master Aadi.

For that, they believed that no human had ever witnessed what they were about to see.

Braden assumed the last one to arrive was Zalastar as he was dragging the remains of the crocs. He threw the first one down into the muck. The second one, he held over his head, the muscles in his arms and back bulging with the effort. He bobbed and shook, turning in a complete circle so all could see. The Lizard Men watching also bobbed in delight, and no sound escaped as they worked their wide mouths.

Besides the splashing as Zalastar danced, it was eerily quiet.

With a final bob, Zalastar held himself tall, thrusting the croc high over his head, then let it tumble from his hands, where it landed next to the other.

Dropping to all fours, he hissed, thrusting his head forward with his tongue shooting far in front of his pointed teeth. Micah looked at Braden, her eyes wide. Braden hoped that Aadi was correct that the Lizard Men weren't going to eat them.

All the Lizard Men, including the small ones the humans assumed were children, dropped to all fours and hissed back. Although the sound wasn't loud, it was fearsome. It struck Braden as a war cry. He reached back to feel the comforting shape of his bow and quiver, caressing it to help his mind calm. Micah held the grip of her sword, knuckles white with the effort.

Zalastar stood up on his two hind legs. The hissing stopped and Lizard Men returned to their seated positions. With a wave of one webbed hand, some figures at the outside of the circle stood up. All eyes turned toward them. One started slapping his foot into a puddle. Rhythmically, it continued. Another tapped a stick on a log, filling the space between the water sounds. The beat was set.

Sawing on a tree with a bowstring made of vine. Scraping of a rock. Tapping of webbed hands on anything nearby. The sawing on the tree assumed a melody, dancing among the rhythm in the glade. Human ears could barely follow the nuances of the sounds. Micah closed her eyes and swayed slightly in time with the beat.

Music wasn't common in the north. Braden had liked what he heard when traveling through the bigger towns, but in the rural areas, there were no instruments. People didn't make the time for them, because there was always something else that was more important. As Braden listened and watched, he saw what the music did for all present. Braden saw the wisdom and beauty of the peace it brought. He saw that Micah was swept up in the sounds. Aadi was in his statue pose, unblinking and unmoving.

Finally, Zalastar broke the rhythm as he stepped carefully to the area where Aadi, Braden, and Micah sat. He bowed low and with one hand, showed the way to the crocs.

'Aadi, I don't know what we're supposed to do. You go first. Show us.' They had checked as they traveled and their mindlink stayed strong. Although it seemed that they had traveled a long way from the road and the horses, it may not have been. When Braden thought about it, this was the furthest he'd ever been away from G-War. Checking in, the 'cat told him they were safe. A number of Lizard Men were nearby in the trees, watching but not threatening.

'They want you two to go first since you made the kills. The Lizard Men aren't often successful at killing crocs. This is a rare treat that you've provided for them. Let's go.' Aadi started to swim slowly toward the crocs, making sure that the humans were with him. *'We'll take a little piece of meat, eat it, and declare it fit for all. I suggest you slice a piece from the tail. I think you'll like that more. Don't try to eat the skin.'*

'Don't eat the skin, he tells us.' Braden rolled his eyes at Micah as he pulled his skinning knife from the pouch at his belt.

'Do you want me to cut a piece for you, Master Aadi?' Micah offered in her thought voice. *'What about the Lizard Men? What would they think if we cut up the crocs and served them?'*

'I honestly don't know. It could be interpreted one of two ways. Demeaning and they'll kill you for it, or an honor and they'll forever welcome you. Let me 'feel them out,' as you humans say.'

'There's no in between? Either we're lifelong friends or dead? Sometimes I wonder about you.' Micah said what Braden was thinking. He liked the idea, hoping beyond hope that the Lizard Men would befriend them. Allies, he thought. He knew where he was only because a four hundred cycle old map told him. It would be nice to have allies confirm where they were and that they were safe.

He didn't know anything about the Amazon, except that it was a dangerous place. Having the Lizard Men as friends might help him and his companions to survive one more turn. Knowing that tomorrow would come was his comforting thought. Knowing that G-War watched as he slept was always the blanket that kept him warm for a restful sleep.

'Master Micah, I believe you have won the hearts of the Lizard Men! They will see your service to them as a great honor.' Aadi bobbed his head and blinked to emphasize his point. Micah smiled broadly. Braden didn't realize how afraid she had been. Although she was used to Skirill, Aadi, and G-War, she had an innate fear of anything mutant. Braden was raised differently and his bond with the 'cat ensured he would look at all creatures, judging them simply by how dangerous they were to him personally. In reality, he was most suspicious of his fellow man.

With their skinning knives in hand, Braden and Micah each took one of the crocs and started to work on it. As Aadi advised, they sliced down the tail and cut out a small piece of meat, which they ate, much to their dismay. They weren't hungry enough for raw meat to taste good, and did not know what the croc was supposed to taste like. It was different enough that it was all they could do not to gag. Aadi took a bite of a piece that Micah offered him. After gulping it down, he asked for another, just to be sure. Braden gave him a piece from his croc and waited while the Tortoid threw it back and swallowed it whole.

He bobbed to Zalastar. Braden and Micah weren't sure how the Tortoid communicated with the Lizard Men, but he spoke their language, whatever that looked like.

With the food declared fit, Zalastar waved his hands and bobbed his head, tongue flicking in and out. The smaller Lizard Men jumped up and pressed forward.

'Children?' Braden asked.

'Yes, yes, the little ones.'

'How can we tell the females from the males?' Micah asked.

'There are no males or females. There are only Lizard Men. The word "Men" is my creation because I don't know what another word would be. They are all the same, for what that's worth.'

Braden found that by rolling the croc over, the skin on the under side was much easier to cut through. Micah followed his lead and soon, they were handing out bits of meat from all different places on the body. It seemed that each Lizard Man had his favorite. They would point with a flick of their tongue and the humans would extract a piece for them.

Time flew by. They ran out of croc meat before they ran out of Lizard Men to feed. Not to be deterred, the last group of Lizard Men stuck their faces into the carcass, licking and eating anything not bone or skin.

The rhythmic tapping, splashing, and bowing continued.

Aadi told them that Zalastar considered this the greatest celebration he had ever seen.

'Time to ask for a favor, then. Can we go back to our friends and how can we get to Sanctuary?'

'Yes, they will take us back tonight. To get to the ruined city, keep following the road. It leads there.'

'Tonight, good.' Lizard Men lived during the night, resting during the daylight. *'Ruined city? Is that what you were keeping from me?'* Braden looked at Micah as they talked over the mindlink. He didn't want to talk out loud and damage the silent calm of the glade.

'It is nothing but ruins, yes, but there is still something to see and areas where you might find what you are looking for. I don't believe in your quest, but I believe in you. I didn't want you to think that I was killing your dream. I wanted you to see and make a decision for yourself.' Micah made her thought voice as soothing as possible.

Braden was angry. *'Could you tell Zalastar that we are ready to go? Our friends are waiting.'* He stormed off toward the edge of the glade, not looking back. The only thing he accomplished was getting more water and mud in his boots.

'Braden, wait. What else am I supposed to say? What do you want from me?'

'How about the truth?' He wanted to yell, but was afraid of harming their newfound position as friends of the Lizard Men.

'I never lied to you. Now listen, you farging crap hole! I joined you when all I wanted to do was kill any man I met. You showed me what it was like to trust someone. You shared your friends with me. For the first time in my life, I'm at peace. The last thing I

wanted to do was to take away your dream. We could find something there for you. I don't know, but it's a bad place. We all go there once in our lifetime so that we know what we don't want to become. It keeps us isolated and you've shown me that isn't a good thing.

'You've changed how I see the world. Keep slopping through the mud like that and I'll come over there and stomp you!'

Braden hadn't set out to change the world, only the part that affected him. The burden of leadership was heavy, and it came with great responsibility. Aadi told him that where he led, others would follow. He had a group that counted on him to make decisions for them all.

She wasn't wrong. Seeing the ancients' city of Sanctuary was important. From there, they could all talk about what to do next. That was the plan.

Micah, Aadi, and Zalastar watched patiently as Braden wrestled with himself. When he realized this, he ushered them past him so they could lead the way.

Micah punched his shoulder as she passed.

"Oww!" Braden wanted to say more, but thought better of it. Micah smiled back at him as she followed Zalastar back into the rainforest.

My life used to be so much simpler, Braden thought. *And far less interesting.*

75 – Safe Now, Safe Forever

The return trip to the road was uneventful.

Skirill and G-War were waiting for them. The horses were still tied to a nearby tree. Braden hadn't wanted them to wander off. They were sleeping standing up, without any concerns. The 'cat was equally unperturbed. Only Skirill seemed anxious, but he was ready to fly in the open skies. It was the middle of the night, as well. Braden asked Micah if she was tired, which she was. So they decided to spend the remainder of the night in place.

Even if they wanted to continue that night, they couldn't see. Zalastar probably would have escorted them further if they wanted, but there was no need. The Lizard Men guaranteed their safety any time they were in the rainforest, and Braden was overwhelmed by the offer.

"Any time? Even cycles from now if we travel through?"

Yes, Master Humans. Any time means for as long as they remember who you all are, which that will be for a very long time. This has been a good turn for you, for us. I am honored to know you both,' Master Aadi said.

With their final bows and silent waves, the Lizard Men melted back into the forest.

Braden rolled his blanket on the ground in the middle of the road. It was the highest point in the area and the most dry. Micah rolled her blanket out as well, seeking a similar dry spot to sleep.

"Thanks, Micah. Thanks for suggesting we serve the Lizard Men. Once again, you delivered allies. It will be nice to go through here without having to worry, whether it's on our way back to Village McCullough or wherever we may go. Are you sure you weren't a trader in a previous life?"

"Don't be insulting. I was a warrior in a prior life."

"I think you're a warrior now. I think the Lizard Men allowed us to serve them because they were afraid you were going to club their heads in like you did to those crocs. That was ridiculous!"

"What can I say? I was mad." She laughed to herself as she put an arm under her head as a pillow.

Mad indeed. Braden was happy she was on his side. He wouldn't like to face her in a real fight.

When the sun rose, a new daylight would come with new challenges. They'd all stretch their wings a bit as they left the Amazon and entered the area where Sanctuary had been built.

Until then, as usual when G-War watched over him, Braden slept well. Not only G-War, but the entirety of the Lizard Men watched over them, too.

76 – Too Much Power

Skirill launched himself from Micah's lap. He couldn't wait any longer. He flew the last of the tree and vine tunnel, low to the road before bursting into the open air.

The rainforest ended abruptly as the ancients' mastery over nature was again demonstrated. The trees grew thickly and within a few paces, there were no trees at all, only dry grasses waving in a gentle breeze. Rolling hills were before them, beyond which, nothing grew, not trees, grass, or even weeds.

"When you came here, where were you?"

Micah pointed. "Probably over those hills, far to the east. We may not be able to see where we were, even from up there." One of the hills rose a little more than the others. Beyond a certain point, everything looked barren.

The Hawkoid soared high overhead.

Aadi looked on wide-eyed.

G-War was asleep in Braden's lap, happy that he was finally dry and in the sun.

They spurred the horses to a trot, covering ground quickly. The area of destruction was immense, all the way to the horizon.

As they reached the top of the largest rolling hill, they looked down on a basin where the city of Sanctuary once sat. It was still there, but leveled. Large debris stuck out, but nature was winning the battle and reclaiming what it once had. Whatever weapons they used, the effects no longer lingered. Grasses grew, not tall but they grew. What they thought was barren was not.

Braden imagined how it looked when it first happened. Thunder, lightning, fire, and even earthquakes. The worst parts of nature brought together at one time, in one place. This confirmed his belief that the ancients were masters of the earth and the sky. They commanded the weather. They commanded the ground. They could grow an oasis in the heart of the desert.

And then they used that power to destroy. Maybe it was an accident, but Braden didn't think so. The ancients had fought, but instead of bows and swords, they used the power of their technology.

And it almost killed them all.

Only those who ran away from the technology had survived.

Was Braden's quest misguided? Did he want to see that kind of power returned to man? He knew what they would do with it. Conquests. Personal power. If only the traders had the power, then above all, trade would go on. Even as a trader, his goal was to become wealthy enough that he could settle down. He wasn't sure anyone could manage the power of Old Tech without being corrupted.

Micah watched Braden struggle to make sense of how he could bring Old Tech to the north without the danger it represented.

"This is what I wanted you to see. I wanted you to make your own decision whether Old Tech should be brought back," Micah said softly.

"Yet you carry a blaster?" Braden said matter-of-factly. He wasn't trying to start a fight. He only wanted to understand.

"This blaster was used to bring fear so that one man could rule. One man, who passed it down, son to son, so they could always rule. Because of this one piece of Old Tech, that family was the definition of evil. No one should ever have that much power over another. I carry it as a prize and a symbol to show that evil can be defeated."

"Why didn't you destroy it?"

She nodded. "I tried. Rocks can't hurt it, it seems. As long as I carry it, no one else can find it and use it."

"But it doesn't have any power..." Braden started.

"The man I took it from had a way to recharge it. If he gets this back, he'll kill everyone in my village. The only reason he didn't before is that we paid him in fish and vegetables. Now it's different. If he brought this and all the men... I'm afraid to think what he would do to my family."

"He won't do anything because we won't let the Old Tech get into the hands of those who would misuse it. We're your family now and we won't let anything happen to you." Max and Pack were side by side. Braden reached out a hand to put on Micah's shoulder.

'Hungry.' They both looked at G-War as he stretched. His claws extended full length from his stretched out front legs, then retracted as he sat upright on Braden's lap.

"The world is yours, Master Golden Warrior of the Stone Cliffs," Braden said, waving one arm with a flourish. The 'cat looked out upon the grassy wasteland, then cocked his head to one side.

'Go that way,' was all he said.

77 – A New Oasis

Braden trusted G-War. With a shrug, he pulled Max's head away from Pack and spurred him to a distance-covering trot. Micah carefully nudged Pack forward, turning his head after he was moving. He joined up with Max shortly.

"You're getting better," Braden told her. She smirked at him. Better wasn't necessarily a compliment. She should be able to ride a horse by now, but still struggled, although she was better than when she spurred Max to a panic as they approached Village McCullough. Then again, she hadn't ridden Max since then. Pack was a pack horse, never intended for riding. She'd have to broach this with Braden, maybe for the return trip through the Amazon. He wasn't watching her as she caught up with him. He was looking at an island of green in the distance.

"Ess, can you take a look over there and see what that is? Can you see what I'm talking about?" Braden said aloud, but knowing that it was his thought voice that the Hawkoid would hear. With a screech from high above them, Skirill passed and continued gliding southwest. He beat his wings to gain altitude as he shrunk to a black dot. Then he disappeared into the distance.

Braden was uncomfortable. A sea of green in the middle of the ruined area made him think of the oasis. That meant Bots. "G, do you sense anything?"

'Deer. Nothing else,' the 'cat said.

"Have you ever seen anything like that?" he asked Micah.

"No. I wonder if there are people?"

"There aren't. G would know. It looks like the oasis where we stayed before our final leg out of the Great Desert. I think there might be Bots there, mechanical creatures created by the ancients. They build. They serve. G doesn't like them because he can't sense them." Braden squinted as he tried to see into the distance.

He watched as beams of light slashed into the sky.

"Skirill!" he screamed, spurring Max into a full run. Pack jogged along behind, losing ground with each step. Micah struggled to stay on his back.

They missed, kind of, whatever they were. I had to go south. I'll fly for a while and circle back to you.' Skirill said, anxiety cracking his thought voice. As an afterthought, he added, *'I'm scared.'*

He didn't need to say it. They were all instantly scared. Braden slowed Max and waited for Pack to catch up. He looked at Micah, who nodded.

"It looks kind of like a Blaster," she said. "We can't fight that."

"Who's using it?" Braden asked, thinking out loud. No one in the caravan had the answer.

He wanted to get closer where he could use his telescope. Micah was right about him. He needed to see things for himself.

Craig Martelle

78 – What To Do

Skirill made it back to them, his tail feathers scorched. He saw Bots in the oasis, more like the Mirror Beast from the first oasis they had come across. He wasn't sure if there were the smaller Maintenance Bots. There were deer, too. A few small buildings stood in the middle of the trees, but nothing like the structure with the rooms where Braden had rested at Oasis Zero One.

They stopped on a small hill between them and the land oasis as they talked, while Braden looked through his rudimentary telescope. He showed Micah how to hold the glass in place with the wrapped stiff hide. Big lens at the front, small at the back. Bring the image into focus by squeezing the middle of the hide while looking through the small end.

They saw what Skirill told them was there. Two Mirror Beasts at the perimeter, buildings standing among the trees. The trees were more like what they'd seen in the rainforest, otherwise, it looked no different from the oases in the Great Desert.

Master Aadi was on the ground, struggling mightily to walk the last few steps to the top of the hill. No wonder he floated everywhere. G-War crouched low, watching.

"Are you sure the light came from the Mirror Beast?" Braden asked Skirill as they crouched by the hilltop.

"Yesss. It was clear. 'irror 'east. They are di"erent 'ro' the desert 'east," Skirill said out loud in his hissing Hawkoid voice. "They ha'e ar's."

"They have arms. Interesting. The desert Beast didn't attack us, so I agree. These are different, Ess, and you have some burnt feathers to prove it. The question is, what do we do now?"

"We leave," Micah said firmly. "We get the crap away from here."

Braden looked at her. She was pragmatic, a survivor, not a coward. He wished he could leave, but he had traveled a long way to get here. Turning around so close to his goal was too much like failure. He didn't like to fail.

Sanctuary was supposed to be destroyed. This oasis said otherwise. It said something survived, something more powerful than the Bots in Oasis Zero One. Braden buried his face in the dirt as he wrestled with himself. What was it about the Old Tech that drew him?

Maybe it wasn't the Old Tech as much as the knowledge it represented. Braden wanted answers. He wanted to know if people survived on Cygnus VI. He wanted to know what went wrong and how could they fix it. He wanted the best of both worlds, an incredible bed to sleep in and land to hunt. He wanted people to smile as the hologram had smiled. Every tidbit he learned about the ancients made him think of more questions.

He needed to know.

"Let's make camp. We can sleep on it," he told Micah. Braden had no intention of sleeping.

79 – All of Us

As the sun disappeared to the west and darkness settled over them, Braden rolled into his blanket, back toward Micah. She did the same thing. Sleep did not come easily to her. Braden rolled back to watch her, waiting for his moment.

He woke with a start. He had fallen asleep and it was now well toward sunrise. Micah was breathing deeply and slowly. She was asleep.

Leaving his blanket on the ground, he carefully adjusted his belt pouch, his long knife, and recurve bow. With one last look at Micah's sleeping form, he carefully walked away.

Two eyes gleamed at him from the darkness.

Golden Warrior of the Stone Cliffs sat near the top of the hill, waiting for him.

Braden leaned down and whispered, "You know I have to do this."

'I know it. I don't support it,' the 'cat said with a sharp edge to his thought voice.

"I'd ask you to come along, but I know that you and Bots don't exactly see things the same way."

'I shall come regardless. It can't do this alone.'

"No, it can't," came Micah's voice from behind him.

"Holy crap! You scared the hell out of me. Don't sneak up on people like that!"

"Don't sneak away and I wouldn't have to. Where do you think you're going?" she asked.

"You know where I'm going. Your real question is why," Braden answered. She waited. He knew she was glaring at him, although he could only see her outline in the darkness of the early morning.

"I need to know, Micah. I need to know why and what. I need to know about Cygnus VI. How can the ancients harness the power of the sun? How do they control the weather? So many questions. They weigh on me."

"The more you learn, the more you want to learn? Remember when you didn't know any of this existed? There was no Cygnus VI. Why does it matter now?" she asked softly as she moved closer to him, the starlight glinting in her eyes.

"I don't want to learn. I have to learn. I have to know," Braden repeated himself, emphasizing his point.

"I don't understand and I definitely don't think this is worth risking all our lives. But I'm in. We're all in. Now don't get us killed!" she directed. Braden shook his head.

"No. I'm not going to risk your lives. This is mine, my risk."

"You should have thought of that before we came here. If you go all the way, so do we. Sometimes you seem really smart and then there's the rest of the time." She leaned forward, smiling, their noses almost touching. With a quick motion, she had him by both arms, pushing him backwards, slamming him on the ground. His bow dug harshly into his back.

She pinned him to the ground. He stopped fighting. She leaned in and kissed him fiercely. His breath caught. She bit his lip as she pulled back.

"I might even like you if you ever pull your head out of your butt." She stood up, then headed back down the hill to their small camp. Braden lay there, wondering what just happened. He wasn't sure he liked it. However he was certain that when they went to the oasis, it would be all of them.

80 – Where You Go, We Follow

At the camp, they ate in silence. Max and Pack got up when they saw that the humans were awake. They grazed contentedly on the grasses of the wasted rolling plains.

Aadi watched everything. *'Fascinating,'* was all he said.

"Everyone can just stop the madness!" Braden blurted out. "Fine. We're all in this together. Here's how it's going to go. Micah and I up front, the rest of you behind us. They already shot at Skirill. At the oasis, they wouldn't recognize you guys to open a door. They see humans differently. I'm counting on that.

"Master Aadi, do you mind if Skirill rides you? It would be too long of a walk otherwise. He can hop down as we get close, if that's okay with you both."

'I've never been ridden before, Master Human. How would he hold on?'

"We can tie a blanket on. Ess can grip the rope?" he asked more than told. The Tortoid blinked a couple times, so they turned to. In short order, the blanket was held tightly in place by a rope wrapped around his body. He floated and swam to show that it didn't restrict him. Skirill beat his powerful wings twice, lifting him into the air so he could glide gently onto Aadi's back. He settled in, one talon gripping tightly.

"They shall sing songs of Skirill's march to battle, a Tortoid as his mighty steed!" Braden laughed. Micah looked on, mouth agape at the view of a Hawkoid riding a floating Tortoid.

'Now, Master Human, we do what we must. No need to poke fun. I swear that you shall never have the pleasure of a Tortoid ride. One turn, it could have kept your feet dry. Master Micah, you are welcome any time should we need to cross a swamp or river.'

"Yes, indeed. Everyone punish the bad Braden. When we all die this morning, you'll feel bad that your last words were so hurtful." Micah stepped forward, making a fist in Braden's direction. "Okay, okay. You all win. When we survive this, and I say when, not if, we'll sit down and talk about how much we can charge children for a Master Aadi ride. Instead of trading, maybe we can start a traveling circus?" They looked at him.

"A circus. Performers who do strange things for money."

Aadi looked at him without blinking and slowly shook his head. Skirill bobbed as he did when he laughed. G-War sat silently by. He rarely found Braden's humor to be funny.

'Life or death awaits us over that hill,' Aadi said in a soft thought voice. *'We go, as friends, on a quest for knowledge. We will succeed together or not at all. Master Braden, lead on. Where you go, we follow.'*

81 – Nothing to Fear, Everything to Fear

They walked toward the oasis, Micah and Braden side by side to block the view of their three companions. They walked boldly in the early morning sun, heads high, eyes alert.

"Here comes one," Braden said more calmly than he felt as one of the strange Mirror Beasts broke out of the trees and headed toward them. It picked up speed quickly. He appeared to hover like the Tortoid, but he didn't have to swim to move.

They stopped, not having to wait long before the Beast arrived. It hovered in front of them briefly. Then in a booming voice that seemed to come from everywhere, it said, "Greetings, Caretaker. Will you require escort to the New Command Center?"

"Caretaker? Again? Why are you calling me that?" Braden asked. He could hear G-War's sigh behind him.

"You carry the band of a Caretaker. You are the Caretaker of Oasis Zero One." Braden dug into his pouch and pulled out the item he had taken from the repair shop. The hologram called it a watch. He strapped it on his wrist.

"Yes, I am," Braden answered boldly. "I didn't know the New Command Center existed. Explain." Braden fell quickly into the role that seemed to resonate with the Mirror Beast. It was wider than they were tall, taller than they stood, with arms that seemed more human than the tentacles of the Maintenance Bots. It shined and glimmered like the Mirror Beast at Oasis Zero Three. He expected it would resist any attack upon it.

"The New Command Center became functional three years ago. Hundreds of years ago, after the last attack, one Bot remained, far underground. It took resources to reestablish infrastructure. Over time, it dug the ore, processed the ore, and built the Bots it needed to build more Bots. It had to build the manufacturing facility from scratch. It built the New Command Center based on the design of the original Command Center."

"You know what happened? You said war. Tell me."

"This unit is a Mark V Security Robot. It is not programmed to teach history. This unit has access to a system which has logged that the event happened. That is all. This unit is programmed to provide security for the New Command Center. Your band allows you access. You may pass."

"Access. To other humans?"

"No. You are the first human to return," the Bot responded in its unemotional, mechanical voice.

"What about my friends?"

"The other human is your guest. She may pass."

"What about my other friends? The ones behind me. You attacked one yesterday. You are not to attack any of them. They are my guests."

"These mutants are not in our system. They could be enemies. Do you wish me to log them into my system as enemies?"

"No. Log them as friends. No harm is to come to them," Braden said firmly, then repeated himself. "They are my friends. They are the Caretaker's friends."

"They will be protected like all creatures known to us and accepted into our system as non-combatants and allies."

"Shall we then?" Braden asked his companions. Only Micah nodded. The others remained wary. Skirill looked back at his scorched tail feathers. He hoped the mechanical creature would stay true to its word.

"Your blaster is in need of repair and charging. Give it to this unit and it will be taken care of it. It will be returned when it is ready." Micah hesitated briefly. The chance of getting it charged was worth the risk of not getting it back. If it was in the hands of the Security Bot, then no other human could get it and misuse it. She handed it over. The Bot took it, turned, and headed toward the oasis at a pace that they could follow.

82 – Everything to Fear, Nothing to Fear

The oasis was similar in style to Zero One, but much larger. The trees seemed natural to this part of Vii, and not strange like the ones in the desert. This oasis didn't have big buildings, though.

The Security Bot took them to a nondescript building, one of three. Braden saw the roll-up door on the building next door which suggested it would be the repair shop. The third building lacked windows. Braden couldn't guess what that building was for.

Once they arrived at the building of the Bot's choice, it left them while it entered the building with the roll-up door.

Braden peeked inside. It was nearly identical to the shop at Oasis Zero One. He walked the few steps back to the building the Bot had guided them to. With a shrug, he stepped close to the door. It opened. They went inside--the humans, G-War, and Aadi with Skirill on his back, still clinging to the rope.

There was nothing in the room except another set of doors. These looked like they slid to the side. Braden stepped close. Nothing.

Micah looked at a protrusion beside the door. It was lit. She touched it and it dinged in response. The doors opened to a very small room. They wouldn't all fit.

"Do you mind staying here, Master Aadi, Ess?" Braden asked.

"We ha'e no 'lace 'etter to go," Skirill answered for both of them. Braden turned back to see the doors close. He tried the button and the doors opened again.

He stepped inside, followed by Micah and G-War. They stood in the room, anxiety rising as the doors closed. G-War panicked and launched his furry body at the doors, claws scratching their surface.

The doors didn't move, but the room did. It started slowly and then picked up speed. It was dropping. They had the sensation of falling, but only briefly. The room slowed to a stop, and the doors opened.

G-War launched himself through as soon as he could fit. Micah and Braden hurried out shortly thereafter.

They were in a huge room. It was dark, but well lit. It was Old Tech. Everywhere they looked, they saw screens like the ones at the oasis. They saw tables and chairs. One complete wall consisted of a hundred windows with fantastic views. Their eyes couldn't take in everything there was to see. Braden looked for G-War.

"G! Where are you?" he called. No answer. He started to fear for the 'cat. He reached out with his emotions, finally touching his friend, who was almost insane with fear. There. He was under one of the tables. His eyes were wide in the darkness. He crouched, his claws extended.

Braden reached out and the 'cat reacted, striking his arm with a claw but not raking it. Blood started to pool in the puncture wounds. "It's okay, G. I'm here. Come. I'll shield you." Braden scooped up the 'cat and held him close. G-War buried his head under Braden's arm. He felt the 'cat relax slightly. Micah reached over and stroked the 'cat's back, purring to him.

With G-War, they walked slowly around the various seats and looked at the screens, but didn't touching anything. Braden looked for a place like the one he used when he talked with the hologram, but there wasn't anything like that.

The wall of windows was actually a wall made up of small screens, melded together. It was like looking through the eyes of a hundred different Hawkoids. He pointed at one screen for Micah. She looked closely.

"That's Max and Pack," she said, fear creeping into her voice. "How can they see them from here? Where is 'here'?"

"I think we're underground. The Security Bot told us that one Bot was underground when the war finished. There has to be a hologram here somewhere." He looked around to no avail.

Without anyone to answer their questions, they were lost as to what to do next. They understood that some of the screens showed parts of the world. Others showed images, like some he had drawn in his rudder.

Braden continued to absently pet G-War as he cradled the 'cat tightly in his arms.

"Time to go. We can't do this to G. Maybe we'll come back, but this is enough for now." They went back to the doors to the moving room and pressed the button. The doors opened and they stepped in. The room moved, upward this time.

When the doors opened, both Aadi and Skirill looked at them wide-eyed. *We are ecstatic that you have returned!'* Master Aadi blinked rapidly as he spoke. Looking at the 'cat in Braden's arms, he asked fearfully, *'What happened to the Golden Warrior?'*

"It's a bit busy down there. Later, we'll be able to describe it. But for this turn, we've seen enough." When the sunshine struck the 'cat's fur, he looked up, then wiggled to let Braden know he was alright to get down. Like putting a baby in a crib, Braden gently put G-War on the ground. His fur stuck up in various places around his body.

Braden dropped to his knees as the 'cat's instantaneous rage consumed him. G-War bolted into the brush, attacking something there. Micah was first after him as Braden struggled to his feet.

She arrived in time to see G-War ripping a rabbit apart. It had probably died with the first slash, but the 'cat needed to expend its energy. He shredded the rabbit, spattering blood across the ground, spreading fur and entrails. The 'cat's slashing slowed, then stopped.

He staggered a few steps, then puked up his smoked venison from breakfast. Braden, back on all fours, heaved up his breakfast, too. Then G-War sat and calmly licked his paw, grooming his face and whiskers.

Micah watched for a few heartbeats, until Braden stood up, wiping his mouth on his sleeve. "Feel like kissing me now?" he asked as he spit to the side. His insides still rebelled at the emotional overload the 'cat had shared. Micah smiled, knowing that Braden's joke meant he was okay. It meant that the 'cat was okay.

Most importantly, it meant they'd survived. Earlier that daylight, she was sure they would not.

They walked to the repair shop. The door obediently opened and they went inside. The Security Bot was nowhere to be seen, but Micah's Blaster was plugged into a device by the wall. The light was green, and as Braden had learned, green was good. So they removed the blaster. She holstered it, being careful not to put her finger on the trigger. She had seen what the blaster could do, although she had never fired it herself. She didn't want to find out while they were inside the building.

Braden looked around for anything small of value. He settled on some of the coated copper strings, then decided against them.

If he showed up in the north and was trading in Old Tech, then others would come here. He didn't want any others here. The ones to be trusted, like Micah, would avoid this place for what it represented. Others would come for that very reason.

83 – Leave or Stay?

Braden hunted the Security Bot down to ask if they were safe to go and then come back. Any of them. The Bot confirmed that they were safe. The humans and their companions would always travel securely in the area guarded by the Security Bots.

Skirill, with some trepidation, took to the sky and winged quickly away, staying low to the ground and flying erratically until he was past the hill. Beyond it, they saw him gracefully climb high and make lazy circles against the blue backdrop of the sunny sky.

Aadi seemed indifferent to it all. Braden suspected he was thinking. They had again experienced a great deal of new information, and the Tortoid had to think it all over before he formed an opinion. G-War was back to himself, although he seemed a little less sure than before. They knew he had to be hungry, so Micah asked Braden to take a deer using his bow. The deer in the land oasis were unafraid of humans. Braden felt like he was shooting sheep in a pen, but they needed the meat. He took a smaller buck with one clean shot at close range.

Working together, Braden and Micah field dressed it. Each grabbing a leg, they dragged it between them as they left the oasis and headed back to their camp.

The rest of the daylight passed uneventfully. It took a good deal of work to gather enough grass to make a fire to smoke some of the meat. G-War ate his fill of the raw venison, as did Aadi and Skirill. Braden and Micah enjoyed the first tender slices once they were cooked sufficiently.

No one talked. Braden finally remembered the wounds on his arm. He used some water to wash them, then a little bit of their precious numbweed to take out the sting. How long had it been since they needed the numbweed last? That was a good sign.

But water was getting in short supply. They needed to get back to the rainforest or bring the horses to the oasis. With Braden wearing the watch-- that is, his Caretaker band--he should be able to get the horses logged into the system. Then they could eat and drink, get refreshed. Same for all of them. They needed the rest. He hoped the companions weren't so traumatized from the experience that they wouldn't go back. At least he and Micah could take the horses.

In the end, they all agreed to go to the oasis. G-War's and Skirill's fear was palpable. Only time would relieve that, Braden thought, along with the humans helping to keep them calm.

Braden wasn't worried. He knew that he would find answers here. He was confident that his friends would not be harmed. His road had been long and dangerous, and he felt that he'd earned this opportunity to learn more. All of them had earned this knowledge.

There was more to do, so much more.

He was Free Trader Braden and they were the Caravan from Warren Deep.

Postscript

If you liked The Free Trader of Warren Deep, please stop by www.craigmartelle.com and drop me a line. This series will continue with at least two more volumes.

If you liked it, write a short review of it on Amazon. I greatly appreciate any kind words. If you have suggestions to make future volumes in this series better, send those to me as well. I'm always looking for ideas. I'll credit people in the acknowledgements for ideas that I incorporate.

Thank you for reading The Free Trader of Warren Deep. This was the lead volume of a series I originally titled as "The Animal Companions." I like that as the animal companions play a key role throughout. I renamed it as the series evolved with Braden and Micah creating a more civilized world based on trust, mutual cooperation, and trade. They encounter enemies of all kinds at every turn.

Braden and Micah's adventures continue in The Free Trader of Planet Vii. Enjoy the first couple chapters, which I've included here. I've also included the cover as I thought you might appreciate what Micah looks like.

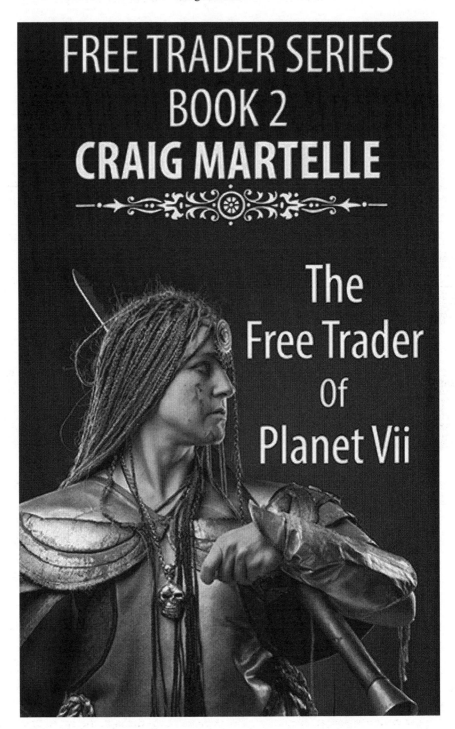

FREE TRADER SERIES
BOOK 2
CRAIG MARTELLE

The
Free Trader
Of
Planet Vii

The Free Trader of Planet Vii

1 – The Companions

The companions found themselves on a hillside, enjoying a breakfast of venison, freshly reheated over a small fire of field grass. Braden and Micah had no luck recounting to the others what they'd seen in the Command Center. The Hillcat simply called it a place of terror and shut down further discussion.

The animal companions were not comfortable inside buildings, and they never would be. Only the humans would make a return trip inside.

As long as the Security Bots left the other members of the caravan alone.

Golden Warrior of the Stone Cliffs was an orange tabby Hillcat. Braden called him G-War. His back was above a man's knee, his body the length of a man's arm, and his claws were as sharp as the finest blades. With his quickness and mutant ability to see a short distance into the future, G-War was one of the deadliest creatures in Warren Deep. Despite all this, his real gift was his ability to mindlink and talk with nearly any creature. The only things he feared were the mechanical creations of the ancients known as Bots.

Skirill was a magnificent Hawkoid who had joined Braden and G-War when they found him, injured from a fight with a mutie Bear. His body was similar in size to the Hillcat, but when he unfolded his wings, they were wider than a man was tall. He could be airborne with one hop and a single beat of his massive wings. His hooked beak was a thing to fear, but his greatest weapon was his claws. He struck from above or behind, ripping and lifting. Thanks to G-War, Skirill could share what he saw as he flew. He didn't miss much as he had the eyes of a Hawkoid.

Aadi, First Master of the Tortoid Consortium, had joined the caravan as they traveled across the Great Desert. He found Braden and the others to be interesting. It was refreshing for him to speak with them, his wisdom otherwise wasted in silence. He floated and swam through the air, with a powerful beak, although his real weapon was a focused thunderclap. The Tortoid could deliver all the sound of thunder into one small space. It usually left the victims unable to move. In the case of the Old Tech Bots, it was more destructive.

Micah had been the last to join the caravan. She was from the area south of the Great Desert, called Devaney's Barren by the ancients. She was running from an arranged marriage because she had killed the groom-to-be while injuring his father, and she had taken their revered blaster on her way out. She believed that they wouldn't allow her to return to her village of Trent. Her body belied an incomparable physical strength. Now that she was free of her village, she found her place as a warrior, although she was learning the nuance of trade.

Braden was the reluctant leader of the caravan and the companions, having fallen into it when he saved a drowning Hillcat ten cycles ago. Since then, he always preferred the company of animals. His parents left the Caravan Guild, ending their careers as Free Traders, and Braden followed in their footsteps, becoming a Free Trader, plying the areas outside the influence of the Guild.

Braden also carried a weapon from the ancients, but this one needed no power beyond his own physical strength. He called it a Rico Bow, although that was an aberration of the term recurve bow. The second curve of the Old Tech material made it possible for him to shoot arrows further and more accurately than any other weapon.

Braden's greatest strength was his vision for a better future. That's why he led the caravan. The companions believed in him because he believed in what was possible. Braden's vision and planning made it possible for the caravan to cross the Great Desert, a feat no one had managed before.

The six companions of the caravan were joined by two horses that Braden had managed to trade for in Cameron, the southernmost town of the Caravan Guild's territory. Max and Pack weren't mutants, but were still equal members of the caravan, and at times, more important. During their passage through the Amazon, Aadi's negotiations with the Lizard Men had saved the horses' lives.

2 – The Power of Old Tech

Braden and Micah gnawed their smoked venison in silence. They'd argued about how to approach the oasis, neither satisfied and no decision made. Micah wanted to leave the companions at the camp while only she and Braden went in. Braden wanted the others to have free run of the oasis where they could eat and drink as they wished.

As the so-called Caretaker, Braden held some sway over the massive Security Bots. He'd found a bracelet that showed time in the ancients' way. This also identified him as the Caretaker of Oasis Zero One and gave him preferred treatment at the New Command Center. He expected that he could tell the Security Bot to log the horses into the system, so they would be free to roam the fertile area while Braden and Micah were occupied underground.

"As long as we are the only ones in the system, I think the Security Bots will protect us," Braden said, thinking out loud.

"Protect us from who?" Micah asked.

"Say that merry band from a certain village with a broken-armed old man show up looking for their blaster…"

"Then I would be happy to shoot them with this very blaster. Maybe we can shoot it before we go back?" Micah suggested, and Braden liked the idea. It was a tool and they needed to know how to use it.

They set up a patch of ground and walked twenty-five strides away. Micah held the blaster in front of her as she had seen the old man do. She pulled back on the trigger using the pointer fingers of both hands. The blaster bucked slightly in her hands. Not knowing what to expect, she had a death grip on it. After firing it, she stood, mesmerized.

The air smelled funny, as if the very sky had burned. A ragged beam of light launched forward, scorching the spot on the ground and many small areas around it. The grasses at the edge started to burn, while the center of the blast site was gone, burned to smoldering cinders.

Braden ran forward and stomped out the fires. The last thing they needed was a wildfire racing across the rolling hills. Braden, smoke swirling around his feet, looked back at Micah.

She still hadn't moved after firing the blaster, her eyes locked on the scorched earth of her target. Braden put his hands up, palms toward her.

"Relax and put the blaster down, Micah," he said soothingly. Slowly, she looked up at him. Her mouth worked, but nothing came out.

Braden let out a whoop of celebration and jumped into the air, pumping his fist as he did so. "Now that's a weapon!"

Micah put the blaster on the ground and stepped back. Braden picked it up and looked at it in awe. He aimed it at the spot, looking around to make sure nothing was coming, and then depressed the trigger as Micah had done.

It kicked in his hands, but he held it firm. It discharged its flame into the ground. Braden held the trigger down, and the blaster continued to throw flame and light forward until Micah grabbed him from behind.

"Let go! Let go!" He realized what she was saying and finally let up on the trigger. "Just pull it once and let it go. What the hell were you trying to do?"

"Sorry. I didn't know. I never saw a blaster fire before and I sure as crap never fired anything like this. I have a bow, remember?" Braden was more than a little miffed at Micah's scolding. She took the blaster from his hands and put it in the holster as she bolted toward their target.

The new fires grew quickly. She tried stamping them out, but the flames were already fierce.

Braden pulled her away and they ran to the camp to collect their stuff. Max and Pack were trying to run from the fires, but they were hobbled. Braden and Micah loosened the bonds while holding their reins, then swung into the saddles. G-War ran the opposite direction, which took him straight toward the oasis. Aadi swam as quickly as he could in the same direction. Skirill was much calmer as he took wing and flew above the mounting chaos of the wildfire.

They kicked the horses to a gallop and raced past Aadi, who was still behind the fleet Hillcat. They pulled up shortly to see the progress of the fire. It moved slowly after the initial rage. When they ripped out the prairie grasses to make their cook fires, they'd created fire breaks. There wasn't much to burn, but what there was, burned well.

Knowing they still wouldn't be able to put out the fire, they turned and continued toward the oasis.

3 – Back to the Oasis

As Braden and Micah approached the oasis, one Security Bot floated gracefully, yet quickly, toward them.

"Add the creatures we ride to your system, Master Security Bot. They are called horses."

"The horses are added," it responded instantly.

"Tell me, what is this place called?" Braden asked.

"It is the New Command Center."

"That's the place at the bottom of the little room that moves. What's the area up here called? We can't keep calling it the New Command Center." Micah looked at Braden. Of all the things to ask, this wasn't on any of her lists.

"The elevator takes you to the New Command Center. The surface area above the New Command Center is called the New Command Center."

"Elevator you called it. Okay. I tell you what, put this into your system. We're going to call this place New Sanctuary."

"I have added that name to the system."

"While we're here, will you protect us from our enemies? All of us?" Micah asked, sweeping her arm to take in Aadi, G-War, and Skirill.

"Yes. When an enemy is so defined in our system, we will protect the Caretaker and his guests. The only enemies currently listed in the system are James Warren and his followers."

"Who is James Warren?" Braden asked, although he knew that he was the founder of Warren Deep.

"James Warren is a bio-geneticist who rebelled against the proper authority of Sanctuary, ultimately waging war on the peaceful people of the south. We were programmed to protect against his forces should they try to seize the capital city. His last known location was north of Devaney's Barren."

"Warren Deep," Braden whispered. He, G-War, and Skirill were all the result of what James Warren had done in the north. That's why muties were treated as enemies in the south. Warren was their creator.

"Master Security Bot. James Warren and his followers are no longer enemies. We achieved peace hundreds of cycles, I mean years, ago. Do you agree that the last known battles were that long ago?"

"I concur. The new information is added to the system. There are no enemies currently listed in the system."

Braden and Micah looked at each other and nodded. The ability to direct the Security Bots was unexpected, but welcome.

"Without enemies, this unit has no tasks to perform," the Security Bot said as it remained motionless.

"Can you put out that fire?" Micah offered, not knowing what they could get from the Security Bot.

"Yes. Is that the Caretaker's command?"

"Yes, please. Put that fire out!" Braden said in his most commanding voice, smirking as he looked at Micah. She shook her head and smiled. Braden's smirk faded. He knew that she could take the bracelet away from him if she wanted. It was by pure chance that he had it, and luck was probably not the best method of picking a leader.

"Okay. Yes, I know. Next time we find a New Command Center, you get to be the Caretaker…"

With a couple beeps, the Security Bot bolted past the horses, scaring them. A second Security Bot appeared from behind the trees of New Sanctuary and headed toward the fires as well. The Bots bracketed the area and without the aid of water, systematically reduced the fires until only smoke remained. They hadn't gone into the flames, but stood apart as they floated back and forth.

"How'd they do that?" Braden asked rhetorically. Micah shrugged, happy the fires were out. She didn't want to be responsible for the wanton destruction of the grasslands as they struggled to grow out of the previous wasteland of Sanctuary.

That must have been one hell of a war. With creatures like the Security Bots, it was amazing that any humans survived at all.

About the Author

I retired from the Marine Corps, got a law degree, worked as a management consultant, and then retired from that. I watched people. I worked with people. I studied how they interacted. It is fascinating when you sit back and take it in without any preconceptions.

In the Free Trader books, you'll see the leadership themes I embrace painted across a variety of backdrops. You'll see successes and failures. Winning is a state of mind that takes determination, humility, and even compromise. When that makes sense, you'll start to understand more about me.

I was raised on Dungeons and Dragons™ along with James Ward's games of Metamorphosis Alpha™ and Gamma World™. I studied World War II and the Civil Wars in America and Russia. I lived in Japan for four years, Korea for a year, and even Russia for a couple years.

I owned Gauntlet Publishing Company. I published the magazine Gauntlet U.S., along with a number of wargame rules and historical studies. That was all a hobby while I worked my day job. I left that all behind to focus on my work as a management consultant, where I traveled a great deal, more than half my year was spent on the road. I don't recommend it.

Through a bizarre series of events, we ended up in Fairbanks, Alaska. I never expected to retire to a place where golf courses are only open for four months out of the year. But we love it here. It is off the beaten path. We watch the northern lights from our driveway. Our dog has lots of room to run. And temperatures reach forty below zero. We have from three and a half hours of daylight in the winter to twenty four hours in the summer.

It's all part of the give and take of life. If we didn't have those extremes, then everyone would live here.

Made in the USA
Middletown, DE
18 September 2016